THE CASE OF THE BORROWED BRUNETTE
THE CASE OF THE BURIED CLOCK
THE CASE OF THE FOOTLOOSE DOLL
THE CASE OF THE LAZY LOVER
THE CASE OF THE SHOPLIFTER'S SHOE
THE CASE OF THE FABULOUS FAKE
THE CASE OF THE CROOKED CANDLE
THE CASE OF THE HOWLING DOG
THE CASE OF THE FIERY FINGERS
THE CASE OF THE HAUNTED HUSBAND
THE CASE OF THE MYTHICAL MONKEYS
THE CASE OF THE SHAPELY SHADOW
THE CASE OF THE GLAMOROUS GHOST
THE CASE OF THE GRINNING GORILLA
THE CASE OF THE NEGLIGENT NYMPH
THE CASE OF THE PERJURED PARROT
THE CASE OF THE RESTLESS REDHEAD
THE CASE OF THE SUNBATHER'S DIARY
THE CASE OF THE VAGABOND VIRGIN
THE CASE OF THE DEADLY TOY
THE CASE OF THE LONELY HEIRESS
THE CASE OF THE EMPTY TIN
THE CASE OF THE GOLDDIGGER'S PURSE
THE CASE OF THE LAME CANARY
THE CASE OF THE BLACK-EYED BLOND
THE CASE OF THE CARETAKER'S CAT
THE CASE OF THE GILDED LILY
THE CASE OF THE ROLLING BONES
THE CASE OF THE SILENT PARTNER
THE CASE OF THE VELVET CLAWS
THE CASE OF THE BAITED HOOK
THE CASE OF THE COUNTERFEIT EYE
THE CASE OF THE PHANTOM FORTUNE
THE CASE OF THE WORRIED WAITRESS
THE CASE OF THE CALENDAR GIRL
THE CASE OF THE TERRIFIED TYPIST
THE CASE OF THE CAUTIOUS COQUETTE
THE CASE OF THE SPURIOUS SPINSTER
THE CASE OF THE DUPLICATE DAUGHTER
THE CASE OF THE STUTTERING BISHOP
THE CASE OF THE ICE COLD HANDS

The Case of the
Dubious
Bridegroom

Erle Stanley Gardner

BALLANTINE BOOKS • NEW YORK

ISBN 0-345-34186-4

This edition published by arrangement with William Morrow and Company, Inc.

Printed in Canada

First Ballantine Books Edition: April 1983
Fifth Printing: February 1989

FOREWORD

THIS BOOK WAS WRITTEN UNDER RATHER UNUSUAL CIR-
cumstances. The last part of it was dictated while I was
in Boston attending a seminar on Homicide Investigation
at the Department of Legal Medicine of the Harvard Medical School.

I had for some time heard about these seminars, which
are sponsored by Mrs. Frances G. Lee of New Hampshire (a Captain of the New Hampshire State Police).
Invitations to attend are as sought after in police circles
as bids to Hollywood by girls who aspire to be actresses.

Despite the fact I had heard so much about these seminars, I was hardly prepared for what I found.

The instructors, under the guidance of Dr. Alan R.
Moritz, are not only brilliant but practical men who are
daily accomplishing feats of crime detection which are
little short of astounding. The department works in connection with both the Boston city police and the state
police of Massachusetts. They have at their command
every facility, every bit of scientific knowledge available,
and they have brains.

Dr. Robert P. Brittain, from the University of Glasgow,
doctor of medicine, criminologist, and barrister, was not
only a mine of information as to practical detective work
on this side of the water, but was able to furnish the latest
information as to British and European police methods of
crime detection. Incidentally, from comments I heard, as
well as from my own observation, I realize that Dr. Brittain, by his presence and character, made an outstanding
contribution to international understanding and friend-

ship at this seminar, and I understand from no less an authority than Captain Lee herself that this was true all during his stay in this country.

The material and methods demonstrated at this seminar were in many instances years ahead of methods now available to the student who has to rely solely upon even the most modern works of forensic medicine and toxicology.

Back of all this, and as the guiding spirit, is Captain Frances G. Lee. I don't believe she has ever overlooked a detail in her life. Captain Lee has reconstructed in small scale (one foot to the inch) some of the most puzzling crimes which have been encountered by police. The detail of these models is absolutely unbelievable. If a state trooper is shown holding a notebook and pencil, you can be sure that the pencil, perhaps half the size of a toothpick, is a genuine pencil containing genuine lead, and that notes in the miniature notebook about the size of one's thumbnail have actually been written with that pencil.

It is not expected that members of the class will be able to solve all of these crimes. They are not "whodunits." They are not like the photographic crimes represented in some of the magazines where the reader is requested to furnish a solution. These are models used to develop and test the powers of observation and concentration on the part of the students. They are expected to point out the significant clues which, when run down, will lead to a correct solution. The observers are expected to notice and remember everything in connection with the crimes which are "assigned" to them.

They then report on these crimes, give their deductions, and state what should be done in order to bring about a correct solution. Not all of these deaths are homicides. Some of them may be suicides masquerading as murders, or murders masquerading as suicides.

They cannot be studied casually; they cannot be solved

...

easily. I mention these matters because subsequently, when students reported on their assignments, I had an opportunity to watch the police mind at work.

Now, I am perfectly willing to concede that these were picked men who were in attendance at that seminar. Attendance is limited to less than two dozen students so that instruction can be highly personalized and a great deal of ground covered in a short space of time. Nevertheless, these men are typical of the highest type of police officer which is being developed in considerable numbers in this country.

It is hard to believe that any group of officers, reporting one after the other, could do the things I saw these men do. They knew what to look for, they knew where and how to look, and when they found something that was significant, they were able to evaluate the reason and advance an explanation. And these homicides have for the most part been conceived with a diabolical ingenuity which would give the proverbial "Philadelphia lawyer" brain-fog within the first few minutes.

We writers like to record the adventures of outstanding, individual detectives, who are generally portrayed as thinking circles around the police. But I am now sure of one thing. I am not going to have any of Mrs. Lee's graduates appearing in my books. Such an officer would not only solve the crime as soon as the hero could, but he just might be a hundred or so pages ahead of the procession.

This is a marvelous work that Captain Lee is doing. It is a progressive work, since a nucleus of highly trained, efficient men can in turn train others, and by the example they set in their work, inspire others to greater efficiency.

The information I received at this seminar is invaluable to me. The people I met are an intellectual inspiration, and I want to take this opportunity to thank these police officers for their splendidly courteous treatment of me: a rank outsider so far as their profession is concerned, and, so far as I know, the only person not a police officer who has ever been invited to take one of these courses.

As for Captain Lee, I have dedicated this book to her as an expression, in some measure, of my appreciation; and in admiration of the manner in which her mind, working with the accurate precision of a railroad watch, has brought into existence the over-all plan of a course in training that is helping to make the competent state police official as much a professional man as the doctor or lawyer. I herewith tender her my profound respect, my deepest admiration, and my eternal gratitude.

ERLE STANLEY GARDNER

Ridgefield, Connecticut
November 1, 1948

CAST OF CHARACTERS

The Case of the
Dubious
Bridegroom

NIGHT CHANGED THE CITY'S SKYSCRAPERS FROM HARD
shafts of steel and concrete to wraithlike fingers etched in
light.

The buildings visible from Perry Mason's office showed,
here and there, oblongs of lighted windows, but for the
most part were illuminated only by floodlights from without.

Perry Mason, wearied after a hard day in court, had
switched out the lights in his office and stretched out in
the big armchair facing his desk. He had intended at first
only to rest his eyes, which had become tired from con-
centrating on the fine print of lawbooks, but fatigue had
asserted itself and he had dropped off into the warmth
of slumber.

Enough illumination came from the street and alley to
show the fire escape outside Mason's window, the desk,
piled with open lawbooks, the quiet figure in the huge
overstuffed leather chair where Mason persuaded nervous
clients to relax and pour forth their troubles.

It had been a hot day, but now a storm was blowing up
and vagrant wisps of wind circling the building swept past
the partially opened window.

Mason stirred restlessly, as though twitched by a sub-
conscious reminder of the pile of work on his desk, and
the necessity of formulating an opinion upon a difficult
legal matter before the next day.

From the dark silence above Mason's window on the
fire escape came the sound of faint motion, then a well-

shod, graceful, feminine foot came groping down the iron stair tread. A moment later the other foot followed.

Slowly, cautiously, a young woman descended the fire escape, until her head was on a level with the landing of the office above.

Lights clicked on in the upper office. A rectangle of light sent rays of radiance out into the darkness.

Mason stirred in his sleep, muttered unintelligibly and flung a restless arm over the arm of the chair.

There was a shadow as a figure moved away from the lighted window above.

The girl on the fire escape hastily descended two more steps, apparently intending to reach the landing in front of Mason's office window.

Then suddenly, as Mason moved his arm again, the girl on the fire escape detected that motion and froze into startled immobility.

A gust of wind, whipping up the alley, billowed her skirts and she instinctively flung down her right hand, fighting against the blowing garment.

The light which sifted in from the street glinted upon reflecting metal.

Mason straightened up in his chair.

The girl on the fire escape turned, started to climb, then stopped, apparently dreading to cross that shaft of light coming from the window of the office above Mason's. The wind freshened. In the distance, thunder rumbled ominously.

Mason yawned, rubbed his eyes, glanced upward, then snapped to incredulous attention as he saw the whipping skirt, the legs of the girl.

He slid out of the chair in a quick, lithe motion and around the desk to the window, peered upward, and said, "Do come . . ."

The girl on the fire escape held a warning finger to her lips.

Mason frowned up at her. "What's the idea . . ."

She shook her head in a frenzy of impatience, motioned imperatively for silence, struggled with her skirts.

Mason beckoned.

She hesitated.

Mason swung one leg out of the office window.

The girl sensed the threat of that motion. She started slowly down the fire escape. Her right hand made a quick, flinging gesture. A metallic object caught the light rays and glittered, then ceased to glitter. She struggled again with her skirts.

"You must have had a free show," she said laughingly, her voice almost a whisper.

"I did," Mason said. "Come in."

Once having decided that surrender was inevitable, she was tractable enough. She slipped a leg over the sill of Mason's window, then, pivoting lightly, jumped into the room.

Mason walked over toward the light switch.

"Please don't," she said in quietly modulated tones.

"Why not?"

"I'd prefer that you didn't. It might—might be dangerous."

"For whom?" Mason asked.

"For me," she said, and then added after a moment, "for you."

Mason surveyed the figure that was silhouetted against the light of the window. "You don't look as though you had anything to fear from the light."

She laughed melodiously. "You ought to know. How long had you been sitting there?"

"An hour or so, but I was asleep."

"You woke up at the crucial moment," she laughed. "That wind caught me unaware."

"I realized that it did," Mason said. "What was it you had in your right hand?"

"A handful of skirt."

"Something metallic."

3

"Oh that," she said, and laughed. "A flashlight."

"And what became of it?"

"It slipped out of my hand."

"Are you certain it wasn't a gun?" Mason asked.

"Why, how absurd, Mr. Mason!"

"You know my name?"

She pointed to the frosted glass of the office door, illuminated by the corridor light outside. "It's all over your door, and I can read backwards."

"I still think it was a gun. What did you do with it?"

"I didn't have a gun. Anyway, the thing that you saw slipped out of my hand and went sailing down into the alley below."

"How do I know?" Mason asked, moving cautiously toward her.

She flung her arms out straight from the shoulder, said, "All right, I suppose I have this coming."

Mason stepped quickly toward her. His hands slid down her body.

For a moment, at that first touch, she winced, then she stood rigidly still.

"Is it necessary to be *that* thorough?" she asked.

"I think it is," Mason said. "Don't move."

"The object of this search, Mr. Mason, is to detect a weapon!"

"Exactly," Mason said. "*I* wasn't the one who made this search necessary. It's going to be sufficiently thorough to assure my protection."

He could feel her muscles stiffen, but she uttered no word, made no motion.

"Finished?" she demanded coldly, as Mason dropped his hands to his sides.

He nodded.

She put down her hands. Lights, reflected from the street, showed her mouth was hard as she walked over to a chair, sat down and took a cigarette case from her purse. "I don't like that sort of thing."

4

"I don't like women to shoot me," Mason said. "You *did* have a gun, you know. I suppose you tossed it down into the alley."

"Why don't you run down and find out, Mr. Mason?"

"I think I can do better than that. I think I can ask the police to make a search."

She laughed scornfully. "That would make a nice story. I can see the headlines in my mind's eye: 'PROMINENT LAWYER CALLS POLICE TO SEE IF THERE IS A REVOLVER IN THE ALLEY BELOW HIS WINDOW.' "

Mason watched her thoughtfully. Light from her match showed the oval of a beautiful face. The hand that held the match was steady.

"And then," she went on, her eyes twinkling with sardonic humor, "there would be a rather humorous story: 'THE LAWYER REFUSED TO MAKE ANY EXPLANATION WHEN POLICE FAILED TO FIND THE WEAPON.—WAS PERRY MASON PRACTICING A JUGGLING ACT WITH A REVOLVER WHEN THE WEAPON SLIPPED OUT OF HIS HAND AND DROPPED DOWN TO THE ALLEY OR WAS HE PRACTICING AT DISARMING CLIENTS?'—It would make quite a story."

"And what makes you think I'll make no explanation?" Mason asked.

"I don't think you will," she said. "It would involve you somewhat, don't you think?"

"Would it?"

"Seeing a woman on the fire escape, forcing her to enter your office, accusing her of carrying a weapon, all with no proof . . . It would leave you open to a suit for damages, wouldn't it?"

"I don't think so," Mason said. "You see, after all, I'd be in the position of having found a prowler who was about to enter my office via the fire escape and . . ."

"Enter *your* office!" she interjected scornfully.

"Weren't you?"

"Of course not."

Mason said, "I'm afraid I'm too busy to waste time

5

with you right now. If you can't make some adequate explanation I'm going to have to pick up that receiver and ask the police to call."

"A new page in your record," she said. "Perry Mason calling the police!"

He smiled at the thought. "I admit it *would* be a bit unusual. Suppose you make the explanation?"

She said, "Haven't I been humiliated enough tonight? Having to stand there while you . . ."

"I was searching for a weapon, you know that."

"Was that your entire interest in the transaction?"

"Yes."

"Then you're even more of a machine than I thought," she flared.

"Well, you'll have to figure it out for yourself."

Mason moved toward the telephone.

She said hastily, "Wait!"

The lawyer turned.

She took a deep drag at her cigarette, exhaled the last of the smoke and then jabbed the cigarette end viciously into the ash tray. "All right," she said, "you win."

"What have I won?"

"An explanation."

"Get going."

She said, "I'm employed in the office upstairs as a secretary."

"Who has that office?" Mason asked.

"The Garvin Mining, Exploration and Development Company."

"You say it glibly enough," Mason said.

"I should. I work there."

The lawyer picked up the telephone book, opened it to the last page of the GA classification, ran down until he found the Garvin Mining, Exploration and Development Company, checked the address, nodded, and said, "So far that seems to be right."

She said, "My employer asked me to come back and

work tonight. He warned me he might be very late. He said he was going to a dinner party, but wanted to do some work just as soon as he was able to break away from the dinner. He wants to get away on a trip tomorrow."

"And so you sat on the fire escape waiting for him?"

She grinned, "As a matter of fact, Mr. Mason, it *was* almost that bad."

"What do you mean?"

She said, "I got up to the office about an hour ago. I waited and waited, and then I got tired of simply sitting there. I had finished with the evening paper and didn't know what else to do. I switched out the lights and went over and sat on the window sill for a while and then, just for the lark of it, I got out on the fire escape and—well, it was dirty out there. I touched the rail and my hand got terribly dirty. That was a nuisance, because I was going to have to go down to the washroom and scrub the grime off.

"But while I was out there, it was—well, it was sort of romantic and exciting, looking out over the city and thinking about all of the heartaches, all of the tragedies, all of the hopes—and then a key clicked in the lock, the door opened. I assumed, of course, it was my boss, and I wondered just how I'd account for my presence out there on the dark fire escape.

"And then the light switch clicked on and *I saw it was his wife!*

"I didn't know what she wanted. I didn't know whether she was there, trying to trap me, whether she thought that—well, I knew how *I* would feel under the circumstances."

"Go right ahead," Mason said.

"So," she said, "almost instinctively, I moved down two or three steps, so that I would be out of her range of vision . . . I could still see into the office. I suppose it was natural curiosity that made me watch to see what she was doing. Well, then she moved over toward the

7

window and I had to start down the steps of the fire escape."

"And the wind blew your skirts up."

She smiled, "And you had a point of vantage, Mr. Mason."

"I did," Mason admitted, then added, "you instinctively put down your hand to hold your skirts in place."

"I'll say! That wind meant business."

"And," Mason said, "the hand held a gun."

"A flashlight," she amended.

"Exactly," Mason said. "I'll be a gentleman and take your word for it. It was a flashlight. And now, if, within the next five seconds, you can make a satisfactory explanation for the flashlight— No coaching from the audience, please— You have only three seconds left—two seconds—one second—I'm sorry."

She bit her lip and said, "The flashlight, you see, was one that I had taken with me so that I could have a light when I went to the parking lot to get my car. I—well, you know, I didn't expect the boss would escort me back to my car, and a woman alone doesn't like prowling around late at night in the back of a lot. After all, Mr. Mason, things *do* happen, you know."

"And so you took the flashlight with you when you went out on the fire escape."

"Strange as it may seem, I did exactly that. It was on the desk, and I picked it up as I went out. It was dark out there!"

"That's fine," Mason said. "So now, if you'll take me down and show me the automobile that you have parked, that will be all there is to it."

"Gladly," she said, getting up from the chair with smooth grace, "I'll be only *too* glad to do that, Mr. Mason. And you can check the license number, my driver's license and the certificate of ownership on the steering post, and then I think that will conclude a very interesting meeting, don't you?"

"Definitely," Mason said. "It's been a pleasure even under such unusual circumstances. As it happens, I don't know your name."

She said, "You'll learn it when you see the registration on the automobile."

"I'd prefer to hear it from you first."

"Virginia Colfax."

"Miss or Mrs.?"

"Miss."

"Let's go," Mason told her.

Mason led the way to the door, opened it and stood aside for the girl to walk out. She tossed a friendly smile at him over her shoulder and, together, they walked down the corridor.

As they passed Paul Drake's office, near the elevator, with the windows lit up and the sign, DRAKE DETECTIVE AGENCY, on the door, the girl made a grimace and said, "I *don't* like that place!"

"Why not?" Mason asked.

"Detectives give me the creeps. I like privacy."

Mason, pushing the elevator button and waiting for the janitor to bring the cage up, said, "Drake does all my work. It's really a very methodical business—just like anything else. After you're familiar with it, it ceases to have romance and glamour. It becomes matter-of-fact. At times I think Paul Drake is completely bored with it."

"I daresay," she said, sarcastically.

The elevator came to a stop. The janitor nodded. Mason placed his hand under the girl's elbow as he guided her into the elevator, said, "You'll have to sign the register, checking out."

She smiled at him, "I'm afraid you're wrong, Mr. Mason. Since the Drake Detective Agency stays open all night, people who are going to that office don't have to sign the register."

"Oh, did you go to them?" Mason asked.

Her laugh held good-natured banter. "Of course. Where did you *think* I'd been? Stupid!"

"We have an understanding that people going to the Drake Detective Agency don't register," the janitor explained. "They keep open twenty-four hours a day, you know."

Mason marked down his own checking out time, said to Virginia Colfax, "You certainly do have a fast mind, a ready wit and a nimble tongue."

"Thank you," she said frigidly.

The elevator stopped at the lobby floor. She swept out, with her chin in the air, and Mason followed.

At the door of the building she stood for a moment with the wind from the approaching shower catching her hair, blowing it back from her ears. The storm was now measurably closer and the occasional rumble of thunder at intervals drowned out the noises of the city street.

She suddenly turned and put her hand on his arm. "I want you to know one thing," she said.

"What?" Mason asked.

She said, "I'm grateful to you for being so decent about everything."

Mason raised his eyebrows.

And with that, she swung her arm up from her side and slapped his face so hard that the sound of her open palm attracted the attention of a group of people who had just emerged from the cocktail lounge a couple of doors down the street.

As Mason stood for a disconcerted moment, she sprinted across the sidewalk, jerked open the door of a waiting taxi and jumped inside.

"Hey!" Mason shouted to the cab driver, "hold that cab!" and started across the sidewalk.

A bull-necked man, with the build of a stevedore and the tailored suit of a business executive, grabbed Mason's coattail. "None of that, buddy!" he said.

Mason whirled on him. "Take your hands off me!"

The man hung on, regarding him with a grin. "It's no dice, buddy, she doesn't like you."

The taxi shot out from the curb and into traffic.

Mason said to the heavy set man, "Let go of that coat or I'll break your jaw."

There was something in his eyes which caused the man to fall back. "Now wait a minute, buddy," the man said, "you can see that the dame doesn't want . . ."

Mason turned toward the curb, looked up and down the street for a cab. There was none in sight.

He turned back toward the big man. "All right," he said, his face white with wrath, "you've played hero in front of your party. I suppose you used to be a great boxer in the good old college days back in nineteen seventeen. If it's any satisfaction to you, your interference has caused a lot of legal complications your mind is too dumb to comprehend. Now get your damn fat face out of my way or I'll push it in!"

The man, abashed, fell back before Mason's blazing fury.

The lawyer pushed contemptuously past him, started back to the office, changed his mind, walked around the corner of the building to the entrance of the alley, then paced down the alley, moving slowly, searching carefully, exploring every foot of the pavement.

There was no trace of either a revolver or flashlight.

Mason walked back to the entrance of the office building, signed the register once more, was taken up to his own floor and stepped into the office of the Drake Detective Agency.

"Paul Drake in?" he asked the girl at the desk.

She shook her head.

Mason said, "I've got a job for him. No great rush about it. Start him on it tomorrow morning. I want to find out something about the background of the Garvin Mining, Exploration and Development Company. I want to know whether a girl by the name of Virginia Colfax is employed there, and I want to know something about the Garvin who runs the outfit. Tell Paul not to spend too much time on it, but to get me the background and let me know when he has something to report."

The girl nodded, and Mason walked on down the corridor to his office, where he again tackled the legal problem of trying to determine whether a statement could be considered as entirely extraneous and inadmissible as hearsay, or whether it could be classed as a part of the *res gestae* and therefore admissible as an exception to the hearsay evidence rule.

The lights in the adjoining buildings winked out one by one, until all the other office buildings were dark. Mason, engrossed in his subject, went on collecting case after case, showing the fine line of distinction between hearsay and *res gestae*.

A vague uneasiness intruded upon his concentration. With his eyes absorbed by the lawbooks, a faint but unfamiliar scent insisted upon reminding him of his feminine intruder.

At length he flung down his book and looked around. There on the floor was a handkerchief grimed with dirt that might have come off a fire escape.

The handkerchief held the scent of a distinctive perfume and was neatly embroidered with the letter "V."

2

∎

AT TEN O'CLOCK THE NEXT MORNING PERRY MASON, appearing before the State Supreme Court, sitting in back, was able, after a masterful thirty-minute argument bristling with authorities, to convince the high tribunal that the statement which had been received in evidence by the lower court was a part of the *res gestae,* and the Court thereupon affirmed a judgment previously awarded in the lower court to one of Perry Mason's clients.

Mason took a taxicab to his office, and shortly after eleven o'clock opened the door of his private office.

Della Street, his private secretary, glanced up from her desk, smiled a greeting, and said, "How did you come out, chief?"

"On top."

"Congratulations."

"Thanks."

"You look tired."

"I was up most of the night."

Della Street smiled.

"Why the smile?" Mason asked.

"Have you, by any chance, seen the newspaper?"

"Yes, I saw the morning newspaper and . . ."

"I'm referring to the early edition of the afternoon newspaper," Della Street said. "You might like to see the Gossip Column."

"Why?" he asked.

She raised two forefingers, rubbing one across the other and said, mockingly, "Naughty, naughty, chief."

"Now what?" he asked.

Della Street placed a folded newspaper on his desk.

Mason noticed a marked section in the Gossip Column on the inside page:

What prominent lawyer, whose name has become almost a byword because of his uncanny skill in defending persons accused of crime, received the mitten in front of his office building last night? Who was the mysterious blonde spitfire who swung one from the hip and left the astonished lawyer groggy while she sprinted across to a taxicab? It must have been someone in whom the attorney had a more than ordinary interest, because only the physical restraint of an athletic bystander prevented the lawyer from dashing across the sidewalk to attempt forcible entry and detainer.

And what was this lawyer looking for in the alley? Did the blonde pitch something out of his office window?

And the party seemed *so* congenial until the haymaker.

This handsome lawyer is the secret of many a heartbreak on the part of yearning debutantes who wish he would give them a tumble instead of being so engrossed in his law business.—Or is it that his office, with its competent employees, seems so attractive that he prefers the business environment to that of the socialites?

In any event, one young woman in this city has registered her emphatic disapproval.

Tut, tut, Mr. M!

Mason's face darkened as he read the column. "Damn snooping buzzard!" he said. "Why do newspapers have to employ people to snoop around in gutters?"

"And alleys," Della Street said.

"And alleys," Mason amended. "How the devil do you suppose he got the information?"

"You forget that you're pretty well known now," she said. "Who was the athletic stranger?"

"A big tub of lard," Mason said. "I should have smashed his jaw. Some fellow trying to show off to the women with him. He grabbed my coat as I went by and gave her just enough time to get out of the way."

"Who was your girl friend?"

"She said her name was Virginia Colfax," Mason said. "Judging from the law of probabilities, I would say that there was possibly one chance in one hundred million that Colfax actually was her last name, but I have a hunch the Virginia part may be all right."

With a wry smile he told Della about the invasion of his office the night before.

"And what did she want?"

"She wanted out. I should have called the police in the first place."

Della raised her eyebrows. "Called the police?"

"Well," Mason said, "I admit it would have looked rather incongruous," and then suddenly he threw back his head and laughed wholeheartedly. "A smart little devil," he said, "and she certainly slipped one over on me. I thought I was escorting her down to the parking lot so she could point out her car to me."

"And something slipped?"

"Something came up unexpectedly, Della—her right hand."

"Why?"

"She was smart enough to know that bystanders would sympathize with a woman who was trying to get away from the pursuing wolf. She apparently knew that a taxi-cab customarily waited in front of our office building, and she knew that there would probably be people on the sidewalk . . . As it was, she had all the breaks. I definitely didn't."

"I'm afraid," Della Street told him, "that it's not safe to trust you alone up here in the office. I told you I'd be glad to come up last night and work with you."

"I didn't want to bother you," Mason said. "I worked pretty late—oh well, it was an adventure, anyway."

Mason opened the drawer in the lower left-hand side of the desk, took out the handkerchief the girl had left behind.

"What do you make of that, Della?"

Della Street regarded the square of linen. "Dirty," she said.

Mason nodded. "She wiped the grime of the fire escape from her hands. What's the scent, Della?"

Della Street clamped a thumb and forefinger on a corner of the handkerchief, raised it gingerly.

"Oh, oh," she said, "your visitor uses expensive perfume."

"What is it?"

"Ciro's *Surrender*, I think."

"I'll try and remember it," Mason said. "What's new in the office, Della?"

"There's a Mr. Garvin waiting outside," Della Street said. "He's anxious to see you. He has offices in the same building, on the floor above us, in fact—the Garvin Mining, Exploration . . ."

"Yes, yes, I know," Mason said, "the Garvin Mining, Exploration and Development Company."

"You've noticed the name on the directory?" she asked.

"Virginia Colfax," Mason said, "was supposed to be a secretary working for that organization. By all means, show Mr. Garvin in. Let's see what *he* looks like. There's a chance he may be the other point of a triangle."

"He's a well-rounded point, then," Della Street said, laughing.

"Heavy?"

"Well-fed."

"How old?"

"Around forty. Well-tailored, manicured. Probably accustomed to getting what he wants when he wants it."

"Well, well! Apparently he has the external appearance of a first point in a triangle. The second could be a jealous wife, and the third a blonde girl with smoldering slate-gray eyes and a—well, you know . . ."

"I believe 'superb figure' is the cliché you're trying to think of," Della Street said as she moved toward the door of the reception room. "I'll bring Mr. Garvin in."

Garvin ostentatiously consulted his wrist watch as he entered the office. "Thought you'd never get here, Mason," he said. "Been waiting twenty minutes. Damn it, I don't like waiting for anyone."

"So it seems," Mason said dryly.

"Well, I'm not talking about this instance," Garvin said. "I mean generally. I've noticed you coming in and out several times, Mason. Never thought I'd have occasion to consult you but—well, that's the way it is."

"Sit down," Mason told him. "What can I do for you?"

Garvin glanced at Della Street.

"She stays," Mason said. "Makes notes, keeps my time straight and my appointments."

"This is a delicate matter."

"I specialize in delicate matters."

"I recently married a mighty fine young woman, Mason. I—well, it's important that nothing happen to that marriage."

"Why should anything happen to your marriage?"

"There are—complications."

"Tell me about it. How long have you been married?"

"Six weeks," Garvin said somewhat belligerently.

"A second wife?" Mason asked.

"There's the rub," Garvin told him.

"Well, let's have it," Mason said.

Garvin settled himself in the overstuffed client's chair, after first unbuttoning his double-breasted coat. "Mason," he said, "how good are Mexican divorces?"

"They have a certain value," Mason said. "It depends on the jurisdiction."

"How much value?"

"Well," Mason told him, "they all have a certain psychological value."

"What do you mean?"

"Technically," Mason said, "when a man has a Mexican divorce and remarries, the authorities *could* get tough about it. Actually they don't do very much about it, where it appears a man acted in good faith, because if they did, they wouldn't have enough jails in the country to hold all the persons charged with bigamy. It would break up all sorts of families, disrupt the domestic life of the state, and, after the state had gone to the trouble and expense of getting a conviction, the judge would usually impose a sentence of probation."

"They're good, then."

"Some good," Mason said smiling. "Of course if you want a careful, exact opinion, it would take study. While it isn't generally known, the Mexican government doesn't want to have its border courts made a dumping ground for our domestic entanglements. It's done a lot to clean up situations which did exist. But our courts are under no legal obligation to be bound by the validity of Mexican divorces."

"Hang it, Mason," Garvin said, "I'm afraid I'm in a jam."

"Suppose," Mason said, "you begin at the beginning and tell me what it's all about?"

"I married a girl named Ethel Carter ten years ago," Garvin said. "She was a mighty sweet girl then. I remember how completely hypnotized I was—and hypnotism is the right word for it, too, Mason, don't make any mistake about that. As it turned out, she was a cold, clever, scheming—well, I hate to use the word that comes to my mind in front of a lady," and Garvin bowed in the direction of Della Street's desk.

Mason said, "Love brings out the best in people. When love leaves, it frequently happens the best is gone. Perhaps there was trouble on both sides."

Garvin shifted his position. "Well, perhaps," he said, "it's barely possible. But what I want you to realize now, Mason, is that she's a holy terror."

"In what way?" Mason asked.

"In every way," Garvin said. "She's—well, she's a wildcat. You know, that old saying about 'Hell hath no fury like a woman scorned.' "

"How long have you been separated?"

"I don't think the separation had so much to do with it," Garvin said. "It was when I remarried. She became absolutely insane with rage."

"By the way," Mason asked, glancing significantly at Della Street, "what does your present wife look like?"

"A beautiful redhead, with the bluest of blue eyes, Mason. You can look right down into the depths. The fair, delicate skin that goes with a redhead of that type. Hang it, she's beautiful! She's a gem. She's a marvel."

Mason broke in, "I get it. While we're on the subject of women, do you by any chance have a woman in your employ about twenty-three or twenty-four, with a good figure, trim, slim-waisted, long-legged, high-breasted, blonde hair, gray eyes . . ."

"In *my* employ!" Garvin said. "Good Lord, Mason, you make her sound like a Hollywood movie actress!"

"She's good-looking," Mason admitted.

Garvin shook his head. "Don't know anyone."

"Know anyone by the name of Colfax?" Mason asked.

Garvin thought. "Yes," he said, "I had a business deal at one time with a man by the name of Colfax, some sort of a mining deal. I can't remember much about it. I have a lot of things on my mind. However, I wanted to talk to you about my first wife."

"Go ahead."

"Well," Garvin said, "we separated about a year ago. Now, there was something strange about that separation. My wife and I hadn't been getting along too well and I'd been—well, I'd been turning to other interests, staying at the club a lot, playing a little poker, going out with the boys. But my wife was not sitting home, pining her life away . . . Hang it, Mason, we'd just reached the point where we'd started to grow apart. Frankly, she bored me and I suppose I bored her. Anyway, when the separation came there were no hard feelings, no tears shed. It was just a plain business matter. I gave her a mine in New Mexico that looked pretty good."

"Any formal property settlement drawn up?" Mason asked.

"Now, on that I admit I made a little mistake. I didn't have it formal, but Ethel had always been pretty square that way. We talked things over and I gave her this mine and we were going to see how it turned out. If it turned out all right, she was going to take that as a complete property settlement; if it didn't turn out so good, I told her we'd make some sort of an adjustment."

"And did it turn out good?"

"I *think* it was all right," Garvin said, "but the point is Ethel went out to New Mexico, stayed at the mine for a while, then wrote me she was going to Nevada to get a divorce. Then after a while I heard in a more or less roundabout way that she had a divorce."

"A letter from her?"

"From one of our mutual friends."

"You've saved that letter, and the letter from your wife?"

"Unfortunately I haven't."

"*Did* she get a divorce in Reno?"

"Apparently not."

"Tell me the rest of it."

"Well, I met Lorraine Evans." His face lit up with a fatuous smile. "I can't begin to tell you about Lorrie, Mason. It was just like turning back the hands of the clock. She has everything that I'd expected to find in Ethel when I first married her. Hang it, I still can't believe my good fortune."

"I know. She's a gem! She's a dream! But now let's get on with it," Mason said impatiently.

"Well, I hadn't bothered about records before, but after I met her and—well, I wanted to be sure I was free, so I wrote to Reno and tried to find records of my wife's divorce, and apparently there weren't any."

"Then what?"

"Well," Garvin said uncomfortably, "I'd acted on the assumption, of course, that there had been a divorce in Reno, particularly after receiving that letter from our friend about Ethel's divorce."

"What did you do?"

"Well, I—I tell you, Mason, I'd naturally acted on the assumption I was a free man and . . ."

"What did you do?" Mason asked.

"Well, I'd gone pretty damn far by the time I found out that there was some question about a Reno divorce . . . I still thought that there was a divorce there, all right, but that the records were missing or something."

"So what did you do?" Mason asked.

"Well," Garvin said, "I went down to Mexico and had a talk with a lawyer there who told me I could establish a residence by some sort of proxy and—well, he made it sound pretty good. Anyway, I got a Mexican divorce and Lorrie and I were married afterwards in Mexico. We followed a procedure worked out by a lawyer in Mexico. He seemed to know his business."

"And then what happened?" Mason asked.

"Well," Garvin said, "I'm worried about Ethel. She's—she's suddenly turned bitter. She wants a property settlement. She wants things that would completely ruin me. She wants—me!"

"And so," Mason said, "you find yourself with two wives on your hands?"

"Well," Garvin said, stroking his heavy jaw, "I hoped it wouldn't come to that, Mason. I'd rather be a happy bridegroom than a dubious one. I hoped that Mexican divorce would be good. I wanted to find out something about it."

Mason said, "I'll look into your Mexican divorce. Where's your first wife now?"

"She's right here, in the city somewhere, but I don't know where. She telephoned me from a pay station. She won't give me her address."

"She has a lawyer?"

21

"She says she's going to handle the property settlement by herself."

"Doesn't want to pay a lawyer's fee?" Mason asked.

"No," Garvin said, "she's smarter than any two lawyers in the country—present company excepted, of course. The woman's damned clever. She was my secretary before I married her, and believe me, she certainly knows her way around when it comes to business—a smart woman."

"All right," Mason said, "I'll see what I can do. It's going to cost you money."

"I expected that."

"By the way," Mason said, "your present wife—was she down at your office last night?"

"Down at the office? My wife? Heavens, no!"

"I thought I saw a light up there," Mason said. "I was looking out of the window, and I noticed light striking the upper landing of the fire escape. I believe your office is directly above mine."

"That's right, it is," Garvin said, "but you couldn't have seen a light in my office. It must have been in the office up above that, Mason. No one works in my office at night."

"I see," Mason said. "Well, I'll look into it. Go into that other office and dictate all the data to Miss Street. Give her all the names, addresses, descriptions, anything else you can think of. And leave a check for a thousand-dollar retainer. We'll get busy on it."

3

■

It was midafternoon when Paul Drake entered Mason's office, walking with a loose-jointed gait that gave him the appearance of extreme indolence.

"Hi, Perry."

"How are you, Paul? You certainly don't look the romantic picture."

"What do you mean, the romantic picture?"

Mason grinned, "I was thinking of the description I heard a short time ago of the private detective. A young woman was very much thrilled with the glamour of your occupation, but there was a shudder that went along with the thrill."

"Oh, that," Paul Drake said in a bored voice as he seated himself in the big client's chair. "It's a hell of a job."

"What have you found out about the Garvin Mining, Exploration and Development Company?" Mason asked.

Drake lit a cigarette, sprawled around in the chair until he had his legs draped over one of the overstuffed arms, the other used as support for the small of his back. "Garvin," he said, "is an impulsive sort of a guy."

"In what way?"

"He married his secretary, an Ethel Carter. They got along fine together. Everything was all hunky-dory until the new wore off, and after the new wore off Garvin started looking around."

"I know," Mason said, "then he married Lorraine Evans."

"In between there were two or three other affairs that didn't terminate in marriage."

"And what about Ethel Carter Garvin?"

"Now there," Drake said, "you have a problem. She's reported to have divorced him in Reno, but there's no record of the divorce."

"And what about the company, Paul?"

"It's a corporation. Sort of a holding company. Garvin is a sharpshooter. He picks up mines and prospects. When he finds something that looks good, he turns it in to the Edward Charles Garvin Company, which is a partnership consisting of Garvin and a dummy. Then the partnership turns it over to the Garvin Mining, Exploration and Development Company at a fat profit."

"How come?" Mason asked.

"Just his way of doing business."

"Income tax?"

"How would I know? You're the lawyer."

Mason said, "If he's on the board of directors of the Garvin Mining, Exploration and Development Company, he's hardly in a position to make a profit on selling stuff to his own company."

"That's where he's smart," Drake said. "He isn't even a member of the board of directors. He's the guy that tells 'em what to do, but he's merely the general manager."

"And owns a majority of the stock?"

"No, apparently he controls the whole thing, however, by keeping the confidence of a widely scattered list of stockholders. You can figure the thing out, Perry. He picks up properties, puts them in his partnership, holds them long enough, until they're developed to a point where the value is pretty well assured. Then he gives the Garvin Mining, Exploration and Development Company an opportunity to take them off his hands at a profit. He keeps the management in his own hands, pays himself a nice fat salary and a bonus based on profits. Where the guy is smart is in operating the company in such a

24

way that the stockholders make a nice profit. As long as they're getting a juicy profit, they don't care very much what happens. Everyone who owns stock in the company thinks Edward Charles Garvin is the last word in acumen as a manager . . . Now, that's all I could find out about it, just offhand. There's no Virginia Colfax in the picture, and I don't get any trace of a blonde-haired gal such as you described."

"Well," Mason said, "it was just an exploratory job when I first got in touch with you. Now it's going to be a real job. Garvin's first wife is somewhere here in the city. I want to find her and put a shadow on her and know what she's doing twenty-four hours a day."

"Okay," Drake said. "I don't know just how long it'll take us to locate her. Depends on whether she's really trying to keep under cover."

"When you get her, don't lose sight of her."

"I won't."

Drake started to get up out of the chair, then, as an afterthought pushed his hand down into his pocket and brought out a folded paper.

"What's that?" Mason asked.

"Proxy for the next stockholders' meeting of the Garvin Mining, Exploration and Development Company," Drake told him. "I got my information from a stockholder about most of the setup."

"How in the world did you ever locate a stockholder in the short time you had to work in?" Mason asked.

"Oh," Drake said, "it's just one of those things—part of the job."

"You interest me, Paul. How did you do it?"

"Well, I have a couple of friends who are interested in gold mining. I rang them up and asked them about Garvin's company. They gave me quite a bit of the background. I asked them if they could put me in touch with a stockholder so I could get the information right from the back door of the stable, so to speak, and one of my

25

friends knew a chap he thought knew Garvin. He rang him up and found that he was a stockholder in the company."

"You didn't interview him?" Mason asked.

"Of course not. I had my friend gently pump him. This guy started talking because a funny thing had happened. He had been out of the state for a while and when he got back, found this proxy in his mail for the stockholders' meeting, day after tomorrow. He couldn't understand it because he'd already sent in another proxy before he left. Proxies have to be on file with the secretary for a period of ten days prior to the stockholders' meeting."

Mason held out his hand, took the proxy, opened it, and glanced through it, then frowned and said, "The man said he'd already sent in a proxy?"

"That's right."

Mason glanced through the proxy, then dropped it on the desk. "That's made out in a peculiar way, Paul."

"How come?"

"This proxy provides that the voting rights are given to E. C. Garvin, holder of Certificate Number 123 of stock in the corporation."

"Well, what's wrong with that?"

"I don't know," Mason said, "but usually a proxy is made out in favor of a certain individual and it's not necessary to tack on a lot of descriptive material . . . And he had already signed one proxy?"

"Yeah. He told this friend of mine he thought they'd sent the second one to him by mistake."

"Okay," Mason said. "We'll let it go at that. Take a look around and see what you can find out about Garvin's first wife, Paul."

Drake slid off the chair and said, "I should have a line on her pretty quick. You don't know whether she's staying in a hotel, an apartment house, or where?"

"No faintest idea," Mason said.

"Know anything about who her friends or associates are?"

The lawyer shook his head.

"You seem to think a detective can pull a rabbit out of the hat just any old time he reaches in," Drake complained. "You might at least give a guy something to work on."

"I can give you a five-hundred-dollar retainer to work on," Mason said.

"Okay," Drake grinned, "tell Della to make out a check and send it along."

Drake crossed the office, opened the door and walked rapidly down the corridor toward his own office.

Mason picked up the proxy, studied it.

"Why do you think that's so important?" Della Street asked.

"Because of a remarkable coincidence," Mason told her, folding the proxy and putting it in his pocket. "Does it occur to you," Mason asked, "that the initials of Edward Charles Garvin are exactly the same as those of Ethel Carter Garvin? Now then, note that this proxy is issued to the E. C. Garvin who holds Stock Certificate Number 123 in the corporation and that *all prior proxies are hereby revoked.*"

"You mean," Della Street asked, "that . . ."

"Exactly," Mason interrupted. "I mean that if it should turn out that the holder of Certificate Number 123 is Ethel Carter Garvin, then every one of the stockholders who has signed one of these second proxies has automatically revoked the proxy that he had previously given to Edward Garvin, and his wife can walk into the stockholders' meeting with a fistful of proxies, put in her own board of directors, fire Edward as general manager, and run things to suit herself."

"Oh, oh!" Della exclaimed.

Mason said, "See if you can get hold of Garvin, Della. We'll find out about this."

Della Street nodded, and, consulting the memo of telephone numbers Garvin had given her when he had made out his check, sent busy fingers flying around the dial of the telephone while Mason devoted himself to cleaning up some of the mess of lawbooks left on his desk from the research he had conducted the night before.

At the end of ten minutes Della Street made her report. "Mr. Garvin can't be reached before the stockholders' meeting. As soon as he left our office, he went off on a trip. He told his secretary he was going to look at some mining properties. My guess is he's on the second installment of a honeymoon."

"Damn him, he could have told me he was planning that," Mason said. "Well, get the secretary and treasurer of the company. Tell him to come down here. I want to see him. Tell him that we're representing Mr. Garvin and I want him down here on a matter of the greatest importance."

"They already know you're representing Garvin," Della Street said. "His secretary put through the check for a thousand dollars."

"All right," Mason told her, "get the secretary and treasurer of the corporation, whoever he may be, to come on down here, and tell him to make it snappy."

A few minutes later Della Street took a phone call from the outer office and said to Mason, "Mr. George L. Denby is in the office, chief."

"Who's Denby?"

"He's the secretary and treasurer of the company upstairs."

"Show him in," Mason said.

Denby, a thin, formal individual, with glasses, gray hair, a loosely fitting suit and cold hands, introduced himself to Perry Mason, shook hands and sat down. He hitched up the knees of his trousers before crossing his legs as he settled down facing the attorney.

Mason said, "I'm representing Garvin."

"I understand so. May I ask if you're representing him as an individual, or did he retain you to look after the interests of the corporation?"

"I'm representing Garvin," Mason said. "I take it he has a diversity of interests?"

"Oh, yes."

"Some of which are in the corporation?"

"Yes."

"Does that answer your question, then?" Mason asked with a smile.

Denby's ice-cold eyes peered out from behind his spectacles. "No," he said.

Mason threw back his head and laughed.

Denby didn't even smile.

Mason said, "All right, I'm representing him as an individual, put it that way. Now then, a certain matter has come to my attention which bothers me."

"What is it, Mr. Mason?"

"Who holds Certificate Number 123 in the corporation?"

"I'm sure I couldn't tell you, offhand, Mr. Mason."

"When's your stockholders' meeting?"

"Day after tomorrow."

"What time?"

"Two o'clock."

"It's a regular annual meeting?"

"Oh, yes."

"What are the provisions in the bylaws about proxy voting, if any?"

"Really, Mr. Mason, I can't answer *that* offhand. I believe the provisions conform to the state law."

"Garvin holds a lot of proxies?"

"I believe so, yes."

"How many?"

"I'm afraid I'm not at liberty to discuss the affairs of the corporation, Mr. Mason—under the circumstances."

"I see," Mason said. "Go up to your office and check

through your files. See how many proxies have been sent in for E. C. Garvin to vote."

"Yes, of course, Mr. Mason, I'll be very glad to check on that."

"And then let me know."

"That, unfortunately, Mr. Mason, is an entirely different matter. It's a matter which concerns the corporation, as well as Mr. Garvin. I would require specific authorization from some officer of the company."

"Get that authorization, then."

"That might not be easy."

"I didn't ask you whether it would be easy—I told you to get it. It's in the best interests of the corporation."

"Of course, it calls for confidential information. Even Mr. Garvin—well, Mr. Garvin, Mr. Mason, is not an officer of the company."

"Who's the president?"

"Frank C. Livesey."

"Is he up in the office now?"

"No. He was in earlier in the day, but he left."

"Get him on the phone," Mason said. "Tell him what's cooking. Suggest to him that he'd better get in touch with me."

"Yes, sir."

"He's listed in the telephone book?"

"I believe so, yes."

"See what you can do," Mason said.

"Very well." Denby arose, said, "I trust you will appreciate my position, Mr. Mason. Of course, I understand that . . ."

"That's all right," Mason told him. "Go right ahead. Let me have what information you can."

As soon as Denby had left the office Mason nodded to Della Street. "Look through the telephone directory for Frank C. Livesey and . . ."

Della Street smiled. "I have already done that. As soon as he mentioned the name I started looking."

"Got the number?"

"Yes."

"See if you can get him on the phone," Mason said.

Della Street whirled the dial of the telephone, her fingers flying over the numbers, said, "Hello . . . hello. Is this Mr. Frank C. Livesey? Just a moment, Mr. Livesey, Mr. Mason wants to talk with you—Mr. Perry Mason, the lawyer. Just hold the phone a moment, please."

Mason picked up the telephone and said, "Hello. Mr. Livesey?"

A cautious voice over the wire said, "This is Mr. *Frank* C. Livesey."

"You're president of the Garvin Mining, Exploration and Development Company?"

"Yes, Mr. Mason. May I ask the reason for your inquiry?"

"Something is going on which I think may affect the corporation. I'm representing Mr. Garvin. I've run into a snag when it came to getting information out of Denby, the secretary-treasurer."

Livesey laughed and said, "You would."

"Meaning he's hostile to Garvin?" Mason asked bluntly.

"Meaning that he's a stickler for formality and red tape," Livesey said. "What's the trouble, Mr. Mason?"

"I don't like to tell you over the phone."

"All right, I'll come to your office at once."

"Do that," Mason said, and hung up.

4

■

FRANK C. LIVESEY WAS A PUDGY, JOVIAL INDIVIDUAL, with a stubby red mustache, popeyes and a partially bald bullet head. The tightness of his clothes indicated that he had put on weight since buying his suit. His figure indicated that this process had been going on for years, but had not affected the optimism which always possessed him when buying new clothes.

He was around forty, and his eyes lit with the appreciation of a connoisseur as he glanced at Della Street.

"Well, well, Mr. Mason, how are you?" he said, with genial cordiality, but his eyes dwelt on Della Street.

He advanced across Mason's office, hand pushed out in front of him, grabbed the lawyer's hand and wrung it heartily.

"Sorry to have kept you waiting, Mason. I'm very sorry indeed. But I wanted to check up on a couple of things before I came down to talk with you. Frankly, Mason, the situation is incredible."

"What's wrong with it?" Mason asked.

"It's incredible, absolutely incredible. Things are in a hell of a shape."

"Tell me about it."

"Well, now, the setup of the Garvin Mining, Exploration and Development Company is a little peculiar, Mason. I can't go into details but Garvin, of course, is the big shot. For legal purposes he likes to keep in the background. On the advice of counsel, he's kept off the board of directors and doesn't hold any elective office. Because of certain deals with a partnership his interests in that are perfectly all right as long as he's only a stockholder, but they might be questioned if he were a director."

Mason nodded.

"But, of course," Livesey went on, "you understand the situation, Mason. We're all of us Garvin's men. In fact, we're—well, I may say we're dummies for Garvin . . . Now, I shouldn't put it that way. That sort of slipped out. But, after all, Mason, you're Garvin's lawyer and you're nobody's fool."

"And, I take it," Mason said, "after I telephoned you, you delayed coming to see me until you could have a talk with Mr. Denby?"

"Exactly," Livesey said. "After all, you're a busy man. There's no use taking up your time talking about something unless I know what I'm talking about. I wanted to find out."

"And did you find out?"

"I did indeed. That woman! That Ethel Garvin! She's smart, Mason. She's smart as a whip!"

"Exactly what has she done?"

"Well, we sent out proxies in the usual form, made out to E. C. Garvin, and I'm damned if she didn't send out other proxies made out to 'E. C. Garvin, holder of Certificate of Stock 123.' Well, you've guessed it, Mason, Certificate of Stock Number 123 was made out to Ethel Garvin four years ago when she and Ed were all hunky-dory and everything was sitting pretty."

"What happened to the original proxies?" Mason asked.

"They're all in order, all right," Livesey said. "They're filed in alphabetical order, just as neat as a pin. You've met Denby. You know how he'd go about it, filing 'em all in order with cross references to the stock ledger and all that."

Livesey threw back his head and laughed.

"But it would certainly seem to me that *someone* would have realized the situation when these other proxies began to come in," Mason said. "Certainly Denby must have known that he didn't send those proxies out, and when a new proxy, made to E. C. Garvin, holder of Certificate 123, came in, you'd certainly think Denby would have checked up on it."

"You would, for a fact," Livesey said. "But the funny part of it is that Denby doesn't know when those proxies came in. They're there all right; they're signed, all right, and they're filed neatly, in apple-pie order. But they must have come in all at once and some filing clerk did the job. Denby swears they never went across his desk. He says he'd have known about them if they had."

"And the stockholders' meeting's day after tomorrow?"

"That's right, and I don't mind telling you, Mason, there's hell to pay. We can't get hold of Garvin. He's off on a second honeymoon, all wrapped up in that new redhead of his. Doesn't want anyone to know where he is. Doesn't want to be disturbed by business. And he is faced with the loss of his whole company! I'm worried. I'm frightened."

"What will happen if Ethel Garvin gets control?"

"What will happen? Good Lord, she'll have the books audited! She'll shake down this, that and the other. She'll put in her own board of directors. She'll sue the Garvin partnership for fraud on a couple of deals that haven't panned out so well. She'll call in the income tax people and point out certain things that we've been keeping covered up. She'd wreck the whole damn business. She'd collapse the whole house of cards!"

"Has Denby checked with any of the filing clerks, to see who filed those other proxies?"

"Well, in a quiet sort of a way he's snooping around. He doesn't want any of the help to know that anything's wrong. He's asking a few guarded questions and . . ."

The telephone on Mason's desk, that had an unlisted number known only to Della Street and Paul Drake, sounded strident summons.

Mason picked up the receiver, heard Paul Drake's

voice saying, "Excuse me for ringing on the emergency line, Perry, but I thought you'd want this right away. I've located Ethel Garvin."

"The deuce you have! How did you do it so fast, Paul?"

Drake said casually, "Just used my head and the telephone. I keep a lot of odds and ends of information such as membership lists of the principal women's clubs. When she was living with Garvin, she was a member of a well-known book study club. I started ringing up all the members on the list, asking them if they knew where I could get in touch with Mrs. Ethel Garvin about a rare book she had been searching for. The second rattle out of the box I struck pay dirt. The woman said Mrs. Garvin had been out of town for a while but she'd happened to run into her on the street and learned she was staying at the Monolith Apartments. I started checking from there, found her hairdresser, and picked up a little gossip."

"Damn it," Mason said, "every time you tell me how you do this stuff it sounds so simple I hate to pay you for it."

"You can go right on paying! You want me to do anything else, Perry?"

"Yes, keep a shadow on her twenty-four hours a day."

Mason glanced out of the corner of his eye at Frank Livesey who was now sitting forward on his chair, his ear craned forward, eyes wide. "Whenever I get hold of a witness in an automobile accident," Mason went on casually, "I don't want to lose sight of her. She's probably the only one who can testify as to which car was first at that intersection. I want to get a written statement from her just as soon as I can clean up some of this other stuff."

There was a moment's silence at the other end of the line, then Drake said, "Some client in the office where he can hear, Perry?"

"That's right," Mason said.

"I take it the first part of that, about putting a shadow

on her twenty-four hours a day, is what you really want, and the rest was a stall?"

"That's right."

"Okay," Drake said, "it's done."

Mason hung up the telephone, said to Livesey, "I'm sorry, but that was an important call. I'm working on an automobile collision case where there were very serious bodily injuries . . . Well, now let's see. Let's get back to this thing. You think there are some skeletons in the closet of the Garvin Company?"

"Well, now," Livesey hedged, "I'm trying to use my best judgment in the absence of Ed Garvin, Mr. Mason, but—well, let's just consider that I've told you everything I can . . . Matter of fact, Mason, I've told you too damn much."

"You're a heavy stockholder in the company?" Mason asked.

Livesey grinned, and said, "Don't make any mistake about me, Mason. I hold one share of stock in the company, just enough to qualify for the board of directors and be president." He grinned at Mason, then added, "The salary's good and the duties of office consist mostly in signing my name and furnishing entertainment for the visiting firemen."

"You don't happen to have anyone working in your stenographic department by the name of Colfax, do you?"

"Heavens, Mr. Mason, I wouldn't know. I don't think so. We keep a few girls busy, not too many."

"This one is a girl about twenty-two or twenty-three, long-legged, slim-waisted, smooth-hipped, high-breasted, with steady, slate-gray eyes, fine blonde hair, and . . ."

"Stop it!" Livesey groaned. "You're killing me. I can't take it. You're breaking my heart."

"You know her?" Mason asked.

"Gosh, no, but I sure wish I did! If she's someone you're looking for, cut me in on it, will you, Mason?"

And Livesey threw back his head, laughed roguishly and then preened his stubby red mustache.

Mason said, "If you have to do quite a bit of entertaining you perhaps have a list of young women who can be called in as partners."

Livesey chuckled. "I see you know a bit about selling stock, Mr. Mason."

"And perhaps this girl's name and address are in your little black notebook. Perhaps she's available for dinner dates, or a dancing partner?"

"Could be."

"But you don't remember her?"

"I wish I did."

"If you should recall her later will you let me know?"

"I will for a fact, Mason. I most certainly will."

Mason said, "What are you going to do about those proxies?"

"Frankly, Mason, I'll be damned if I know. It looks as though there's going to be a regular free-for-all at that annual stockholders' meeting and I'm frank to tell you I haven't the faintest idea what to do about it."

Mason said, "If you know of any way to get in touch with Garvin, you'd better go to work on that angle."

Livesey looked glum.

"And in the meantime," Mason went on, "you'd better investigate your own organization and see if you can't find who filed those new proxies."

"I'd give a lot to know that one," Livesey said. "It looks to me as though someone was double-crossing us."

Mason said, "I wish you'd check your entire organization and find out if anyone was working last night about eleven o'clock. See if anyone was in the office."

"I'll do that."

"And then let me know," Mason said, standing up to indicate that the interview was over.

"Okay, thanks," Livesey said.

He heaved himself up out of the big chair, and

seemed reluctant to leave. Twice as he walked toward the door, he hesitated as though about to turn back and attempt to renew the conversation, but he reached the door, turned, smiled, bowed, caught Della Street's eyes, gave her a special smile and then backed out into the corridor.

Della Street waited until the door had closed, then made a little grimace. "God's gift to women," she said, and then added bitterly, "put that in quotes and sign it Frank C. Livesey."

Mason laughed. "He's probably Santa Claus to a certain type of party girl."

"A certain type," Della said, "but he's forgotten that Santa Claus only picks the chimneys where stockings are hung."

Mason smiled, picked up his phone, dialed Paul Drake's number, and then, when he had the detective on the line, said, "Here's another job for you, Paul. That fool client of ours seems to have decided this is a good time to take himself out of circulation.

"He can't be very far because he must be planning on attending that stockholders' meeting day after tomorrow. But he's out with his new wife on the second installment of a honeymoon.

"I want him. Find out what car he's driving, get the lowdown on the places he likes to go, see how much baggage he took and—hell, find him, that's all."

"Okay," Drake said in a bored voice, "if a client wants to pay me money to find him, it seems a cockeyed way to spend his money, but I should worry about that."

"And let me know at once, no matter what hour of the day or night it is," Mason went on.

"Okay, you'll hear from me," Drake said and hung up.

MASON PARKED HIS CAR IN FRONT OF THE MONOLITH Apartments, a brick-faced corner building with severely plain lines. Paul Drake's man, on duty in a car parked across the street, was apparently a rather harassed individual looking through the classified section of the newspaper in search of apartments available to renters of average income. He didn't even look up as Perry Mason swung open the car door, crossed the curb and entered the apartment house.

The man at the desk regarded Perry Mason with polite curiosity, but a complete lack of cordiality.

"Mrs. Ethel Garvin," Mason said.

"Does she expect you?"

"Tell her it's about a proxy."

"Your name?"

"Mason."

The man turned to a switchboard, and, with the obvious condescension of one who is engaging in a menial work which he is quite certain is beneath his dignity, plugged in a line, waited a moment, then said, "There's a Mr. Mason to see you about a proxy, Mrs. Garvin . . . No, he didn't say . . . Shall I ask him? . . . Very well.

"You may go up," the clerk said, pulling out the telephone connection. "Room 624."

"Thank you," Mason said.

Mason entered the elevator, saw that it was designed so that it could be manipulated by an operator during the daytime and turned on to automatic by night, said, "Six, please," and waited.

The woman who was running the elevator, a big woman with sagging muscles and a general air of weariness, put down the magazine she was reading, glanced expectantly down the corridor, hopeful of more customers before she closed the door. She was seated on a folding chair and her hips seemed to spread out over each side. A look of extreme weariness was stamped upon her countenance.

"Sixth floor," Mason repeated.

She made no response, but leaned forward to peer once more down the corridor. Then, after an interval, she reluctantly closed the door, and the cage rattled upward to the sixth floor.

The operator opened the door, promptly picked up the magazine she was reading, resumed her place in the story and waited for a call to some other floor.

As Mason stepped out of the elevator and turned to the left, the buzzer on the elevator was calling for the ground floor.

The operator glanced up at the signal, then resumed reading for a few lines before closing the door and taking the cage back down.

Mason followed the corridor, checking the numbers until he came to 624.

He knocked, and the door was promptly opened by a woman somewhere in the thirties who wore a clinging black gown and who smiled graciously.

"Mr. Mason?" she asked, her voice melodiously cordial.

"Yes."

"I'm Mrs. Garvin. You wanted to see me about a proxy, Mr. Mason?" She smiled and the smile was one of warm friendliness.

"Yes," Mason said, "a proxy covering voting privileges in the Garvin Mining, Exploration and Development Company."

"Won't you come in, please?"

"Thank you."

40

Mason entered the apartment. She gently closed the door behind him and said, "Do sit down, Mr. Mason."

While her figure did not have the lines of early youth, it had, nevertheless, maintained the slim-waisted symmetry which comes with a disciplined diet. There was about her face and about her eyes the calm, self-contained look of a woman who has coordinated her life with the greatest care and makes every move as the result of some carefully preconceived plan.

"*Do* sit down, Mr. Mason."

Mason seated himself by the window.

Mrs. Garvin sized him up, then seated herself across from him, crossed her knees, settled back on the davenport, and said, "What about the proxy, Mr. Mason, was there something you didn't understand about it?"

Mason said, "The designation of the person named in the proxy was a little different from the wording in previous proxies, wasn't it?"

She threw back her head and laughed.

Mason waited for an answer.

The laugh became a smile, a roguish, tantalizing smile. "My, Mr. Mason," she said, "did you take *all* the trouble to come up here in order to talk with me about that unfortunate matter of the wording?"

"Yes," Mason said.

"You shouldn't have done that," she said in a tone of voice that indicated she might well have added, "silly boy!"

She shifted her position, sliding her right arm along the back of the davenport. "Really, Mr. Mason," she said, and laughed again.

Mason sat quietly waiting.

She said, "And it must have been difficult for you to have found me. Tell me, Mr. Mason, how did you go about doing it?"

"I hired a detective," Mason said casually.

41

Her entire body stiffened into wary attention. "You did *what?*"

"Hired a detective to find you," Mason said.

"For heaven's sake, why?"

"Because I considered it important."

"And why?"

Mason said, "Just what did you intend to do with your proxies, Mrs. Garvin? Did you intend to take control of the corporation away from your ex-husband?"

"My husband!" she flared.

"Oh, pardon me. I thought you had been divorced."

"Just who are you?" she asked.

Mason said, "I'm an attorney. I have offices in the same building as your husband."

"Are you—did he hire you to come here?"

"Retain is the word one uses in connection with an attorney," Mason said.

"All right, did he *retain* you to come here?"

"Not specifically."

"Then why are you here?"

"Because I'm representing his interests."

"And what do you want?"

"Primarily," Mason said, "I want to know what *you* want."

She said, "As it happens, Mr. Mason, I see no reason why I shouldn't answer that question."

"That's fine."

She indicated a carved wooden cigarette case. "Care to smoke, Mr. Mason?"

"Thank you."

The lawyer took the cover from the cigarette case, extended it to her. She took one and leaned foward for Mason's match. Her eyes glanced up at him with steady appraisal while he was holding the light to her cigarette. Mason lit a cigarette of his own, resumed his chair, thrust his long legs out in front of him, crossed his ankles and said, "Well?"

She said, "Mr. Mason, let's be frank with each other. I think you're going to prove rather a dangerous antagonist."

"Thank you."

"How did you find out about me?"

"I told you, I hired a detective."

"How did you find out about the proxies?"

"That," Mason said, "is another matter."

She tapped the toe of her foot on the carpet, then, with a graceful, feline shrug of her shoulders, squirmed herself into a comfortable position on the davenport, adjusted a cushion to suit herself, and, with a flash of stocking, elevated her legs so that she was half reclining. She took a deep drag of the cigarette, blew a long stream of blue cigarette smoke toward the ceiling. "Interesting, isn't it?"

"Very," Mason said.

"My darling husband," she said, "has accumulated himself another woman. He wanted to trade me in on the new model but something happened and he got all mixed up with the pink slip. I'm afraid I'm still his and the defect in title may be with the new model."

"And so?" Mason asked.

"And so," she said, "Mr. Mason, I intend to show my claws—just a little bit."

"And, specifically, what do you want?"

"I want him."

"You mean you would like to hold him legally, whether he wants to be held or not."

She half closed her eyes and studied him thoughtfully, then she said, "I'm going to tell you something, Mr. Mason."

"Go ahead."

"Perhaps," she said, "because I rather like your face; perhaps because I happen to feel philosophical. Are you married?"

"No."

43

"When a man possesses a woman," Mrs. Garvin said, "he has acquired a very peculiar possession. It is, in a way, an emotional mirror, a sounding board, an animated echo of his emotions. He gets back exactly what he gives.

"During the honeymoon, while he looks upon her as an angel, she looks upon him as a god. There is a period of mutual, worshipful admiration. Then, as the glamour wears off and the man realizes that he has acquired a working partner, he gets in return a working partner."

"Go on," Mason said.

Her eyes glittered slightly under the half-closed lids.

"Then," she said, "a man sometimes begins to fret. He begins to chafe at restraint. He begins to be a little restless, because he has lost his freedom. He then does either one of two things. He begins to cheat a little bit, in a quiet, awkward manner, or he begins to nag. In any event, he shows that his wife has become something less than his most prized possession."

"And then what?" Mason asked.

"Then," she said, "he gets paid back in exactly his own coin. If a man is wise, he'll take as much freedom as he feels that he needs; if a wife is wise, she'll give a man as much freedom as he needs to keep him happy. Then the home life will be happy. The man may lie to his wife; he may cheat a little, but he'll always value her as a prized possession. But when he starts regarding her as a ball and chain, she can slam the door of the prison very, very tight, Mr. Mason, lock the door and throw away the key."

"Which is what you have done?"

"What I am going to do, Mr. Mason."

"And just how do you propose to do it?"

She said, "You're a lawyer. You've found out about my little trick with the stock proxies, haven't you, Mr. Mason?"

"Yes."

"Just what do you contemplate doing?"

"On behalf of your husband, I intend to see that any proxies that were fraudulently signed are held to be invalid."

"So that my husband will then be here and assume control of the stockholders' meeting, as usual?"

"Yes."

"I think you are very clever, Mr. Mason. I think that perhaps you know your way around the law. I think perhaps you can do that. However, if you do, I am going to do something that will enable me to achieve my goal by a different method."

"What?" Mason asked.

"Perhaps," she said, "you would care to listen."

She was careless of her legs as she changed position on the davenport, drew the telephone to her, said to the switchboard operator downstairs, "Will you please get me the district attorney's office?"

After a moment she said, "I want the complaint division, please."

After another moment she said, "This is Mrs. Ethel Garvin talking. I am the wife of Edward Charles Garvin, who has gone through a bigamous marriage ceremony and is now living with another women. He has deserted me and is openly cohabiting with this woman as his wife. He did, I believe, go through the formality of an invalid, fraudulent and entirely spurious Mexican divorce. I desire to swear to a complaint against him, charging him with bigamy. Could you give me an appointment for some time tomorrow morning?"

There was a moment's silence, then she smiled and said, "I am aware that you would prefer not to stir up the question of these Mexican divorces, but, as it happens, *I* am the one who is stirring it up. I insist upon swearing to a complaint charging my husband with bigamy. What time may I have an appointment, please?"

Again she listened, then smiled and said, "Ten-fifteen. Thank you very much. And for whom shall I ask? . . .

Yes, Mr. Stockton, yes. The deputy in the complaint department, yes. Thank you very much. At ten-fifteen promptly I'll be there."

She hung up the telephone, turned to Mason. "Does *that* answer your question?"

Mason smiled. "Do you think it will answer yours?"

She regarded him frankly for a moment, then said quietly, "I'll be damned if I know, Mr. Mason, but when I get in a fight I keep moving. You've called my hand and now I'm going to lead my trumps. How many tricks I can take I don't know, but I certainly intend to find out."

"And you really intend to file a complaint against your husband, charging him with bigamy?"

"Mr. Mason, if it's the last thing on earth that I ever do, I intend to charge my husband with bigamy. I'm going to prosecute him to the limit."

"Once you start something like that it's hard to quit."

"Who wants to quit?" she asked, her eyes flaming. "Mr. Mason, will you kindly tell my husband what I said about a man finding in a woman a reflection of his own thoughts? Mr. Mason, my claws are going to be very, very sharp."

Mason said, "Didn't you lead your husband to believe that you had secured a divorce?"

"I am not responsible for what he believed."

"But you told him you were getting a divorce, didn't you?"

"Mr. Mason, a woman quite frequently tells a man a lot of things when she is trying to renew his passion, his love, his regard for her. For instance, she may tell him that she's about to commit suicide; she may make all sorts of threats, all sorts of statements, all sorts of promises."

Mason said, "Under the circumstances, I'm afraid you're going to cost your husband some money."

"I'm afraid I am."

46

"Perhaps not entirely in the way you intended," Mason said.

"What do you mean by that?"

Mason met her eyes. "I mean," he said, "that I'm pretty good at fighting, too. I mean that sooner or later I'll know every place you've been since you left your husband. We'll know all about you. We'll know . . ."

She smiled archly. "Mr. Mason, I don't care how many detectives you employ you'll never know *all* that I've done during the last six months. And even if I had turned my bedroom into a dormitory, you wouldn't have any defense against a prosecution for bigamy. I'm smart enough to know that, Mr. Mason, and you *should* be.

"And now, if you'll excuse me, Mr. Mason, I have other things to do. There are other telephone conversations which I'd prefer you didn't listen in on. *Good* afternoon, Mr. Mason."

Mason arose. She escorted him to the door, said somewhat wistfully, "I wish I'd retained you before Edward did. However, that can't be helped. I'm afraid you're going to make a lot of trouble."

The lawyer stepped into the corridor. "And I'm quite certain *you* are."

Her eyes were suddenly hot with emotion. "You're damn right I am," she said, and closed the door.

6

■

EDWARD C. GARVIN STOOD ON THE PORCH OF THE LA Jolla hotel, looking out over the path that the moonlight made in the waters of the Pacific Ocean.

The second Mrs. Garvin stood beside him.

"Lorrie, darling," Garvin said enthusiastically, *"this* is something like . . ."

"Yes, dear."

"We're embarking on a perpetual honeymoon. Do you love me, darling?"

"Of course."

"Sweetheart, look at me. You keep looking out at the ocean."

She turned to him with a complacent, indulgent smile.

"Say something," Garvin said.

"What?"

"You know what. Say 'I love you.'"

"Oh, Edward," she said impatiently, "you're becoming sophomoric."

"Darling, don't you *feel* the romance? Don't you feel the charm of our surroundings? Here we are away from business. No one knows where we are. We're all alone, out here, standing on the brink . . ."

"And I'm hungry," she broke in.

He laughed. "All right, I'll feed you. Only I don't feel that I want to share you with anyone tonight. Let's have something served in our room."

"Oh, it's terrible down here. They don't have the facilities for room service that they have in the bigger hotels, Ed. Let's go out and get a good hot steak with some shoestring potatoes and French fried onions. There's a very nice restaurant back at the center of town. I noticed it when we came through, and I've eaten there before."

"Very well," Garvin surrendered, "if you want it that way. I *had* hoped we could have dinner on our private balcony, looking out over the water."

"With the moisture creeping in and getting the wave out of my hair?" she demanded. "There's almost a fog." Her laughter was light and all but impatient. "Come, come, Ed, you're getting altogether too romantic. Let's

48

have a cocktail and a steak. Shall we go now? You won't need a hat, dear."

"Just as you say, Lorrie. How about *your* hair? Shall we put the top of the car up?"

"No, we'll leave it down," she said. "I like it better that way. I'll tie a scarf around my hair."

They descended the stairs to the lobby, crossed the lobby to the parking lot where Garvin had left his big convertible. He walked around the car, held the door open for his wife, then walked all the way around the long hood to the door by the driver's seat.

"I'm famished," Lorraine said. "Please hurry."

"Yes, dear, we'll be on our way. You're sure you don't want the top up?"

"No, this is all right."

Garvin started the car. The motor purred a smooth rhythm of easy power. He backed the car out of the parking place, spun it around, made a perfunctory stop at the edge of the highway, waited for a break in traffic, then slipped the clutch back in and the car shot ahead like an arrow, swept into a turn and gathered speed as it headed down the highway.

They drove to the café. Garvin parked his car, got out and hurried around behind the car, to open the door on his wife's side.

He gave her his hand. She put her own hand lightly in it, jumped to the ground with a swirl of skirts.

Tires sounded a screaming protest as a motorist braked his big, heavy car to a sudden stop.

They turned around, and Lorraine Garvin regarded with awakening interest the tall man who slid out from behind the steering wheel of the convertible machine with its top up and strode across toward them.

"Good heavens!" Garvin exclaimed. "It's Perry Mason!"

"The lawyer?" his wife asked.

"That's right."

Mason came toward them. "I've had the devil of a time finding you, Garvin. A twenty-four-hour search."

Garvin drew up with dignity. "Darling," he said, "may I present Mr. Mason. Mr. Mason, my wife."

Mason bowed, said to her, "I'm very pleased to meet you," and to Garvin, "I must see you alone and at once."

"The reason you had the devil of a time finding me," Garvin said somewhat coldly, "is that I didn't want to be found."

"So I gathered," Mason said. "However, you picked a bad time for it. Now give me five minutes, please."

"I'm not interested in business at the moment, but anything you have to say can be said now and here."

"When's your stockholders' meeting, Garvin?"

"Tomorrow at two o'clock in the afternoon. I shall be there, Mason, make no mistake."

"You have enough proxies to control that meeting?"

"Of course I have. Come, come, Mason, this is no time to be talking business. Furthermore, your car is blocking traffic and . . ."

Mason said, "Your wife has sent out a flock of proxies in her own name. Remember that her initials are also E. C."

"His *former* wife," Lorraine said coldly.

"There seems to be some question about that, too," Mason said. "Get back in your car. You're going to Mexico."

"*I'm* going to have a dry Martini and a steak," Lorraine said.

"We're dining tête-à-tête," Garvin explained.

"Oh come, darling, let Mr. Mason join us, and he can talk while we eat."

Garvin shook his head. "I'm in no mood to discuss business tonight."

Mason said, "Ethel has sent out proxies made out in the name of E. C. Garvin, holder of Certificate of Stock

Number 123. She may have enough proxies to give her complete control of the meeting."

"But she can't. I have *my* proxies."

"That were superseded by her later ones," Mason said. "She took good care to see that hers went out *after* yours had been returned. The proxies contain a clause that all prior proxies are revoked."

"Good Lord!" Garvin said. "She'll ruin me!"

"Well, she's not going to ruin my *dinner*," Lorraine snapped.

"Furthermore," Mason went on, "in order to make certain that you won't be at that stockholders' meeting tomorrow, she has gone to the district attorney's office and sworn to a complaint charging you with bigamy. They're trying to arrest you right now. Apparently she . . ."

"Mason, Mason, for God's sake!" Garvin interrupted. "Don't discuss that matter now!"

"Then give me a chance to discuss it in private," Mason snapped. "I've been scouring the state for you for the last twenty-four hours. I wasn't doing that just for fun, you know."

Lorraine bristled. "What's that about bigamy, Mr. Mason?"

Mason said, "You may as well face the facts. Garvin, you can run away from business, but there are other things you can't run away from. This is an issue you're going to have to face and face fast."

"Edward," Lorraine said coldly, "do you mean there's any question about the validity of our marriage?"

Garvin looked uncomfortably at Mason.

Mason said, "I'll give the facts to you straight from the shoulder. There's all sorts of doubt about the validity of your marriage. In all probability, Ethel Carter Garvin is the only one who has any real claim to being Garvin's wife."

"Edward," Lorraine said, "you told me that she had divorced you."

"I thought she had."

"Thought!" Lorraine exclaimed. "Why, of all the . . ."

"Just a minute," Mason said. "Raising your voice isn't going to help matters any, and this is no place for recriminations. I'm going to move my car. I suggest that you follow me. I may be able to help you."

"How?" Garvin asked.

Mason said, "Let's go to your hotel. You can get a bite to eat there if you have to have it before you start for Mexico. Get your bags packed, throw them in the car and get started for the border."

"Why the border?" Garvin asked.

Mason said, "You were divorced in Mexico."

"Well?" Garvin inquired.

Mason grinned. "Your Mexican divorce may not be recognized in California. Your Mexican marriage would be valid only in the event that the divorce was valid. But in Mexico, since you have a Mexican divorce and a legal marriage thereafter, you're husband and wife."

There was a moment of silence, then Lorraine Garvin said, "Well, don't stand there like a dumbbell, Edward. Can't you realize what Mr. Mason is saying? Get that car backed out of the parking place. Let's get to the hotel, get our bags and get the hell out of here!"

7

■

MASON'S CAR FOLLOWED GARVIN'S CONVERTIBLE ACROSS the bridge below San Ysidro.

The lights of Tijuana below the far end of the bridge

52

were an aura against which the steady stars for the moment pitted their brilliance in vain.

Garvin piloted his car down the wide main street and into a parking place where there was opportunity for Mason to run his car in beside theirs.

The lawyer got out, crossed over to Garvin's open convertible and said, "Well, here we are. You're now husband and wife once more."

"Dammit, Mason," Garvin said irritably, "tell me what I'm up against."

Mason said, "I don't know. I'm going to find out as much as I can. The best way to spike her scheme on these proxies is to have enough friendly stockholders there in person to control the meeting. A proxy is always revoked when the person who gave it is present at the meeting.

"That means you've got to give me a list of big stockholders who are friendly and I've got to phone them. I've prepared papers for an injunction which I can file in court tomorrow morning if I have to, but getting your friendly stockholders to attend the meeting in person is the best way. And I'm not entirely satisfied your president and your secretary-treasurer aren't in on the scheme.

"So the next time you plan to skip out and leave business behind, let your lawyer know where you are. I had detectives scouring the country for you. One of them finally located a filling station attendant in La Jolla who remembered your convertible and said you'd been asking about a hotel. So I drove down."

Lorraine Garvin said, "Well, I'm starved. Personally I'm going to have something to eat right now."

"There's a restaurant two doors down," Mason told her. "You can find a place to stay here tonight. Tomorrow you can go on down to Ensenada if you want."

Garvin said, "You folks start on. I want to put up the top on the car."

While he was undoing the fastenings which held the

53

cover of the top in place, Lorraine came close to Mason, said in a low voice, "I'm afraid you're too strong, too resourceful, Mr. Mason. Somehow I just can't feel afraid."

Her hand squeezed his arm.

She looked over at Edward Garvin, said, "He's nice, but frightfully newlywed, if you know what I mean."

"How would *I* know?" Mason asked.

She said archly, "How would *I* know how *you* know?"

Garvin raised the top of the convertible, came to join them.

"When can we come back from Ensenada?"

"Any time you want to face a bigamy charge," Mason said.

"And where does that leave me?" Lorraine asked, thoughtfully.

Mason smiled. "In the United States," he said, "you are an interloper, a corespondent, a mistress, a woman living without legal status, in a state of sin. Here in Mexico you are a lawfully wedded wife."

"That's the damnedest thing!" Lorraine said angrily.

"Isn't it?" Mason agreed. "Such are the ramifications of international law. When you go to the United States, Garvin, you're married to Ethel; you are probably also guilty of bigamy. When you are here in Mexico, you are lawfully wedded to your present companion, and Ethel Garvin is nothing more than an ex-wife who has no legal status."

"I think that's the most absurd damn thing!" Garvin blazed. "I suppose I should build a big house, with the International Border running through the bedroom. I could have triple beds in the room. Ethel could be . . ."

"Edward," Lorraine said frigidly, "don't be coarse."

"I'm not coarse; I'm mad," Garvin yelled. "Damn it, I'm on a honeymoon and I don't even know whether I'm a bridegroom!"

"Get just as mad as you want to," Mason told him,

"but it doesn't affect your legal status. I'm trying to get it straightened out. Now let's eat."

Mason led the way to the restaurant, ordered large, tender steaks and when they were finished said, "There's a new hotel I know here, the Vista de la Mesa. Let's stay there and tomorrow morning you can give me the names of some of the large stockholders who are loyal to your interests, Garvin, and we'll run up a telephone bill."

Garvin said, "Mason, *I'll* telephone stockholders. I want you to make a property settlement with Ethel. Do the best you can. Start with fifty thousand, and . . ."

Lorraine said hastily, "Edward, dear, don't you think you'd better let Mr. Mason be the one to determine the figure? He'll get as low a settlement as possible."

"I want action," Garvin said. "I'm impatient when I want something. How will you locate her, Mason?"

"Through detectives," Mason said, looking at his watch. "I can telephone her tonight and make an appointment for tomorrow morning."

"You have her telephone number?" Garvin asked.

"Yes. She's in 624 at the Monolith Apartments. There's a switchboard there and I can get them to ring her. She was a little difficult when I talked with her yesterday. She thought she had a trump card in that bigamy prosecution. However, when I tell her that you're safely ensconced here in Mexico, where she can't touch you with the bigamy charge, and tell her that you're planning on transferring your property interests, buying a large hacienda in Mexico and living there—well, *that* will give her something to worry about."

Garvin's eyes lit up. "That's a splendid idea, Mason! It's a pippin! That's going to knock her for a loop!"

Mason said, "I'm taking it for granted that Ethel has acquired other romantic interests of her own."

Lorraine's eyes lit up. "Of course she has! Edward, *we* should have thought of that."

Mason said, "From what I've seen of her, she's a good-looking woman who likes to have people admire her. She has a way of doing things so that she shows just enough leg to keep people interested and . . ."

Garvin laughed. "That's Ethel, all right. That's the way she used to be with me. I remember when she was my secretary she . . ."

"Edward!" Lorraine said.

"Pardon, my dear."

Mason said, "Well, before we start talking any cash figure with her, we'll spend some money on detectives and find out a little more about what *she* was doing with *her* time during that period when you didn't hear from her."

"I guess she must have been more in love with me than I thought," Garvin said somewhat thoughtfully. "It was my second marriage that turned her into a hell-cat. She probably felt there was hope of a reconciliation before that."

"Don't be so certain, Edward," Lorraine said, puncturing his ego in well-chosen words. "It was only that when you married me, she saw an opportunity to squeeze money out of you by filing a bigamy charge. You leave things entirely in the hands of Mr. Mason."

The Hotel Vista de la Mesa was back from the main street, a high-class, low, rambling hostelry which had apparently just been completed. The adobe wall which surrounded the place and which had been freshly whitewashed, had an arched entrance and, farther along, an exit. The two big cars crunched up the graveled driveway one behind the other, came to a stop before an eye-pleasing combination of 'dobe bricks, red tile roof, whitewashed walls and green cacti showing in a pastel color combination against the 'dobe.

The woman who was seated behind the desk beamed at them with friendly cordiality.

"We want two rooms," Garvin said. "One for myself and wife and one for my companion."

"But certainly," the woman said in English, "weeth connecting bath?"

"*Separate* baths," Garvin said.

"But that weel be more expensive."

"That's all right. We want the best you have in the house."

Her eyes glistened. "Ah, the señor! He's accustomed to the best, no?"

"Yes," Garvin said.

"And the best here you weel get, Señor. I have two beautiful connecting rooms, but if you do not want to share the bath then you must take both rooms. The room for the other señor must then be in the other wing."

"That will be fine," Garvin said, and, picking up the pen, registered for the three of them.

"How about the cars?" Garvin asked.

"Oh, the cars you leave heem right there in the driveway. No one evaire steals a car from the Vista de la Mesa."

"You have a watchman?" Mason asked.

"No, no watchman, but in thees country you are among honest people, no? But, as a precaution—just as a precaution—you lock the car and you leave the keys weeth me. I put them in the cash drawer. And then, if it should be necessary to move the cars in the morning before you are up, the yard boy can do it and you do not need to be disturbed, and your cars are safe."

Mason said, "Okay, I'll lock up the cars, bring in the keys. And how about the baggage?"

"Unfortunately," she said, "I have no boy on duty tonight. You see, the place ees new. Soon I close up. I have one more room. Only one left. When that is rent, then, poof, I turn out the lights, close up the place and go to bed. No?"

And she smiled again.

Mason turned toward the door, "All right, Garvin, I guess we're elected to bring in our own baggage."

Lorraine said, "All *I* need, dear, is just that little overnight bag."

"Yes, darling."

She smiled at Mason. "I can't begin to tell you how relieved I am to feel that matters are in *your* hands."

"Thanks," Mason told her, "have a good night's sleep."

"I weel show the señora to her room while the señores are getting the baggage, no?"

Lorraine smiled and nodded.

The woman came out from behind the desk. "I am the Señora Inocente Miguerinio," she said. "A hard name for Americans to remember, no?"

"It *is* difficult," Lorraine agreed, good-naturedly.

"But I am running the fine hotel. For so long Tijuana has needed a fine first-class hotel, clean, nice, cool, comfortable. You come with me, Señora."

And the Mexican woman, amply fleshed, rolled ungirdled hips in a seductive, leisurely walk as she led the way through a door in the rear of the office.

Garvin, hurrying out after the baggage, seemed resentful of even the brief few minutes' separation from his wife. While Mason was getting his own bags out of the car, Garvin tugged impatiently at the door of the baggage compartment, pulled out a suitcase and an overnight bag, said, "Well, Mason, I'll be seeing you in the morning."

"What time?" Mason asked.

"Not too early. I . . ."

"Remember, we have a lot of telephoning to do," Mason said.

"Well," Garvin conceded with a sigh, "eight o'clock."

He slammed the car door and started up to the porch.

"Want me to take your keys in?" Mason asked.

"I have them with me," Garvin said. "I'll give them to

the Señora what's-her-name as I go in. Good night, Mason."

"Good night," the lawyer said, and watched Garvin hurry through the entrance, a bag in each hand.

Mason locked his own car, took the ignition keys from the lock, and paused for a moment to admire the stars. The moon had vanished in the west now, and the stars were blazing in steady brilliance through the dry, clear air. The lawyer, who had been working under such great nerve strain for the past few days, stood still in contemplation of the calm tranquillity of the heavens, then he climbed the steps to the porch, entered the lobby, and waited for Señora Inocente Miguerinio to return from showing Garvin to his room.

When the smiling hostess came rolling back into the room Mason said, "Now if you'll show me my room."

"Oh but yes, thees way, please."

Mason followed her through the same door, turned to the right, down the north wing of the building. Señora Miguerinio flung open a door and stood smiling as Mason surveyed the large, commodious room with its comfortable bed, the waxed tile floor, heavy red drapes, shaded floor lamp, and the comfortable mission style furniture.

"See," she said, "a room on the corner weeth windows on both sides—no?"

"Oh, fine," Mason said.

"Thees window, Señor, ees on the patio. That is why the drapes are drawn. You pool thees rope to open and close the drapes—no? But the windows on thees side, Señor, thees open out on nothing—nada. You have here no need for drapes. You can dress, you can undress, nobody looks—no?"

"No," Mason said, smiling.

"You are comfortable—yes?"

"Yes."

Mason handed her the car keys. "Here are the keys to my car."

"You said you weel have the keys to both cars."

"Didn't the other man give you his keys when he came in?" She shook her head. "I should have the keys. Sometimes Pancho has to move the cars in the morning so early ones can get out."

Mason smiled. "He simply forgot about the keys. His car's all right. Let it alone."

"That other man," she said, "he has other things to think of—no?"

And she threw back her head and laughed with a jolly abandon which started her shaking like jelly on a plate.

Mason nodded, put down his bag, said, "Is it possible for me to make a telephone call from here?"

"A telephone call, but certainly. Right in the lobby are two booths. You do not notice them?"

Mason shook his head. "I didn't see them."

"They are not what you call conspeecuous, but they are there—no? You come weeth me. I weel show you."

Mason closed the door of his room, followed her into the lobby and saw two doors which might well have opened into rooms, except that each had painted on it a small picture of a telephone.

"Unfortunately there ees no telephones in the rooms," she said, "but perhaps the guests down here prefer to sleep anyway. Thees is Mexico, Señor. We do not work all during the day and all during the night the way you people do. When we come home from work in Mexico we are done—no?"

Mason, preoccupied with his thoughts, merely nodded.

He entered the phone booth, found a conventional pay station, closed the door, and put through a station-to-station call to Paul Drake's office. He had to wait in the close confines of the booth for some ten minutes before he had Drake's office on the line.

"Drake there?" he asked. "This is Mason calling."

"Yes he is, Mr. Mason. Just a moment."

60

A moment later there was a click and Drake's voice said, "Hello, Perry, where are you?"

Mason said, "I'm staying at a new hotel in Tijuana. A nice little place called the Vista de la Mesa."

"Can I call you there?"

"Not very well. It's a pay station here and they close up the joint. I guess they roll up the sidewalks in this end of town. I'm going to bed and get some sleep. This is a pay station. Just a minute and I'll give you the number."

Mason read the number from the disk on the telephone and Drake said, "Okay, I have it. Now wait a minute, Perry, I've got something for you."

"What?" Mason asked.

"You wanted us to find out all we could about Ethel Garvin. Well, we've struck a lead that may prove promising."

"What?"

"She had a mine in New Mexico. She played around with that for a while and . . ."

"I know all about that," Mason said.

"Then she went to Reno. She took up a residence there, apparently intending to get a divorce. Something made her change her mind. I haven't found out yet what it was, but while she was in Reno she became more or less involved with a man by the name of Alman B. Hackley. Does that name mean anything to you?"

"Not a thing," Mason said.

"Well, he has a cattle ranch up there. Apparently he's a pretty rich chap and quite a playboy. Women went ga-ga over him and Ethel Garvin seems to have fallen in line.

"She was 'taking the cure,' as they call it in that country, and was living at a dude ranch. She did quite a bit of riding and this chap, Hackley, had the adjoining cattle ranch. All of the dude girls who were living at the guest ranch and getting local color along with their six weeks'

61

change of husbands were nuts over him. Ethel somehow got the inside track. He and Ethel Garvin were together a lot."

"Anything serious?" Mason asked.

"Depends on what you mean by serious," Drake said, "but *something* happened. She didn't go ahead and get her divorce. She stayed there six weeks and didn't file. She stayed seven weeks, eight weeks, ten weeks, still didn't file, and then all of a sudden Hackley up and left."

"Sell his ranch?" Mason asked.

"No, he still has this big ranch there, but he came to California. Now here's a funny one, Mason."

"Okay, what is it?"

"He bought property near Oceanside, about fifty miles north of San Diego. Does that mean anything to you?"

"Not a damn thing so far," Mason said, "except that I want to find out something about this Hackley. What's his full name Paul?"

"Alman, A-l-m-a-n, Bell, B-e-l-l, Hackley, H-a-c-k-l-e-y. I've got men searching the records in San Diego and making arrangements to get one of the deputy assessors to go up to the office and open up the assessment rolls. We'll have him located within an hour or two."

"For heaven's sake, Paul, how did you locate him in California?"

"I thought he might be here so I traced the new car registrations. It's something we do all the time."

"Well, Hackley will keep until morning," Mason said, "I'm going to get hold of Garvin first thing in the morning and we're going to get some of the big stockholders of his company to attend the meeting in person. That will supersede all proxies."

"You located him in La Jolla all right?" Drake asked.

"That's right. Your man had a good hunch there. I was just about to cover all the hotels when I happened to see them getting out of their car in front of a restaurant right in the center of town. Tell Della where I am and remember to call me here in case anything of prime importance turns up—but you can't get me until sometime in the morning. I don't know just when. They close this place up tight at night."

"Okay," Drake said, "I was just about to turn in, myself, Perry. I've got things running along smoothly and my investigators are right on the job. You don't want me to make any approach to any of the parties, do you?"

"No, just keep digging up information."

"Well, I . . . hold everything, Perry, here's something just coming in."

"Okay, what is it?" Mason asked.

"A bulletin on this Hackley, and where his ranch is located—you got a pencil there, Perry?"

"I'll have one in just a second," Mason said.

He took a notebook from his vest pocket and a small automatic pencil, opened the book, and placed it on the shelf under the coin slot of the telephone. He said, "Okay, Paul, go ahead. What is it?"

Drake said, "You go to Oceanside and right in the center of town there's a road that turns to the east, with a sign giving the distance to Fallbrook. You turn on that road for about two miles until you come to a mailbox right on the side of the road—the north side. It has the name Rolando, R-o-l-a-n-d-o, C. as in Charles, Lomax, L-o-m-a-x, stenciled on it in black letters. There's a driveway about three hundred feet beyond that mailbox. You follow it for about a quarter of a mile and it brings you up to Hackley's house. He purchased it recently, bought it already furnished."

"Okay," Mason said. "Now you have a shadow on Ethel Garvin?"

"That's right. I have a man sitting in an automobile and watching the place."

"Okay," Mason said. "I guess that'll do the job all right. I'll call you in the morning, Paul."

Mason hung up the telephone, left the booth, and said

to Señora Miguerinio, who was back at the desk, "Can you tell me the number of my friend's room? I want to give him a last word before he goes to sleep."

"But certainly. It ees down that corridor to the left. It ees right across the patio from your room. The two rooms on the corner, numbaire five and numbaire seex. No?"

Mason said, "I'll just run down and tap on the door. Too bad there isn't a phone."

"No, no phone. You see we close at night so we can't have service at a sweetchboard—no?"

Mason nodded, went down the corridor, and tapped on the door of number six.

There was no answer.

Mason raised his voice, said, "Garvin, just a minute," and knocked again.

Garvin opened the door a crack. "What is it, Mason?" he asked, trying in vain to keep his irritation from registering in his voice.

Mason said, "I've just had a telephone message from Paul Drake, my detective."

Garvin opened the door a little wider. "Yes, what is it?"

"I think we've found out the reason your former wife didn't bother you for a while. His name is Alman Bell Hackley. At present he's living on a ranch about two miles east of Oceanside. He owns a big cattle ranch in Nevada and apparently is quite a Romeo. The girls at the dude ranch which adjoins his property were all ga-ga over him."

"What a break!" Garvin said, unable to keep the enthusiasm from his voice. "That's the sort of stuff we want! Is he living there at Oceanside now, Mason?"

"On this ranch," Mason said. "I have directions how to get there."

"What are they?"

Mason gave him the information he had received from Paul Drake. Then he added, "I won't do anything with him tonight, but tomorrow we'll start looking him up a bit."

Garvin's right hand came pushing out through the door. "Mason," he said, "I knew I could depend on you. You're doing a fine job. It just illustrates what I say. When a man wants a doctor or a lawyer, he wants a *good* one!"

From the interior of the bedroom, Lorraine's voice said, "We'd better not make *any* offer until we've found out about this new evidence. Don't you think so, Mr. Mason?"

"I think so," Mason said. "See you in the morning. Good night."

"Good night," they both called.

Mason turned away from the door. Garvin closed it and shot the bolt.

Mason, in order to get to his own room, had to retrace his steps through the lobby.

As he entered the lobby, Mason found that the bright lights had already been turned off. A single desk light gave illumination to the counter. The lights on the outside had been switched off. There was no sign of Señora Inocente Miguerinio.

It was at that moment that Mason realized he had left his automatic pencil in the telephone booth.

Feeling his way cautiously in the dim light across the lobby, Mason opened the door of the booth and was just retrieving his pencil when he heard the voice of a woman in the adjoining phone booth coming through the thin partition.

"Yes, dear," Mason heard her say. "You guessed right ... Yes, dear, across the border in Tijuana."

There were more words Mason couldn't hear, then the woman's voice was raised a bit, "Yes, darling ... No ... I'll do it ... My eyes hurt from watching ... "

Mason gently left the booth, making a note for future reference to be careful of the tin walls which separated the two artistic, but acoustically dangerous telephone booths.

Mason found his room, closed the door, and started undressing.

A clock in the patio chimed melodiously, a full set of rich, throaty chimes, then struck the hour—ten o'clock.

Mason switched out the lights, opened the windows on the west which faced out to what the Señora Inocente Miguerinio had so drastically described as nada, and got into bed.

8
■

FROM SOMEWHERE OUTSIDE THE WEST WINDOW THERE came a series of metallic, strident sounds emanating from some semi-tropical bird Mason could not, for the moment, place.

But, to add to the strangeness of the phenomenon, the bird seemed to have the habits of the woodpecker and kept up a steady tapping against the side of the building.

At length Mason's irritation triumphed over the forces of slumber. The lawyer threw back the covers, sat up in bed and scowled at the window through which could be seen the dry, barren landscape, the first rays of early morning sun turning the mesa to gold.

At that point the lawyer realized that the steady, persistent tapping was not on the side of his room and was not made by a bird, but was a quiet, persistent *tap-tap-tap-tap* on his door.

In bare feet he padded across to the door and opened it.

A wooden-faced Mexican boy stood on the threshold. "Señor Mason?"

Mason nodded.

"Telefono," the boy said, and moved away, sandaled feet sliding along the waxed red tiles of the floor.

"Hey, come back here," Mason said. "Who is it? What . . . ?"

"Telefono," the boy called over his shoulder, and kept on walking.

Mason laughed, then he put on trousers and coat over his pajamas, and, without bothering with socks, thrust his bare feet into his shoes, and in a state of unlaced disarray marched down the corridor to the lobby.

The lobby was deserted but the door of one of the telephone booths was standing open, and the receiver was off the hook and on the shelf.

Mason entered the telephone booth, picked up the receiver, and said dubiously, "Hello."

An impatient voice said, "Is this Mr. Mason?"

"Yes."

"Mr. Perry Mason?"

"Yes."

"Los Angeles is calling. Hold the line, please."

Mason reached out and pulled the door shut. A moment later Paul Drake's voice on the line said, "Hello, Perry?"

"Yes," Mason said. "Hello, Paul."

"I've had the devil of a time getting you," Drake said. "I've been trying ever since five o'clock this morning. I couldn't get any answer down there until just a few minutes ago. Then they said they could get you but the talk was in Spanish and had to be relayed, translated and garbled. Why the devil don't you stay someplace where there's telephone service?"

"What's the trouble?" Mason asked.

Drake said, "I am up against something that I thought you should know about. One of my men made a mistake.

It's an understandable mistake, but nevertheless it's resulted in a botched-up job."

"What happened?" Mason asked.

"We've lost Ethel Garvin."

"The devil you have."

"That's right."

"How did it happen?"

Drake said, "It's a long story if you want it the long way and the easy way. If you want it the short way and the hard way we lost her, and that's that."

Mason thought for a moment, then said, "Give it to me the long and easy way . . . No, wait a minute, Paul. The wall between this telephone booth and the next one is thin as paper. Just a moment, let me check. Hold the line."

Mason put down the receiver, opened the door of the telephone booth, jerked open the door of the adjoining booth, saw that it was empty, then returned to the telephone and said, "Okay, Paul. I was just checking—I overheard snatches of a telephone conversation last night through the wall of the adjoining booth. Now, tell me what happened."

"After ten o'clock," Drake said, "I cut down to one man. By that time there wasn't much doing, and not many people going in and out of the apartment house. I told my man to keep an eye on anyone who looked as though he might be important, simply to check license numbers on the cars, times of arrival and times of departure.

"That's where I made my mistake, Perry. I tried to have one man do too much work.

"My man, of course, had his car parked in a good spot right across from the front door of the apartment house. There isn't a garage in the neighborhood and the tenants leave their cars on the street."

"Go ahead," Mason said, impatiently.

"You wanted it the long way," Drake said. "I'm giving

it to you. Here's what happened. A rather well-dressed man, driving a Buick, circled the block, cruising around, evidently looking for a parking place. From the way he acted my man didn't think he lived in the apartment house. The chap finally found a parking place, turned out the lights, and hurried across to the apartment house. For some reason my operative had a hunch he was about the type that might be calling on our party. He was well dressed and seemed in a hurry, as though he might be trying to keep from being late for an appointment. Putting two and two together, my man decided to go get his license number.

"As I have explained, my man didn't dare to drive around to check up on that license number for fear he'd lose his own parking place, so he jumped out of the car and walked rapidly down the block toward the Buick.

"Well, he'd just got to the Buick when a taxicab swung around the corner and came to a stop in front of the Monolith Apartments. Ethel Garvin must have been in the lobby, waiting. She stepped out of the apartment house door and into the taxi, and they were off—as luck would have it, of course, in the wrong direction.

"My man sprinted back to his car, jumped in, but was in too much of a hurry to start the bus while the motor was cold, managed to flood the carburetor, and—well, what the hell. He lost her. He knows it was a Yellow Cab, but because it went in the wrong direction, he couldn't get the number, and that's that.

"He hurried to a phone and reported at once to the office. My night man got on the job, covering the Yellow Cabs, trying to find where she'd gone. It took us fifteen or twenty minutes to get that information. By that time it was too late. She'd gone to the garage where she keeps her car, a snappy club coupe that can make miles per hour. She didn't even mention where she was going. She had an overnight bag with her. She was wearing some sort of a dark outfit, a jacket and a skirt, and my man thinks she had a little hat tipped over on the left side, but he can't really be certain about that."

"What was the time?" Mason asked.

"Ten-nineteen."

"My man started checking in the apartment house. He claimed it was a cab *he'd* ordered. The clerk at the switchboard insisted *she'd* telephoned for that taxi, then had come downstairs to wait for it. He said she'd been in the lobby for some three or four minutes. He's not particularly communicative. In fact right now, what with one thing and another, he's damned suspicious of the whole setup. Trying to pry information out of him would be like trying to pry into a locked safe with a toothpick."

Mason frowned and gave that information consideration.

"You still on the line?" Drake asked.

"I'm here," Mason said. "Did you keep the apartment house covered?"

"Sure."

"Then she hasn't been back?"

"No. Now, wait a minute," Drake said, "we've got one piece of information out of the clerk that I forgot to tell you. She came downstairs to the lobby, and while she was waiting for the taxicab she took two dollars over to the clerk and asked him if he could give her some quarters, two dimes and a nickel. She didn't want anything larger than quarters. . . Now, there must have been some reason for that."

"I get you," Mason said. "She was going to telephone from a pay station."

"That's right, she had a phone call to make, long distance."

"That's interesting," Mason said.

"Now, unfortunately," Drake went on, "my night secretary is a little too thoughtful sometimes. She knew that I was tired and needed rest and she wouldn't let them call me until around five o'clock this morning. I have a night manager on duty who's a veteran and who did all of the usual things. He got busy with the garage, got a description of her automobile, the make, model, license number, and all that, and found out that the gas tank was only about half full when she took it out. That may mean something.

"When I got on the job at five o'clock this morning," Drake said, "I put another operative in a car and started him for Oceanside. I told him to take a look in a very quiet discreet way around Hackley's house down there and see if he could find any trace of the car. If he couldn't, to circle around Oceanside and see if any of the stations that were open all night had remembered about servicing a car of that description. It may give us a lead. I should be hearing from my man pretty quick now."

"Okay," Mason said. "It looks as though you've done the best you can. Anything else?"

"That's all to date."

"Stay with it," Mason said. "I'll be right here. I guess I can arrange to have them call me—it's pretty early and no one seems to be stirring, but call me back if anything develops, and if I don't hear from you, I'll call you in an hour."

"Okay," Drake said. "I'm sorry, Perry."

"It's all right," Mason told him. "That's one of the things that you just can't guard against."

"I'll call you if anything new turns up," Drake promised.

The lawyer hung up, looked around the lobby, could find no one, went to the front door, opened it and looked out into the driveway and parking space.

There were some half dozen cars in addition to Mason's and Garvin's in the driveway. The wooden-faced Mexican boy who had aroused Mason was sitting on the upper step soaking up the morning sunlight.

"What's *your* name?" Mason asked.

"Pancho," the boy said, without looking around.

Mason took a dollar from his pocket, stepped forward, and the young man promptly shoved out an expectant palm. Mason dropped the dollar.

"Gracias," the boy said, without getting up.

Mason smiled, "You're not so dumb as you look. If you answered that telephone, found out what my room number was and called me, you're a pretty smart boy. You sit right there and listen for that telephone. If it rings again, answer it. If it's for me, you come and call me quick. Understand?"

"Si, Señor."

"Now, wait a minute," Mason said. "You got me all right? You understand English?"

"Si, Señor."

"Okay," Mason said. "If the phone rings again and it's for me, you get another dollar."

Mason retraced his steps through the lobby to his room, showered, shaved, put on clean clothes and was just ready to inquire about breakfast when he heard sandals in the corridor, and a gentle *tap-tap-tap* on the door.

Mason opened the door.

The same boy stood in the corridor. "Telefono," he said.

"Momentito," Mason said, grinning.

The boy paused.

Mason took another dollar from his pocket.

The boy's face lit in a smile. "Gracias," he said, and shuffled off down the corridor.

Mason followed along behind, found the door of the telephone booth open, took the precaution of making certain the adjoining booth was empty, then picked up the receiver, said "Hello," and waited again until he heard Paul Drake's voice on the line.

"Hello, Paul," Mason said. "What's new?"

Drake's voice came over the wire so fast that the

words seemed to telescope each other in rattling their way through the receiver.

"Get this, Perry," Drake said. "Get it fast. We're sitting on a keg of dynamite. My man found Ethel Garvin."

"Where?" Mason asked.

"Oceanside. About two miles south of town, sitting in her automobile parked about fifty or seventy-five feet off the road on the ocean side, dead as a mackerel, a bullet hole in her left temple. From the angle, there's not much chance the wound could have been self-inflicted. She's slumped over the steering wheel and it's rather messy, quite a bit of blood and all that. The window by the steering wheel is rolled down, and the gun, apparently the one with which the crime was committed, is lying on the ground directly beneath the window.

"She *could* have twisted the gun around and managed to fire the weapon herself by holding it upside down, but it's an unnatural position and an unnatural angle for a woman to fire a gun in a suicide attempt."

"What about the police?" Mason asked.

"That's just the point," Drake said. "My man's on the job. He discovered the body. No one else knows it's there—yet. My operative managed to notify me. He's notifying the police but he's notifying them the long way around, calling the sheriff's office in San Diego. It's outside of the city limits of Oceanside, so technically he's within his rights in calling the sheriff's office and the coroner . . . Now get me on this, Perry. My man was too smart to touch the gun or disturb any of the evidence but he's sure been taking in an eyeful. It looks as though two cars had been parked there, side by side, and the other car had driven away—and by bending down my man was able to get the number on the gun. It's a Smith and Wesson .38 and the number is on the tang which crosses the grip on the gun. It's S64805. I'm working my head off trying to trace that gun before the police get all the information. We *may* be just one jump ahead of them."

"Okay," Mason said. "I'm on my way. Get one jump ahead of them and stay one jump ahead of them."

"Garvin and his wife are there with you?"

"Here," Mason said, "but they're not with me."

"What do you want to do about them?"

"Hell," Mason said irritably, "I don't want to do anything about them. I want them to stay right here. Garvin can't get across to the United States without being arrested on a bigamy charge. I don't want to have that happen."

Drake said, "I've had a little trouble getting this call through. I guess on account of getting a call across the border. . . Now, I took it on myself to do something, Perry, that I hope is all right."

"What?"

"I called Della Street as soon as I got the flash and told her to jump into some clothes, grab her car and beat it down to Oceanside just as fast as she could. . . Now my man's playing pretty dumb down there. The way he put the call in and everything there's a pretty good chance there'll be a delay. When he called the sheriff's office in San Diego, he was going to make it sound like a suicide, sort of a routine affair. The sheriff's office probably has some deputy in Oceanside. They'll telephone that deputy to go out and cover the thing. Then the deputy will find it looks like a murder and call back to the sheriff's office and all in all it will be some time before the sheriff and the coroner get there. The body won't be moved until the coroner's office arrives. Now, that's going to give you a chance if you hurry."

"Hell's bells," Mason said, " 'hurry' is my middle name. I'm glad you got Della started. I may want some notes taken."

"I told her to look around and cover everything she could," Drake said. "You should be able to get there from Tijuana just as soon as she can get on the job from Los Angeles, maybe sooner, depending on traffic conditions, and in view of the delay in my getting this call through."

"Okay," Mason said. "I'll get going."

He hung up the receiver, ran down the corridor to his room, threw things in his bag, then sprinted out for the lobby.

Pancho was seated on the front steps.

Mason said, "Pancho, I have two friends here, a Mr. and Mrs. Garvin. They're in Rooms 5 and 6. When they get up, tell them that I had to go away on business, tell them that someone we both know is dead, and that they're to wait right here until they hear from me. They aren't to go anywhere. Tell them to wait right here. You understand?"

"Si, Señor."

Mason said, "I haven't paid my hotel bill. Here's twenty dollars. See that the woman who runs the place gets the money for my room, will you?"

"Si, Señor."

"Okay," Mason said. "I'm on my way."

He flung his suitcase into the car, opened the door, jumped in and was fumbling with the ignition switch when Pancho emerged from the office, grinning, and said in excellent English, "Your keys, Mr. Mason. You leave them in the cash drawer in the desk so that as yard boy I can move the cars in the morning if necessary— only my aunt, Señora Inocente Miguerinio, is very careful to take all of the cash out of the cash drawer when she goes to bed."

Mason grinned, took the keys and said, "You do speak good English, don't you, Pancho?"

"What the hell do you think I go to school for?" Pancho asked.

9

■

PERRY MASON SLOWED HIS CAR AS HE SAW THE LITTLE group ahead.

To the north, the outlying buildings of Oceanside showed white in the morning sunlight. To the west of the highway was a flat mesa and then, beyond that, the sparkling blue of the ocean, lying calm and tranquil under a cloudless sky.

Mason parked his car to one side of the road.

A uniformed traffic officer was making a valiant attempt to keep the traffic moving, but it was possible for cars to be driven off to the side of the road and parked.

Mason approached the group, and a deputy sheriff warned him to stay back. "The coroner hasn't got here yet," he said. "Get back and keep back."

Mason fell back, then as the officer moved away, inched forward.

Paul Drake's man, picking Mason out from the crowd, sidled over toward him and said, "I'm Drake's operative. I found the body. Anything I can do for you, Mr. Mason?"

Mason led him off to the outskirts of the group. "You looked around a little?"

"Sure I looked around," the detective said. "I didn't do anything illegal, and didn't leave any fingerprints, but I looked around."

"What about the gun?"

The man opened a notebook and said, "Here are the numbers on the gun."

Mason checked the numbers from the ones he had written in his notebook, said, "Paul Drake gave them to me over the phone. How many shells were fired?"

"Only one. It's a .38 Smith and Wesson, double-action revolver. All the chambers were loaded and the hammer is resting on the one cylinder that was discharged. Shot in the left side of the head."

"Powder burns?" Mason asked.

"I believe so. The hair's singed. I couldn't look too closely."

"Was she wearing gloves?"

"Yes."

"Anything else of interest?"

"One thing that may be important," the man said. "The ignition switch was turned off on the car. I turned it on long enough to look at the gasoline gauge. The gas tank shows that it's completely full."

"Did you check the gasoline stations in Oceanside?"

"That's right."

"Find out which one of them filled her tank?"

"I checked every one that was open all night. None of them remember it."

"Well, check again after you get away from here," Mason said. "It's important. I'm going to take a little look around here and see what I can find."

The lawyer moved in as close to the car as the deputy would permit him, then started slowly moving around the car, looking it over.

The body was slumped down to the right of the steering wheel. A gloved hand had protruded through the space between the spokes of the steering wheel, and, as the body had slumped, the tension had pulled the arm tight against the spokes.

Drake's man followed Mason.

"Headlights on when you found the car?" Mason asked.

"No, it was just like you see it now. It could have been suicide."

"But why the devil," Mason asked, "should she have driven all the way down here to pull off to the side of the road and commit suicide? Moreover, a woman who is going to commit suicide isn't concerned about having the gasoline tank filled on her automobile."

Mason walked around the car once more, looking it over, noticed that there were numerous spots on the windshield, caused by night-flying bugs which had been picked up and smashed by the windshield as the car speeded through the night.

"Any chance she could have been killed some other place and the car driven over here?" Mason asked.

"I haven't thought of that."

"You haven't seen my secretary, Della Street?"

"I don't believe I know her."

"A good-looking . . . here she comes now."

Della Street, driving rapidly from the north, slowed her car. The traffic officer motioned that she was to keep moving. She nodded, smiled, drove on for a ways, then parked her car and started walking back.

"Any tracks around the car when you got here?" Mason asked, keeping an eye on Della Street.

"None that I could see, not around that particular car. It's evidently a place where couples come for a little necking. You can see that a lot of cars have been in here from time to time and have made a regular roadway in here from the highway. From the way the tracks look they customarily park and turn around. . . But there weren't any tracks, not any that I could see, except car tracks. . . Of course, it's all trampled out now. There have been a hundred people in here at various times. They come and gawk and hang around until the cops chase them off and . . ."

Della Street, looking compact and competent in a neatly tailored skirt and jacket came up to join them. "Hi, chief," she said.

"Hi, Della. Sorry you had to get up so early. Do you have a notebook?"

"Right in my jacket pocket."

"This is Paul Drake's man. He was telling me about tracks—go right ahead. This is my secretary."

"Well, like I was saying, it's a place for picnics and necking, a nice little strip of mesa. Now over on the left a car had been parked and there were tracks in the dust walking away from it, but most of them were obliterated before the police got wise and kept the crowd back.

"Now I left a few tracks of my own around this car. I did a little snooping, all right. But I told the police I had to see whether she was dead or drunk, or if anyone else had been in the car with her. But there weren't any tracks around the car when I got here. If anyone else had been in that car, he sure didn't leave tracks when he got out."

A siren sounded, coming from the direction of San Diego. A car with two red spotlights became visible in the distance as it speeded along the highway. The deputy sheriff called out, "Where's the man that discovered the body? Hey, you, come over here!"

Drake's man left Mason's side, moved over toward the deputy.

Mason said to Della, "I think I've got all I can get here. You look the thing over from a woman's viewpoint. I'm going to telephone Paul Drake. You meet me at the airport."

Mason called Drake's office from Oceanside. "You get anything on that gun yet, Paul?"

"I'm working on it," Drake said. "I have the name of the original purchaser."

"Who?"

"A Frank L. Bynum, who lives in Riverside. I'm having my men find out about him. We haven't been able to contact him as yet."

"Okay," Mason said, "I've picked up Della. I'm going

to charter a private plane and fly back. There's something cockeyed about the case. It looks as though she'd driven at a fast rate of speed all the way down the coast road. Her windshield is smeared up with places where bugs have hit it, and, believe me, when they hit they hit hard. Just spattered all over the windshield."

"Well, of course she was going fast," Drake said. "She wouldn't have started out at that hour and given my shadow a slip merely in order to take a little pleasure ride."

"That isn't the point," Mason said. "She had a full tank of gas. It must have been filled in Oceanside, although so far none of the service stations have identified her. They may not remember the car but when they look at the body it could be different. However, I don't think it will be.

"Now, if you can tell me why a woman should go tearing madly down the highway to fill up her tank with gasoline at Oceanside, then drive off the road and commit suicide, I'll give you a furlined fountain pen.

"And if, on the other hand, you can tell me why a woman should tear down the coast road in order to drive suddenly off the road to a parking place usually used by couples who are out for a little necking, and wait there to get shot, I will again give you the second prize consisting of a twenty-one jewel watch which runs backwards."

Drake laughed and said, "It's too much for me, Perry."

"Use your head," Mason said. "See what it means? She filled the tank where she didn't get any windshield washing thrown in. Get me?"

"Oh, oh! You mean at a ranch?"

"At a ranch gasoline pump, Paul. You know what I mean."

"I get you, Perry. Want to go call on him?"

"Not yet. We'll run down that gun first. You'll probably have a lead by the time I get back. Della's covering the corpse from a woman's angle and I'll get a plane and have the motor all warmed up. We'll be in soon. Try to have that gun angle all worked out by the time we arrive. I'd like to keep one jump ahead of the police on that."

"Okay," Drake said. "We should reach Bynum any minute now."

Mason chartered a plane, waited for Della Street at the airport. "Find out anything?" he asked as she joined him.

"Yes. She wasn't wearing a hat. There was no sign of a hat in her car. Drake's man thinks she was wearing a hat when she started out. That may be very significant."

"Perhaps she took it off and then just forgot it," Mason said.

"Perhaps, but women aren't likely to do things like that. Here's something else. Someone in the crowd said a person living in the nearest house had noticed a car parked there, with the lights on. Now, when Drake's man found the car the lights were off. The lights remained on for what this witness thinks was five or ten minutes. They shone right in his bedroom and bothered him. He didn't hear any shot."

"It could have been another car the neighbor saw."

"That's the point," Della Street said. "It could have been a necking party."

"Necking with the lights on?" Mason asked.

Della Street laughed, said, "Well, I'm giving it to you for what it's worth."

The pilot approaching them said, "Okay, the plane's all ready if you folks want to get in."

Mason and Della Street climbed into the small cabin job. The pilot taxied down the field and took off.

Mason said, "Drake's located the original purchaser of the gun, a Frank Bynum at Riverside. He'll have something definite on that by the time we arrive. We'll call him just as soon as we get to the airport in Los Angeles.

I'd like to beat the police to the evidence on the gun if we can."

They were silent while the plane tossed in rough air over hills near San Juan Capistrano, then they watched the country slowly flow past them, the built-up districts becoming more and more numerous, until finally they were over the city and the plane was slanting down to a landing at the airport.

"Get Paul Drake on the line while I settle up with the pilot," Mason said, and Della Street, nodding, hurried away toward a telephone.

Mason paid off the pilot, hurried toward a bank of telephone booths at the airport. He knew as soon as he saw Della Street's face through the glass door of the telephone booth that she had received definite news on the gun.

Della Street pulled the door back and said, "Frank Bynum has been contacted. He said he gave the gun to his sister for her protection. She lives in the Dixieland Apartment Hotel, apartment 206. Drake wants to know if you want him to call on her."

"Tell Paul Drake to keep that Bynum chap sewed up so he can't telephone and that I'll call on her myself," Mason said. "You take a cab to the office, Della. Call Edward Garvin at the Vista de la Mesa Hotel in Tijuana. When you get him on the line, first get a list of stockholders whom you can call to be at that meeting this afternoon. After you've done that, tell him what's happened. Tell him to be sure to stay in Mexico. Don't let the police bring him back to identify the body or anything else. That bigamy charge is still pending, and he can be arrested on it if he sets foot in the United States. And tell him not to open his mouth to any newspaper reporter. Don't give him too many details about his wife's death. Just tell him the bare facts. I'm on my way."

And Mason sprinted for a taxicab.

The Dixieland Apartment Hotel was one which had no

central switchboard, no clerk on duty, but a list of tenants on the outside was flanked by a row of buttons.

Mason found the name, Miss V. C. Bynum, and held his thumb over the button on the right.

A few moments later the little telephone receiver hanging from a hook by the door made a noise, and Mason picked it up and said, "Hello, yes, I'm looking for Miss Bynum."

"Who are you and what do you want?" the voice asked.

Mason decided to resort to subterfuge.

"A package with twenty-three cents postage due on it," he said. "Want to come down and pick it up?"

"Oh, just a moment. I'll come down or . . . would it be too much to ask you to come up to apartment 206? I'm just dressing and I . . . if you *could,* please."

"Okay, I'll bring it up," Mason promised.

The electric buzzer signaled that the door was being unlocked, and Mason pushed the door open and entered a long, dimly lit lobby.

Apartment 206 was on the second floor. Mason ignored the elevator, climbed the stairs and went down the corridor counting doors.

When he was still a few feet away from 206, the door opened and revealed the young woman whom he had seen on the fire escape and who had said her name was Virginia Colfax. She was wearing a robe thrown over her shoulders and held in the middle with her left hand. Extended, in her right hand, was twenty-three cents.

"Where's the package?" she asked, then, suddenly recognizing Perry Mason, she drew back with a sharp, involuntary exclamation of dismay.

Mason said, "The package is one you threw away and then picked up later."

He took advantage of her utter confusion to push his way into the apartment.

"You! . . . *How* did you find me?"

83

Mason closed the door behind him, said, "We may not have long to talk, so let's get to the point. When you were on the fire escape you threw away a gun when you saw that you were discovered."

"Why I . . ."

"I went down into the alley, looking for that gun, afterwards," Mason said, "and couldn't find it. You must have either had an accomplice waiting there or tossed it somewhere where I couldn't find it and then you came back and found it later."

She was rapidly regaining her composure now. She said, "I'm dressing, Mr. Mason. I . . ."

"I want to know about that gun."

"If you'll sit down," she said, "until I finish dressing. After all, the apartment is rather cramped. I'll take my clothes, go in the bathroom and . . ."

"Tell me about that gun," Mason said.

"I've told you there wasn't any gun."

"The gun," Mason went on, "was given to you by your brother, Frank L. Bynum, who lives in Riverside. Sometime this morning that gun was used to kill Mrs. Ethel Garvin. Sooner or later, you're going to have to get on a witness stand and tell a jury all you know about that gun and what you were doing out on the fire escape, spying into the office of the Garvin Mining, Exploration and Development Company. Now might be a good time for a dress rehearsal—sort of a warm-up, so that you can get your story in shape."

"Mr. Mason, I . . . that gun . . . Ethel Garvin—Good God!"

Mason said, "Yes. Go on, let's hear the story."

She seated herself as though her knees lacked the strength to hold her up.

There was a moment's silence. Then Mason said, "If you killed her, you hadn't better talk to me or anyone else until you've seen your lawyer. But if there's any other

84

explanation, I want to know it. I'm trying to protect Edward Garvin."

"He's . . . he's your client?"

"Yes."

"How does *he* enter into it?"

Mason shook his head impatiently and said, "Quit stalling. How do *you* enter into it?"

"I . . . I don't."

"What about that gun?"

"The gun was stolen several weeks ago," she said. "I used to keep it right here in this bureau drawer. Look, I'll show you right where I had it."

She crossed over to a drawer and said, "See, it was right here in this corner."

Mason didn't even move from his chair. He took out a cigarette case, snapped it open and offered her a cigarette.

She shook her head in refusal and kept pointing at the drawer. "See, you can see the place right here in this corner where I kept it. The cardboard box still has traces of oil on it. I didn't want it to get against my clothes. It was oily, and—my brother, you know, read so much about the recent crime wave and about girls being molested. He thought that it would be a fine thing for me to have something with which to protect myself. He told me I should never answer the door a night and . . .'

"When did you have the gun last?"

"I tell you I don't know. I used to notice it here in the drawer when I'd open the drawer to get my things. You see, I keep my stockings and some underthings here in this drawer. A short time ago . . . oh, I don't know, perhaps three or four weeks . . ."

Mason said, "The other night when I surprised you on the fire escape, you had a gun in your hand. You knew that I'd discovered you. You tossed the gun down into the alley. You pulled a fast one on me for a getaway. I went back and looked in the alley for the gun. It wasn't there. If it was, I couldn't find it. I remember there were some boxes and barrels of trash, and wastepaper. I gave those only a cursory glance. I thought the gun would be lying on the pavement. It wasn't there. Now, what happened to that gun?"

"I tell you it was stolen and . . ."

"And I saw you with it in your possession two nights ago," Mason said.

"Can you swear it was the same gun?"

Mason smiled and said, "No, Miss District Attorney, I can't swear it was the same gun, but I can swear it was *a* gun, and then the police are going to want to know a *lot* more about it."

She hesitated a moment, then said, "Mr. Mason, I simply don't know who has that gun, that's all there is to it. You're right about one thing. I did have it, and I threw it away."

"What were you doing out on the fire escape?"

"I was spying on someone in the office of the Garvin Mining, Exploration and Development Company."

"Who was it?"

"Frankly, I was staked out there so I could investigate certain nocturnal activities in the office. Imagine my surprise when the office door opened and the person who came in wasn't the one I expected, but a woman—a woman who I have since learned is the first wife of Edward C. Garvin."

"What did she do?"

"I didn't have an opportunity to find out *all* she did. Your interference upset that. But she had a handful of papers which I now believe were proxies. She was opening the drawer of the proxy file when your activities took me off the job—and, unfortunately, kept me off the job."

Mason thought that over.

"Why were you watching the office in the first place? Whom were you after?"

She knuckled her eyes, yawned prodigiously.

"I believe he's the secretary and treasurer. His name is Denby."

"Do you know him?"

"Yes."

"How well?"

"Not well. I just know him when I see him."

"Why were you spying on him?"

"Because my mother has every cent of her money invested in that company and I was afraid something was going wrong."

"Now we're beginning to get somewhere," Mason said. "What made you think something was going wrong?"

"I thought there was something—well, something shady going on."

"What made you think that?"

She said, "Mother received a proxy in the mail. She always gave proxies to Mr. Garvin. I guess everyone did. The stockholders were satisfied with the company. It made money and—well, I guess that's all they wanted, to have it make money."

Mason said, "Come on, quit beating around the bush. You knew something was in the wind. You were out on the fire escape with a gun in your hand. You weren't carrying that gun just as an ornament; you were carrying it for some particular specific purpose."

She said, "I was simply carrying it for my own protection, Mr. Mason. As a matter of fact, I've been carrying that gun in my purse whenever I've been out late at night. I'm employed as a stenographer and sometimes I work late at night. The car line is three blocks from here. I have to walk from that car line to this apartment house. The way things have been going—well, you read in the papers about the way girls have been attacked and—well, I carried the gun. That's what my brother gave it to me for. I suppose I shouldn't have carried it without a permit, but anyway you want to know the facts, and those are the facts. It's just that simple."

"And why did you take the gun out of your purse and have it in your hand when you were out on the fire escape?"

"Because I was scared. I didn't know what would happen if I were caught."

"And what were you doing out on the fire escape?"

"As I'm telling you, Mr. Mason, my mother had received the usual proxy and had signed it, and then as we were casually discussing the company, she just happened to tell me that she'd received another proxy and signed it. I couldn't understand why they would have sent out *two* proxies, but didn't think much about it until she mentioned that the proxy had been just a little different in its wording from the way they usually came out; that the proxy listed the certificate number of Mr. Garvin's share of stock. Well, I started wondering about that and I went down and asked the girl who had charge of the office about the date of the stockholders' meeting and a few questions, and then told her who I was and asked her if I could see my mother's proxy."

"And what happened?"

"Well, she went over and asked this Mr. Denby about it, and Mr. Denby came over, all smiles and courtesy, and told me, certainly, he'd be only too glad to let me see the proxy my mother had signed. He went to the files and took out what must have been the first proxy. It was made out just that way, to E. C. Garvin. There was nothing on it about any certificate number."

"So you went back out and climbed out on the fire escape and . . ."

She said, "You're trying to make it sound absurd, aren't you, Mr. Mason?"

"Well, it does sound a little fishy to me, to tell the truth."

She struggled to fight back a yawn, then, putting her

hand over her mouth, surrendered to the yawn. Her eyes seemed heavy from lack of sleep.

"Go ahead," Mason said.

"You can call it a woman's intuition if you want to. I don't know what accounts for it, but in any event I've always followed my hunches. When I was up there, looking things over, I saw that the Drake Detective Agency was in the building and there was a sign on the directory board stating that it was open twenty-four hours a day and that persons who went to the Drake Detective Agency did not need to register with the elevator operator after hours.

"I kept thinking that over and finally decided I'd go up and talk with the Drake Detective Agency. Then I had a brilliant idea. I remembered a landing of the fire escape was outside the window of the office of the mining company. I got off at Drake's floor, found the stairs, walked up *two* flights, located the landing to the fire escape, went out on it, crept down one flight and found I was on the landing just outside the window of the office I wanted.

"The window was open just a little bit. It wasn't locked. I was wrestling with the temptation to go in when all of a sudden a shadow formed against the frosted glass on the outside of the door. I could see that someone was coming in . . . There was a night light in the corridor and it showed the shadow of some person fitting a key to the door of the office.

"I was in a panic. I was—well, Mr. Mason, I'd just made up my mind that I was going to go in and take a look at the proxy file from which Mr. Denby had removed Mother's proxy when he showed it to me. I actually had one leg over the sill."

"Go on," Mason said.

"Well, I backed up fast and started down the fire escape. Then this person came in and switched on the lights and I realized that the lights were streaming out through the window and that I would be plainly visible.

Well, I started down the fire escape and then you moved and I saw you, and my skirts blew up, and—well, frankly, Mr. Mason," she said, smiling disarmingly, "I was in what *I* would consider one hell of a fix."

Mason said, "You seem to me to be a very determined young woman."

"I am and I'm—Mr. Mason, I'm sorry, I'm downright sorry about what I did—slapping your face."

"You should be. I owe you one for that."

She laughed. "You were so darned decent about—well, about everything. I didn't feel that I could tell you all about what was happening and what I was doing there and—well, I felt you wouldn't believe me even if I did try to explain and I was desperate."

Mason said, "You're telling me all about this quite readily now."

"The circumstances are entirely different. You've found me. I suppose that means—oh, I'll bet I know!"

"What?" Mason asked.

"You found that gun," she charged. "I wondered what happened to it."

"Suppose you tell me a little more about the gun?" Mason invited.

"I didn't throw it down in the alley. I made a motion with my hand, as though I was going to throw it, but I didn't. I made that motion and then whirled around and put the gun on the fire escape right next to the wall on the landing. I intended to go back and get it later—but when I had a chance to go back it was gone. I supposed you'd figured out what must have happened and had gone back and found it. You must have done that, traced the numbers, found my brother had bought it and—so *that's* the way it was!"

Mason said, "How did you know the gun was gone, Virginia?"

She shifted her eyes for a moment, then turned back

to face him squarely. "I led with my chin on that one, didn't I?"

"I'm interested in knowing," Mason said.

She said, "I was back there last night as well as the night before. All last night, in fact. That's why I'm so damn sleepy this morning. This business of working all night—and I almost froze to death last night. I'm telling you, Mr. Mason, I looked longingly down in your office and thought I'd give almost anything to get warm."

"You stayed out there all night *last* night?" Mason asked.

"All night."

"Suppose you tell me a little more about that?"

"Well," she said, "I waited until the scrubwomen had left. Then I did just as I'd done before. I went up to the floor where Mr. Drake's office is. The janitor who operates the night elevator knows me by this time and we're palsy."

"So you got off at Drake's office, and then what?"

"Walked up two flights of stairs, went out to the landing on the fire escape, crawled down and took up my position. I looked for the gun, and it was gone. That frightened me."

"Go on," Mason said. "Let's have the rest of it. I think I know now why you're talking so glibly."

"What do you mean?" she asked.

"Never mind," Mason said. "Go ahead."

"That last sounded like a crack."

"I guess it was," Mason told her, "but go ahead. Let's have your story first."

"Well," she said, "I was prepared for what might happen. This time I was bundled up against wind and rain. I even had on what we call in Idaho my 'long-handled underwear,' and I had a heavy sweater and a leather coat over the sweater, and a ski cap—oh, I was all dolled up for a long wait. I'd taken those extra clothes in with me in a bundle."

"And you stayed there all night?"

"All night."

"Didn't you think it was a little unlikely anyone would come in after—oh, say, one or two o'clock in the morning?"

She said, "I wasn't taking any chances, Mr. Mason. That stockholders' meeting is at two o'clock this afternoon. I'm going to be there and I'm going to protect my mother's interests. And I'm here to tell you there's something very funny going on in that company. The whole thing is crooked."

"What makes you think so?"

She said, "That man, that secretary and treasurer, I think his name is Denby—he was in the office all night doing things."

Mason's eyes showed interest. "What sort of things?"

"I don't think I should tell *you* all this, Mr. Mason. After all, I don't know just what your position might be. You might—for all I know, you might be representing somebody on the other side."

Mason said, "Nevertheless, you're talking. You've already said enough. Let's find out what actually happened. Just what did Denby do?"

She said, "For one thing, he did a lot of dictating. I thought at first it was only a little overtime work, but he sat there and dictated eighteen records to the Dictaphone dictating machine that he has by his desk. And I was kicking myself for being a sap—feeling that I was just stranded out there on the fire escape while this poor loyal company official was trying to catch up on the work that needed to be done before the stockholders' meeting—and then I began to get suspicious."

"Why?"

"Well, he started going through files, taking out papers and putting them in a brief case, and it was the way he acted, his manner. It was like that of an absconding cashier. And then he opened the safe and took out some

92

more papers and put those in his brief case. Then he started going over the books and making notes of figures from different pages and—well, just the way he acted, Mr. Mason, it made me suspicious."

"How long was he there?" Mason asked.

"He was there when I arrived, and he stayed there the whole blessed night, Mr. Mason, and I mean the whole blessed night. He kept up a steady stream of dictation.

"When it began to get daylight, there I was, plastered out there on the fire escape. I felt terribly conspicuous. People could see me from the other buildings. So I— well, I just climbed up the fire escape and walked up and down the corridors of the building, trying to get warmed up. Then I wrapped my extra clothes up in a bundle and about the time the elevator started running regularly, so that I wouldn't be too conscpicuous, I took the stairs down to the floor by Drake's office, pressed the buzzer and when the cage came up for me I got in, went down and came home. I took a hot bath and swigged a lot of coffee and guess I managed two or three hours' sleep. But I was so worried about that stockholders' meeting today I—well, I set the alarm clock early. I've got to go up there and do *something* to protect mother's interests."

"You mentioned Idaho," Mason said. "Do you live in Idaho?"

"I have lived there."

"Worked there?"

She said, "Mr. Mason why do you want to pry into all of my private affairs?"

Mason laughed, "You slapped my face. That gives me some rights."

She said, "All right, if you want to know the truth, I've worked around quite a bit in Idaho. I'm a girl who likes adventure and variety. I've—I've worked in mining camps and I've worked in gambling places."

"Do they have gambling in Idaho?"

"No more," she said, "but they did up until a few years ago. They had it in the mountain districts, all sorts of gambling—roulette, crap games and things of that sort. I have a knack of being rather cool and collected and seeing what's going on and yet I—well, I have what they call a pleasing personality, and they tell me I'm easy on the eyes."

Abruptly she moved over, to sit on the arm of Mason's chair, smiling down at him. "And I know a grand guy when I see one," she said softly. "I guess working in those gambling places is what gives a girl an opportunity to know human nature. You get so you can size people up.

"And you're all right, Mr. Mason. You're just a darn good scout. Of course, being in gambling places that way, people feel that if—well, if a girl works in those places they can make passes at her, and it used to make me so damned mad when people would take liberties with me simply because I was trying to hold down a very exacting job—and believe me, Mr. Mason, those jobs *are* exacting.

"Well, that's why I felt so angry when you said you were going to search me. And then you were so nice about it. I—really owe you something for that."

She smiled at him, placed her hand on his shoulder, bent down so her face was close to his and said, "You know, really . . ."

She was interrupted by the banging of peremptory knuckles on the door.

She jumped off the arm of Mason's chair, pulled her robe smoothly around her.

Knuckles again pounded on the door.

Virginia Bynum looked at Mason with dismay in her eyes.

The knuckles banged once more with heavy insistence.

"Who . . . who is it?" Virginia Bynum asked.

94

"This is Sergeant Holcomb of Police Homicide. We're making a checkup. Open up."

Virginia Bynum, her face drained of color, moved over to the door, turned the knob and opened it.

Sergeant Holcomb, pushing his shoulder against the door, shoved her back, entered the room, then stopped short at the sight of Perry Mason.

Mason said, "Good morning, Sergeant," then turning to Virginia Bynum, said, "Well, I guess this is where I came in."

"Wrong again," Sergeant Holcomb said, "this is where you go *out!*"

10

∎

PAUL DRAKE SLID INTO HIS FAVORITE POSITION IN MASON's big chair and said, "Well, I'm gradually beginning to get some facts pieced together, Perry. It's a mess."

"What have you found, Paul?"

Drake said, "This man, Hackley, is going to be a tough nut to crack, Perry. Apparently, the police don't know anything about him, but to my mind he's the key factor in the whole situation."

"Anything about the time of death?" Mason asked.

"As nearly as the doctors can tell from a post-mortem examination, which, of course, hasn't been completed as yet, it happened right around one o'clock. That's taking body temperature of the corpse when it was found, considering rigor mortis and a few other things. Police are making a tentative guess on the time as one o'clock this morning."

Mason said, "She left her apartment at ten-nineteen, is that right?"

"That's right. Of course, the medical authorities can't fix the time of death with stop-watch precision. She could have been killed as soon as she got to Oceanside or it could have been an hour later."

Mason said, "She had her tank filled with gasoline. A murderer would hardly have killed her and then filled the car with gas. She must have done it, herself."

Drake nodded.

"And because she didn't get any windshield service, it wasn't done at a service station."

"You think she stopped at his ranch?" Drake asked.

"I'm virtually certain of it."

Drake lit a cigarette, studied the smoke which drifted up from the end of it with thoughtful contemplative eyes, said slowly, "The police have some theories about the killing, Perry."

"What are they?"

"They don't think she was killed at the place where the body was found."

"No?"

"No. They think she opened the door and let someone get in. He was driving the car. She was sitting over in the righthand seat. Then this person picked an advantageous moment, whipped a revolver out, shot her in the side of the head, pushed the body over to the far side of the car and then drove it down to the place where the body was found. Then this murderer, whoever he was, got out and, after he'd left the automobile, pulled Ethel Garvin's body over so that it was behind the steering wheel, making it look as though she'd been shot while she was driving the car."

"Wait a minute," Mason said. "That doesn't coincide with the facts, Paul. Your man looked around for tracks when he got there and couldn't find any leaving the automobile. Of course, it wasn't the best ground in the world for tracking but, nevertheless, he should have been able . . ."

"I know," Drake interrupted, "but get this, Perry. Another car had apparently been parked down at the place where the body was found. When this man drove up with the car containing Ethel Garvin's body, he was very careful to inch the car into exactly the proper position so that he could open the door of one car and step into the other car. Then he drove away in the other car after pulling the body over behind the steering wheel and dropping the gun."

Mason said impatiently, "That's a goofy way to commit a murder."

"Don't be too certain it wasn't done just about that way," Drake said. "The evidence checks, Perry."

"What sort of evidence?"

"Well, to begin with, this getaway car was driven down there and parked."

"How can the police tell it was *parked?*"

"They can't be absolutely certain, but that's what they *think*. They can see where someone got out of the car and walked across a patch of soft dirt and then over to the highway, but they can't find where anyone ever walked back to the car."

"Go on," Mason said.

"Apparently that gun can be traced to Garvin."

Mason sat bolt upright in his chair. "What's that?" he asked.

Drake said, "The police traced that gun to Frank Bynum. He told them about giving it to his sister, Virginia. The police were right on your heels in getting hold of Virginia. She stalled around for a while and then told them a story about watching the office of the mining company in order to protect her mother's investment. She even told them about you catching her out there on the fire escape and making her come in. She said that's when she left the gun. She thought you had seen the gun, so she made a motion as though she was throwing it down in the alley and then she swung around to come down the fire escape, gave you a glimpse of legs and, using her body as a shield, put the gun on the platform of the fire escape. She said she thought she could depend on you to be looking at the legs instead of the gun."

"Tut, tut," Della Street said in mock reproach.

"I was, too," Mason admitted. "Go ahead, Paul. Then what happened?"

"From there on," Drake said, "the police have an interesting trail. It seems that the next day Garvin entered the office right after he'd consulted you. He walked over to the window and stood there, moodily gazing down into the alley below the window. Then something caught his eye and he said to George L. Denby, the secretary-treasurer, 'Denby, what the devil's this out on the fire escape?' "

"Go ahead," Mason said. "So far it sounds to me like a scenario."

"Well, it all checks," Drake said. "Denby went over and looked out of the window and said, 'My God, Mr. Garvin, it's a gun!' Frank Livesey, the president of the corporation, was there, and he came over. The three of them stood looking, and then Livesey got out of the window, onto the fire escape, and picked up the gun. He looked it over and said, 'It's fully loaded,' and handed it to Denby. Denby looked it over, then handed it to Garvin. Garvin did a little detective work. He said, 'There isn't a speck of rust on it. If it had been left out there very long it would have been rusty. Someone must have been out on that fire escape with a gun. I wonder who it could have been.'

"They had some talk back and forth, and Denby wanted to call the police, but Garvin said he'd think the matter over. He didn't want to have any disadvantageous publicity just before the stockholders' meeting."

"Go ahead," Mason said. "The thing is really getting interesting now. We have a gun, which subsequently turns out to be a murder weapon, with the prints of three men on it."

"All of them legitimately placed there," Drake said. "But here's the thing. Livesey was on his way out to get a cup of coffee. He said he'd arrived early that morning to do some work on the records so everything would be ready for the stockholders' meeting, and Garvin said something to this effect: 'Livesey, I'm just about ready to leave with my wife on a little trip. I'm going to take a short vacation before that stockholders' meeting, just get away from business for a little while. My car's parked down there in front—the big convertible. I wish you'd open the glove compartment and put that gun in there. I want to look it over. It's certainly a nice weapon.'"

"Then what?"

"Livesey went down to get his cup of coffee, looked around to make sure no one was watching him, popped the gun in the glove compartment, went out and got his coffee and came back. They talked for a while, and Garvin left some last-minute instructions. Then he and Denby rode down in the elevator together. I believe, by the way, Perry, these last-minute instructions had to do with having his secretary put through a check for a thousand-dollar retainer to you.

"So that's the story of the gun," Drake said. "Denby remembers riding down in the elevator with Garvin and just as he walked away he saw Garvin check the glove compartment to make certain the gun was there. Then Denby got in his own car and left.

"The girl would be the one that the police would normally go to work on, but she says she has a perfect alibi, that *after* she entered your office, you searched her very thoroughly . . ."

Della Street gave a low whistle.

"All kidding aside, Paul, this young woman had been prowling around my office," Mason said. "For all I knew, she was sneaking down the fire escape, ready to take a pot shot at me as I was lying there, sleeping. I certainly didn't intend to invite her into the office, then have her pull a gun and start working on me."

"I don't blame you," Drake said.

Mason said to Della, "Get Edward Garvin on the phone, Della."

Della Street put through the call.

"How about the time element?" Mason asked. "Have police been checking up on what everyone did, why, where and when?"

"You mean as to an alibi for the time of the murder?"

"Yes."

"They've done a little preliminary checking. Understand, Perry, the police don't take me into their confidence. I have to pick up what I can from pumping newspaper reporters and getting tips here and there."

Mason said. "You always manage to do pretty well, Paul. What are the police doing?"

"Well, to begin with, they checked on Denby. Denby was up here all night working on the books, dictating some correspondence and getting data ready for the stockholders' meeting. He says he worked all night. He looks like it. And he had a whole night's dictation on his secretary's desk when she arrived this morning. What's more this story agrees absolutely with a story he told Livesey when Livesey rang him up earlier and before anyone knew that Mrs. Garvin had been murdered. It also agrees with the story that Virginia Bynum told the police a half hour or so later when they located her, by tracing the numbers on the gun. She was watching from her station on the fire escape again last night. They've asked her to describe just what she saw, and her story really gives Denby an alibi. She describes everything he did. Not that the police figure Denby has any motive."

"The story Virginia told me and told the police is fantastic—but some fantastic stories are true. What about Livesey?" Mason asked.

"Livesey's a bachelor. He was at home in bed. He says, unfortunately, he can't furnish any alibi because he was sleeping alone and what would the police suggest in the line of preventive measures in the future. The police suggested matrimony."

"They would," Mason said.

"But, of course, the one the police want to talk with now," Drake said, "is Garvin. They understand he's going to be here for the stockholders' meeting and as far as anyone knows he's simply out on a second honeymoon with his wife, so the police are planning to come down like a thousand tons of brick when he . . ."

"Here's your call, chief," Della Street interrupted.

"Garvin on the line?"

"Yes."

Mason picked up the receiver, said, "Hello, Garvin. Mason talking. I want to ask you some questions. I want you to be very, very careful about your answers."

"Good heavens, Mason," Garvin said, "this is awful! This is terrible! This is the *worst* thing . . . Why *did* you leave this morning? Why didn't you wake me up?"

"I thought you didn't want to be disturbed."

"My God, Mason, something like that happens and you simply get up and leave—Mason, I want to come back up there. I want to find out what this thing is all about. I want to . . ."

"You stay right there," Mason said, "and keep your shirt on. Now, don't worry about that stockholders' meeting at two o'clock this afternoon. Della has been working over that list of names you gave her, and we have a bunch of staunch and loyal supporters of yours coming in here in person. That will throw all proxies they've signed out the window. We're going to be able to control the stockholders' meeting all right."

"But I want to be there, Mason. I *must* be there. If I should lose control of that company . . ."

"You just sit tight," Mason said, "and quit worrying. Don't do anything. Don't talk with anyone. Don't stir out of the hotel until I can have a chance to see you, and if anyone should find you, then don't answer any questions. Simply refuse to say a word until you've seen me."

"But, hang it, Mason, that will put me in a false light."

"I can't help that, Garvin. There are a lot of angles to this thing that you don't know anything about yet. Now listen carefully. I want you to answer questions, and I want you to be very careful about your nouns."

"What do you mean, nouns?"

"I mean nouns," Mason said. "A noun is an object. Now listen to this. The other morning when you were standing in your office you looked out of your window and noticed something on the fire escape, some object?"

"On the fire escape?"

"Yes, a metallic object, something heavy."

"Oh, yes, I remember. Why, yes, I pointed out this . . ."

"Careful," Mason warned. "Let's keep the conversation on an ambiguous note, if possible, and remember that the walls of that telephone partition you're talking from are paper-thin. The front door is all right but the wall between that and the other telephone booth is just like paper. Now, what happened to that object?"

"Livesey crawled out of the window and picked it up. We talked about it and I . . . I told Livesey to put it in the glove compartment of my car. He said he was going out to get a cup of coffee, and I wanted to look the thing over—to tell you the truth, Mr. Mason, I'd entirely forgotten about that . . . that object. It must be in the car now."

"Go out and take a look and see if it is," Mason said.

"Right now?"

"Right now. Just leave the receiver off the hook and go out and take a look. I'll hold the line. Your car's still in front?"

"Yes."

"Now, wait a minute," Mason said, "this is important. You didn't turn your car keys in to the woman who runs the hotel last night?"

"No, I forgot. I intended to. I put them in my pocket and . . . but it was all right. They didn't need to move the car."

"That's all right. The keys stayed in your pocket all night?"

"Why, yes, of course."

"The car wasn't moved?"

"No, certainly not."

"And the doors were locked?"

"Yes."

"You're certain?"

"Why, of course. The car's just where I left it last night when I went to bed."

Mason said, "Go on out and take a look and tell me if that object is still there."

"All right," Garvin said. "Hold the phone."

Mason waited, holding the phone, drumming impatiently with his finger tips on the edge of the desk for some fifteen seconds until he could hear over the phone the noise made by Garvin's pounding feet as he hurried back toward the telephone. There was the sound of the receiver being moved, then Garvin's excited voice, "It's gone, Mason, it's gone!"

"All right," Mason said, "now *when* did it go?"

"My gosh, it *must* have been taken before we left Los Angeles. No one could have taken it out here."

"Are you sure?"

"Well, of course—hang it, Mason, how do I know? All I know is that it's gone—I know that Livesey put it in there."

"Did you look in the glove compartment after . . ."

"Yes. Right after I came downstairs I looked in the glove compartment to make certain that Livesey had put it there. It was there."

"And when did you next look in the glove compartment?"

"Just now. That's the only time I've had it open . . . Wait a minute, no. Hold everything, Mason, Lorraine looked in there shortly after we got started. I told her to open the glove compartment and get out my sunglasses. I wanted to put them on."

"Where's Lorraine?"

"Right here. Right out in the lobby. Just a minute."

"Don't get excited and say anything where people can hear you," Mason cautioned. "Get her in the phone booth with you."

"Okay."

Mason could hear the sound of a door opening and low-voiced conversation. Then Garvin said, "She's here."

"All right," Mason said. "Ask her if she remembers looking in the glove compartment for your dark glasses and . . ."

"I already have," Garvin said. "She says that she got my glasses out of the glove compartment all right, but that an object such as you mention was *not* in there."

"But you know it was in there when you came downstairs?"

"Yes."

"And did you drive the car away immediately then?"

"I . . . no, wait a minute. I went into the cigar counter to get some cigars and I shook a game of twenty-six with the girl at the counter. Then I got in the car and drove out and picked up my wife. She had the baggage all packed and we got started right away."

Mason said, "All right. Sit tight. Hold everything until I get down there. I'll be there before dark."

11

■

GARVIN WAS PACING THE FLOOR OF THE LOBBY OF THE Hotel Vista de la Mesa when Mason arrived. Garvin jerked around at the sound of the opening door as though he had been pulled by a string, saw Mason's face, and then his own features lighted up in a genial smile.

"Thank heavens you're here, Mason," he said. "I thought you *never* would get here. What's new?"

Mason said, "We've just come from the stockholders' meeting."

"How did things go?"

"Like clockwork," Mason told him. "Some man by the name of Smith started a revolt but it died aborning. The stockholders put the same board of directors in office for another year, elected all the same officers, and the directors organized, after the stockholders' meeting, for the new year, employed you for another year as general manager at the same salary and bonus, and I gather that everything you've done has been duly ratified."

"That's fine," Garvin said. "Now tell me about Ethel, Mason. My heavens, this is awful. I've been having the damnedest ideas. What happened? Did she commit suicide?"

"Apparently not. Apparently it was murder."

"But who could have killed her?"

"That's a question that's bothering the police. Where's your wife?"

"In her room."

Mason said, "Suppose we all go down there. I'll get Della Street."

Mason called Della Street from the limousine; then, together with Garvin, they walked down the corridor. Garvin tapped on the door of the room and Lorraine's voice called, "Come in."

Garvin opened the door and said, "Well, he's here, Lorrie."

"Thank heaven!" she said, and came toward him smiling cordially, giving him her hand. "Mr. Mason, I can't begin to tell you how much it means to me to have you *here*. I've been worrying and Edward has been simply frantic."

"Thank you," Mason said. He presented Della Street to Mrs. Garvin and said, "The stockholders' meeting and the meeting of the new board of directors is all out of the way. Everything moved along smoothly. There was no trouble at all. I had thought perhaps that there might have been an organized revolt planned, that the substitution of Ethel's name on those proxies wasn't simply a piece of isolated, personal skulduggery. I thought that perhaps it might mask something more sinister. As nearly as I could tell from checking the names of the stockholders, there were a lot of stockholders present who weren't ones that *we'd* called.

"Della Street called that list you gave her this morning and nearly all of them showed up. I guess there was enough friendly stock there to control the meeting; but, for the life of me, I don't know why some of those other people showed up. It was a peculiar situation."

"Anyhow, we can quit worrying about *that*," Garvin said. "It probably was all right. Let's get down to news of this tragedy, Mason."

Mason said, "I'm going to be blunt about this thing,

Garvin. You're not a widower. That doesn't affect your status as having committed bigamy when you went through that marriage ceremony in Mexico. I don't want you to go back to the United States. I know that it may look a little callous for you to stay over here and refuse to go to the funeral of your ex-wife, but nevertheless I want you to play it that way. There are a lot of things I can't tell you about right now."

"I *want* to know the details," Garvin said. "Good Lord, Mason, I've been biting my fingernails down to the knuckles. Tell me, how did it happen?"

Mason said, "I had a detective shadowing her. She left her apartment at ten-nineteen. She probably received a telephone call from someone shortly before she left. She ditched my shadow. The next contact we had was when we found her sitting in her car about two miles south of Oceanside on a mesa, a vacant lot. Someone had shot her with a .38 caliber revolver. One shot on the left side of the head.

"Now that .38 caliber revolver is probably the same one that you found out on the fire escape a couple of days ago. I'm going to have to ask you some questions. They're going to hurt but we've got to go through with it. The police are going to ask you those same questions. I want to hear your answers before the police hear them."

"Go right ahead. Ask anything you want," Garvin said. "As far as that revolver is concerned . . ."

"I think I've checked up on the revolver pretty well," Mason said. "What I want to check up on now is *you*."

"On me?"

"Yes."

"What do you mean?"

"Where were you last night?"

"Where was I? Why, you were with me. You drove in here. You went across the border with me. You . . ."

"You went in your room and then what did you do?"

"I went to bed."

"You stayed in there all night?"

"Why, yes, of course."

"Didn't go out for any purpose?"

"No, certainly not."

"How about it, Mrs. Garvin?" Mason asked. "Can you swear to that?"

"Why, certainly," she said indignantly.

"Now, don't get hot under the collar," Mason warned. "I'm simply closing the thing up so the police won't find any loopholes. Now, did you folks go to sleep, say around midnight?"

"Probably before that."

"Do you sleep soundly?"

"I don't sleep too soundly," Garvin said. "My wife is quite a sound sleeper."

"That's bad," Mason said.

"I don't see anything bad about it," she said.

"You can't give him an alibi."

"I certainly can. As it happens I woke up—oh, right around one o'clock. Edward was snoring. I told him to roll over on his side. I had to speak to him twice before he did, but he rolled over on his side and then quit snoring. I went back to sleep. I will admit that I sleep very heavily, but at times I'm an intermittent sleeper. I didn't know anything after that until about half past two or quarter to three. I woke up then and was awake until after quarter past three."

"How do you know about the time?" Mason asked.

She said, "I heard a clock chime the hour at one o'clock and when I woke up and was awake for about half an hour I not only heard the clock chime three o'clock but I looked at my wrist watch. In fact, I got up and took a glass of water and an aspirin. I had a slight headache and felt a little restless. Then I went back to sleep."

Mason heaved a sigh of relief and said, "Well, that's fine. I just wanted to be sure that you have an absolute ironclad alibi. Now let's get back to the question of that gun . . ."

"That gun definitely was *not* in the glove compartment, Mr. Mason," Lorraine Garvin said. "I looked in there to get some sunglasses for Edward."

"When was that?"

"Very shortly after we'd left Los Angeles. It had been a little cloudy, and then the sun came out and was quite brilliant and Edward wanted his dark glasses. I opened the door of the glove compartment and the glasses were in a case toward the back of the compartment. Now that you mention about the gun, I remember thinking that everything had been pushed toward the back part of the glove compartment and wondered why. It was as though some other object had occupied the front of the compartment for a little while. But it certainly wasn't there when I got those glasses. There were just some maps and a small flashlight, a pair of pliers, and this case with Edward's sunglasses."

"No gun?"

"Definitely not."

Mason said to Garvin, "But you're certain the gun *was* in the glove compartment?"

"It certainly was, and I guess the only time when it could have been removed was when I was out in front of my house waiting for my wife. She had the baggage all packed and I went in and got the baggage and then . . ."

"And then we had a bottle of beer," Lorraine said. "You remember that you wanted to have some beer. You said you were thirsty so we went back to the icebox and had a bottle of beer."

"That's right," Garvin said.

"And during this time the car wasn't locked up?"

"Heavens, no," Garvin said. "As a matter of fact I almost didn't shut off my motor. Lorraine said she had the baggage all ready and I went in and got it and it wasn't until after I got in the house that I thought about the beer. Lorraine joined me. We went back to the ice-box, opened a bottle and split it in two glasses. Now someone *could* have taken the gun out at that time."

"Someone who had followed you for that specific purpose?" Mason asked.

"I don't think so, Mason. I doubt if anyone could have done that. It would have been more apt to have been kids in the neighborhood."

"It wasn't kids in the neighborhood," Mason said. "Whoever got that gun, got it for a specific, deliberate purpose. That was the gun that was used in killing your former wife."

"They're absolutely certain about that?" Garvin asked.

"They will be as soon as they recover the fatal bullet and then shoot a test bullet through the gun and make a series of tests with a comparison microscope. But you can gamble a thousand to one that it was that gun which did the job."

"That, of course, complicates things," Garvin admitted. "I suppose police might even discover my fingerprints on that gun."

"You handled it?"

"I handled it, Denby handled it, and Livesey handled it. And whoever put it out on the fire escape must have handled it. In other words there must be quite a few fingerprints on it."

"I suppose so," Mason said. "The police aren't taking me into their confidence."

"The body was found near Oceanside," Lorraine Garvin said significantly.

"That's right," Mason said. "We haven't interviewed Hackley yet. The police don't know anything at all about him. I'm going to have a car drive me back to Oceanside. Paul Drake is going to meet me there."

"Paul Drake?" Lorraine asked.

"The detective who's been working with me. The one who located Ethel Garvin for me. He's a good man."

"Well," Mrs. Garvin said, "I can't help but say that *I* consider it highly significant that she drove to Oceanside —if that is where her lover is living."

"We don't know he's her lover. We don't know very much about him," Mason said. "He may be a tough nut to crack. The only satisfaction we have to date is that we know about him and the police don't. It is, of course, significant that she went to Oceanside. There are a couple of other angles in the case that indicate she may have gone to keep an appointment with this man, and . . ."

From the patio outside came the sound of the voice of Señora Inocente Miguerinio.

"Thees place ees very old," Señora Miguerinio said, "muy viejo—old, you understand, like the ruinas. My father, and before him my grandfather, have owned thees place. Now I have feex heem up so the turista have a place to sleep, no?"

"I see," a man's voice answered.

"An old estate, a hacienda," Señora Miguerinio went on.

The masculine voice said, "I am glad to know it. Two years ago when I was here, I did not notice it."

"Of course you deed not notice. Ees so much ruin that my father make a board fence so he ees hid, no?"

"No," the man said.

Señora Miguerinio's laughter was like bubbling water. "Ah, well, the turista love to stay in my old Spanish house, inside ees very old, ees what you call quaint, no?"

"Yes."

"Si, Señor, ees quaint. You speak my language, no?"

"No, only a few words."

"You weel come in and sit down, no?"

"Yes, thank you."

Mason glanced at the grinning Garvin, frowned and placed his finger to his lips in a gesture for silence.

The man's voice came through the open window. "You have a Señor Edward Garvin and his wife staying here? He owns that big convertible in the driveway."

"Oh, but certainly. The Señor Garvin, and the Señora. She ees beautiful, with the hair like red gold. And they have their fren' the Señor Perry Mason weeth them."

"The devil!" the voice exclaimed in irritation.

Mason walked over close to Garvin. "That voice," he said, "is the voice of Lieutenant Tragg, of the Metropolitan police force. And if you don't think *he's* a smart cookie, just stick around."

Señora Miguerinio said, "They are een these rooms now. Five and seex. If you are a fren' of theirs they weel be glad to see you, no?"

"No," Lieutenant Tragg said.

They heard a door close, then steps in the hallway, knuckles on the door. Mason opened the door.

"Well, well, Tragg! How are you?"

"Mason!" Tragg exclaimed. "And the estimable Miss Street. Well, Mason, I'm certainly glad to see you. I don't get to see you very often these days."

"It's been a while," Mason admitted. "Lieutenant, shake hands with Mr. Edward Garvin."

"Glad to know you," Lieutenant Tragg said.

Mason turned toward Lorraine Garvin at the far side of the room. "Mrs. Garvin, may I present Lieutenant Tragg of the Metropolitan police—Homicide Squad."

Her smile was a wan motion of tight lips. Of a sudden, she seemed to be cowering by the closet door. "How do you do, Lieutenant? I'm very pleased to meet you."

Tragg said to Edward Garvin, "You've heard about your wife?"

"Yes, I was shocked, surprised. I . . . I hardly know what to do."

"There's a good chance she was killed in Los Angeles and transported to Oceanside. That's why I'm interested in the case. Now if you want to help," Tragg said, "you can come on back and make arrangements for the funeral and while you're back we'll . . ."

"Arrest him on a bigamy complaint that was issued yesterday by the district attorney's office," Mason interpolated.

Tragg turned to Mason, said, "Now, that wasn't necessary."

"I merely wanted him to know what the score was," Mason said.

"Now look," Tragg said, in the voice one used to an obstreperous child, "I want to talk with Mr. Garvin. I'm not going to hurt him, and he certainly has nothing to conceal, but there are *some* things about his wife's death that I want to uncover. He can help me."

"That's fine," Mason said. "We'll both help."

"I can get along without *your* help."

"Come, come, Lieutenant. Two heads are better than one."

"We're getting into the field of a different proverb now," Tragg said, smiling. "At this point you can refer to the good old proverb that too many cooks spoil the broth."

"Didn't Ethel Garvin commit suicide?" Mason asked.

"She did *not* commit suicide," Tragg said. "The bullet in her head produced almost instant death."

"Well?" Mason asked.

"She was shot while she was in the right-hand seat of the car. Someone drove her for some little distance, then parked the car and pulled and hauled the body over until it was in the driver's seat. He then pushed the left arm through the spokes of the wheel, shut off the lights and ignition and drove away in another car."

"That had been following?" Mason asked.

Tragg shook his head and said, "Frankly, Mason, I don't think so. It looks as though the murderer had gone to a certain spot and had parked the getaway car. Then he'd gone out and joined his victim, shot her right in the head at close range, then driven the car for some little distance, perhaps quite a few miles, to the point where his own car had been parked and was waiting for a getaway. The murder may well have been committed while she was in Los Angeles. The murderer drove Ethel Garvin's car up as close to his own car as he dared, then got out, stood on the running board of his own car, pulled the body over behind the steering wheel, fixed everything the way he wanted, then stepped into his own car and drove away."

"Unless, of course, he had an accomplice waiting," Mason said, "which would make it a two-man job."

"Which would make it a two-man job," Tragg told him, "but for certain reasons, we don't think that it was. We think that it was a one-man job."

"How come?"

"Well, to begin with, if there had been an accomplice waiting in the getaway car, the tendency would have been for the murderer to have driven the car with the body in it to a stop and then the getaway car would have driven alongside. Actually it was the other way around. The murderer even had to back once in order to get the car with the body in it in exactly the position that he wanted. Then he got over into the other car."

"That's good deductive reasoning," Mason said.

Tragg turned to Garvin. "Now, I know this is a painful subject," he said, "but if your wife was murdered, I know you'll do everything in your power to clear it up. Despite the fact that you'd been separated, despite the fact there was some friction between you, you *would* want to clear it up, wouldn't you?"

Garvin hesitated.

"Let's put it this way," Tragg said, his eyes cold as ice, "you wouldn't want to put yourself in a position of seeming to protect a murderer, would you, Mr. Garvin?"

"Of course not," Garvin said hastily.

"I thought not," Tragg told him. "Now then, if you'll just come back across the border we'll . . ."

"What about this bigamy warrant, Tragg?"

"I tell you, that's out of my jurisdiction. That's between this man and the D. A. But whether he comes back with me or whether he doesn't isn't going to help matters any. He's a defendant in a bigamy rap. I don't know what the D. A. will do. He may dismiss the case now that the complainant is dead. He may just keep on continuing or he may let the guy plead guilty and apply for probation. I'm not interested in bigamy; I'm interested in a murder."

"That's the difference between us," Mason said cheerfully. "I'm interested *both* in the murder and in the bigamy charge."

"Well," Tragg said irritably, Mason's manner forcing him to lose his good nature, "don't think that this man has any choice in the matter. He's faced with a rap for bigamy. We can get him out of Mexico any time we want him out. There's an easy way and a hard way. I'm asking him to come the easy way."

"We prefer to go the hard way," Mason told him cheerfully.

"Now, don't be like that," Tragg said to Mason. "You know we can bring this man back any time we want him. We can nail him on an absolutely dead-open-and-shut bigamy charge. He has no possible defense to that and we can get him extradited from Mexico to face it. I thought we could expedite this murder investigation by not having to go through all that red tape."

Mason said, "You face an interesting situation on that bigamy charge."

"Phooey!" Lieutenant Tragg said. "Don't hand me that line of double-talk, Mason. You know as well as I do that the Mexican divorce this man had isn't worth the paper it's written on. You also know that the Mexican marriage is a bigamous marriage."

115

Mason said, "There's some interesting law involved, Lieutenant. Section 61 of our Civil Code provides that a second marriage made during the lifetime of an undivorced spouse is illegal and void from the beginning."

"That's what I was telling you," Lieutenant Tragg said.

"On the other hand," Mason said, "Section 63 of the Civil Code also contains some very interesting language."

"Such as what?" Tragg asked.

Mason took a piece of paper from his pocket, on which he had copied Section 63 of the Civil Code.

"Listen to this, Lieutenant: 'All marriages contracted without this state, which would be valid by the laws of the country in which the same were contracted, are valid in this state.' "

Tragg said, "What are you getting at? That marriage in Mexico wasn't any better than the divorce."

"Exactly," Mason said, "but Mexico recognized the divorce."

"Well, what if it does?"

"Notice that language again," Mason said. "I'll read it to you once more." He again held up the paper and read, *"All* marriages contracted without this state, which would be valid by the laws of the country in which the same were contracted, are valid in this state."

Tragg tilted his hat back and scratched his head. "I'll be damned," he said.

"There you are," Mason said. "The marriage is legal in Mexico. Therefore, it's legal in every other country, particularly in the state of California, because the California law specifically so provides."

"But look here," Tragg said. "It'll be possible to prove that these two people left California in order to perpetrate a fraud on the marriage laws of California and . . ."

Mason smiled, and shook his head. "Read the case of McDonald versus McDonald, 6 California (Second) 457. It's also reported and discussed in 106 A. L. R. 1290 and is reported in the Pacific Reporter in 58 Pacific (Second) Page 163. That case holds squarely and fairly that where people leave California for the sole purpose of contracting a marriage, in defiance of the laws of California, and go to another state, and, as a part of that general scheme, a marriage is contracted in that state, that marriage is valid. It is a legal and binding ceremony in California, regardless of the fact that such marriage is not only contrary to the *laws* of California but contrary to the underlying policy of the laws of California."

"Well, dammit," Tragg said, "the divorce in Mexico is no good in California, you have to admit that."

"I don't admit it, but I'm willing to concede it for the purpose of the argument."

"Then the marriage has to be bigamous."

"The marriage is as good as gold," Mason said.

"You mean that this man has two wives and . . ."

"He doesn't now," Mason said, "but until an early hour this morning he did have. He's in the rather unique position of having committed legal bigamy and having had two perfectly legal wives."

"You're nuts, Mason. You're pulling a lot of double-talk and a lot of fast legal stuff in order to get me mixed up. You may be able to put up a good razzle-dazzle for a jury, but that's all it is."

Mason said, "Tragg, I'm telling you, the minute this man sets foot in Mexico, he's married to this woman standing here at his side. I'm willing to concede that when he goes back to the United States, he *may* be held to have committed bigamy. That's why I don't propose to have him go back to the United States. He's living here with his lawfully wedded wife.

"Now, Mexico will grant extradition for a crime that is a crime against the laws of the United States, but it's not going to grant extradition for an act performed under the laws of the Mexican government which is perfectly legal here but which *could* be held to be illegal in California."

Tragg said irritably, "You make the thing sound so damn convincing that . . . That's the trouble with you, you've built up a reputation because you *are* able to make things sound so convincing."

"You don't want to go back to the United States, do you, Garvin?" Mason asked his client.

Garvin shook his head.

"There you are, Tragg," Mason said.

Tragg took a small fingerprint outfit from his pocket. "Well," he said, "I take it you'll at least be willing to do whatever you can to help us clear up that murder case."

"What do you want?"

"I want your fingerprints."

"Why?"

"I think I found one of your fingerprints on the weapon with which the crime was committed."

"You don't need to bother about that," Mason said. "I can tell you very frankly, Tragg, that my client handled that gun—that is, if it's the gun we think it is."

"What gun?" Tragg asked suspiciously.

"A gun," Mason said, "that was left on the fire escape outside of the window of the Garvin Mining, Exploration and Development Company. That gun was handled by Mr. Garvin and was, in fact, placed in the glove compartment of his automobile. Someone removed it from the glove compartment before he had left Los Angeles."

Tragg threw back his head and laughed. "You do have the most naïve, ingenious explanations! You admit your client put that gun in the glove compartment of his automobile?" Tragg asked.

"It was put there for him," Mason said.

Tragg turned to Garvin. "You admit you put that gun in the glove compartment of your car?"

"He admits someone else put it there," Mason said.

118

"I'm taking *to* Garvin," Tragg said irritably.

"I'm talking *for* him."

Lorraine Garvin said, "Well, I know very well that gun was *not* in the glove compartment after we left Los Angeles. Someone took it out."

"*How* do you know?" Tragg asked.

"Because my husband had left his sunglasses in the glove compartment. After we got going he asked me to get them out for him. I opened the glove compartment and took out the dark glasses. If there had been a gun in there I *certainly* would have seen it, and if I'd seen it, I naturally would have demanded to know what Edward was doing with a gun."

"And you're sure there was no gun in there?"

"Absolutely certain."

"After all," Tragg said, suavely, "by that time your husband could have removed it from the glove compartment. He might have put it anywhere."

Lorraine glowered at Lieutenant Tragg and said, "If you're not going to believe any statements made by a person, what's the use of asking him to submit to an inquiry and answer questions?"

Tragg grinned, and said, "It's the way we solve murder cases sometimes. You have to admit, *Mrs.* Garvin, that a man who would commit murder would be perfectly willing to tell a falsehood."

"Well, I can tell you one thing," Lorraine snapped, "my husband might have taken that gun but he never could have used it. He was here with me all night."

"*All* night?" Tragg asked.

"Yes, all night."

"You didn't sleep a wink?"

"Well, I know I woke up around one o'clock and he was lying in bed right beside me and snoring. I was awake from around quarter to three to three-thirty and he was there."

"You looked at your watch to check the time, of course," Tragg said sarcastically.

"I *listened* to the time."

"You listened?"

"Yes. They have a clock—just listen for yourself."

She held up her hand for silence. The musical chimes of the big clock in the lobby melodiously tolled a preamble, and then after a pause, chimed the hour.

"Okay," Tragg said. "If you'll swear to those times . . ."

"I'll swear to them."

"And if you're not mistaken . . ."

"I'm not."

"In that event I'm all finished," Tragg said, "except that I want to get Mr. Garvin's fingerprints. I want to see whether or not he left a fingerprint on that gun. Any objection, Garvin?"

"Certainly not," Garvin said. "I'm only too eager to do anything I can to help clear this matter up."

"Except return to California," Tragg said.

"So far as that is concerned, I am not going to subject my wife to a lot of vulgar curiosity, nor am I going to walk into a trap that was set for me by . . ."

"Go on," Tragg said, "by whom?"

"There's no need mentioning her name now," Garvin said with dignity. "She's dead."

"All right," Tragg said, opening his fingerprint outfit and taking the cover off a blank ink pad, "let's have your hands and we'll get the fingerprints. At least we'll accomplish that much."

Garvin extended his hands. Tragg carefully took fingerprints, marked them with the name, date and place, then grinned cheerfully. "That's fine. I hope you enjoy your stay in Mexico."

He bowed, said, "Glad to have met you, Mr. and *Mrs.* Garvin. You'll hear from me later." Then he opened the door and was gone, as though suddenly in a great hurry.

■

12

It was dark by the time the limousine returned Perry Mason and Della Street to San Diego. Mason stopped long enough to telephone Paul Drake.

"Okay, Paul," Mason said. "Della and I are leaving San Diego. We'll go to Oceanside and have dinner there. Then we'll meet you and go on out to see what we can do with Hackley."

"He's going to be a tough nut," Drake warned. "I've been getting a little more dope on him. He's considered pretty hard."

"That's fine," Mason said. "I like 'em tough. When can you get to Oceanside?"

"I'm ready to start right now."

"All right," Mason told him. "Della and I will pick up our cars at the airport and then go get some dinner. You can cruise slowly along the main street until you find us . . . you can't miss my car. I'm driving the convertible with the light tan top."

"Okay," Drake said. "I'll find you."

"We're on our way," Mason told him, and hung up.

The limousine purred smoothly along the coast route until it reached Oceanside. Mason had the driver take them to the airport where he and Della Street picked up their respective automobiles, paid off the limousine, and drove back to the center of Oceanside where Mason found two parking places near a restaurant.

They entered the restaurant, enjoyed a leisurely dinner, and were chatting over after-dinner coffee and cigarettes when Drake walked in, looked around, spotted them, waved his hand and came over to join them in the booth.

"What's new, Paul?" Mason asked.

"I could use a cup of coffee," Drake said, "and a piece of that lemon pie. I had a late lunch but I'm beginning to get hungry . . . Hang it, Perry, there just isn't any easy way out of Los Angeles. You have to fight traffic no matter *what* you do."

"I'll say," Mason told him. "What's new in the case, anything?"

"The police have found Edward Garvin's fingerprint on the murder weapon," Drake said.

"Why not? Garvin admits that he handled it. What else is new?"

"Not very much. I got a little dope on this Hackley. He was mixed up in some gambling. I didn't find out too much about it but people who know him think he's dangerous."

"Well, that's fine," Mason said. "We'll go look him over. We should be able to give him quite a jolt. He doubtless thinks that no one is ever going to connect him with Ethel Garvin."

Drake said, "Well, I'll have that piece of pie and a cup of coffee before the shooting starts anyway."

They waited until Drake had finished, then left the restaurant. Mason said, "We may as well all go in one car. Let's get in my bus. It has a wide front seat."

"That's an idea," Drake said. "Put Della in the middle. It will give me an excuse to put my arm around her. I haven't made even the preliminary approaches to a pretty girl for so long I've forgotten how."

"Don't think *I'm* going to educate you," Della said. "I have no time to waste with amateurs."

"Oh, it'll all come back to me readily enough," Drake said reassuringly.

They climbed in Mason's car, swung away from the curb, turned east on the Fallbrook road and drove slowly until they found the Lomax mailbox. Then Mason slowed and located the driveway.

"Easy enough to find when you have the directions," he said.

"It sure is."

"The police haven't any lead on Hackley, Paul?"

"I don't think so. I don't think it's even occurred to them to check back on Ethel's stay in Nevada."

The rutted driveway led past an orange orchard for about a quarter of a mile and up to a neat California bungalow which loomed dark and somber.

"Looks as though he's either out or has gone to bed," Drake said. "What do we do? Bust right in?"

"We bust right in," Mason told him. "If he's home we try to get him on the defensive and get him started answering questions. In other words, we pull a complete razzle-dazzle, if we have to."

"Do we tell him who we are?"

"Not if we can avoid it. We just give him names, no more."

"Okay," Drake said. "Let's go!"

Mason drove the car up to the front of the big house, braked it to a stop, waited a moment to see if there were any dogs.

A big, black German shepherd walked on tiptoe around the car, his mane bristling, his nose busily inquiring as to the identity of the late visitors.

"Don't take any chances on that dog," Drake warned. "Blow the horn and let's get someone to come out here and escort us in."

Mason said, "I'd rather try the doorbell, and catch him entirely by surprise. That dog looks intelligent."

"That doesn't mean anything."

"It does with a dog," Mason said, and opened the door of the car.

The dog immediately bristled in hostile silence.

Mason looked down, and caught the dog's eye. "Look,"

he said, as though addressing a human being, "I want to talk with the master of the house. I'm going to get out of this car and walk in a direct line right up to the porch and ring the bell. You can follow along behind me to make certain I don't make any false move. How's that?"

With the last two words, Mason raised his voice. Then, without an instant's hesitation, stepped to the ground.

The dog lunged forward, keeping his nose within a half inch of Mason's legs as the lawyer walked around the car and up to the porch. "It's all right," Mason assured Della Street who was watching with apprehensive eyes. He dropped his hands so that the open fingers were where the dog's cold nose could explore them.

The lawyer walked up to the porch and pressed the bell button. He could hear the sound of chimes inside the house.

He waited a minute, then pressed the bell button several times in quick succession.

From the dark interior of the house there was the sound of slow, deliberate footsteps approaching the door. A light switch clicked on, then another. A door opened and through the glass in the window Mason could see the figure of a man in a double-breasted gray suit. The man shifted his right hand to a position near the left lapel of his coat. The lawyer caught a glimpse of a revolver in a shoulder holster.

The dog, facing the door, elevated his tail, the tip of it waving to and fro.

A bolt shot on the inside of the door. The man opened the door for an inch or two, a safety chain holding it in that position. A porch light clicked on, outlining Mason in brilliance.

"Who are you?" the man asked. "What do you want?"

"I'm looking for Alman Bell Hackley."

"What do you want with him?"

"I want to talk with him."

"What about?"

"Some properties he has in Nevada."

"Nothing is for sale."

"Do you want to hear what I have to say, or not?"

"If you have any business with me, go back to the hotel at Oceanside. Call on me after ten o'clock in the morning." He started to close the door. Then, something about the dog's attitude caught his attention, and he said suspiciously, "Say, how did you get past that dog?"

"I'm not past him. I just got out of the car and . . ."

"He's not supposed to let anyone out of a car after dark."

"He made an exception in my case," Mason said.

"Why?"

"Ask the dog."

The man frowned, said, "Just who *are* you anyway?"

Mason said, "I'm trying to find out something about Ethel Garvin."

Hackley's face became rigidly immobile.

"Know anything about her?" Mason asked.

"No," Hackley said, and slammed the door.

"She was murdered early this morning," Mason called through the closed door.

There was no response, but, on the other hand, Mason heard no sound of steps in the corridor indicating the man had turned away from the door.

"And she stopped here and had her gasoline tank filled," Mason shouted.

There was a pause, then the door jerked open.

"What was that you said?" the man demanded.

"I said she stopped here sometime around twelve-thirty o'clock in the morning and had her gas tank filled."

"You're drunk or crazy, I don't know which, and I don't give a damn. Now get back in your car or I'll tell the dog to tear a leg off."

"Do that and I'll sue you for damages and wind up owning your Nevada ranch," Mason said.

"You talk big."

"Go on," Mason told him. "Tell your dog to tear off a leg and see what happens."

"What do you want?"

"I want to talk about Ethel Garvin."

There followed a long moment during which the slender, sinewy man behind the door met Mason's eyes in thoughtful appraisal. Suddenly he reached a decision, removed the safety chain from the door and said, "Come in. If you want to talk I'm willing to listen.

"And before you leave you'll tell me exactly what you meant by saying Ethel Garvin, whoever *she* is, stopped here at twelve-thirty o'clock this morning. Come right in, Mr.—?"

"Mason," the lawyer said.

"All right, Mr. Mason, come in."

Mason turned back toward the car, "Come on Della, and Paul," he called.

"What about that damned dog?" Drake called irritably. "Can't you put him in the house?"

"The dog remains where he is," Hackley said. "He won't do anything unless I tell him to."

Della Street opened the door of the car, slid out to the ground, walked confidently toward the porch where Mason was standing. The dog turned to regard her, gave a low-throated, ominous growl, but made no move.

Drake, who had put one foot on the ground, heard the growl, promptly returned to the automobile and slammed the door.

"It's all right," Hackley called, and then to the dog, "Shut up, Rex!"

The dog ceased growling, regarded Della Street's confident approach with hard-eyed appraisal, then slowly waved the tip of his tail. Drake, observing that Della Street made it all right, opened the door once more, placed his right foot on the ground tentatively, followed it with his left foot, and took two or three cautiously diffident steps toward the porch.

The dog bristled, growled, then suddenly made a lunge for Drake.

Drake whirled, raced back into the car just as the snarling dog flung himself against the door, his teeth snapping at the metal.

Hackley opened the door, ran out on the porch, yelled, "Rex! Down! Damn it, Rex, get down!"

The dog looked back over his shoulder, slowly and reluctantly sank to a crouching position on the ground.

"Here," Hackley shouted. "Come here. Come here to me!"

The dog turned and came toward Hackley as though expecting a beating.

Hackley said, "Damn you, I told you not to do that. Now you get down, and stay down."

Hackley walked over to the car, said to Drake, "Come in. He won't hurt you."

Drake looked past Hackley at the dog, said, "If that dog makes a pass at me, I'm going to shoot him."

"You won't have any trouble with him as long as you get out and come in, and move confidently," Hackley said. "But don't ever start running from a dog, and don't ever act as though you were afraid."

"Stand still and let him tear a leg off, I suppose," Drake said, sarcastically.

"The others didn't have any trouble," Hackley pointed out.

"The trouble I had," Drake told him, "was enough to make up for all three of us." He eased himself out of the automobile, followed Hackley to the porch.

"Come in," Hackley said. "Rex, get the hell back out of the way." He aimed a half-hearted kick. The dog, deftly avoiding his kick, stood watching Drake with lips that curled back from his fangs.

Hackley said, "Come on in. Let's go inside, sit down, and talk this thing over in a civilized fashion."

He said to Mason, "All right, let's get this straight. Your name's Mason. Who are the others?"

"Miss Street, my secretary," Mason said.

Hackley's bow was a model of polite deference. "Miss Street," he said, "I'm very pleased to meet you."

"And Paul Drake," Mason said.

"How do you do, Mr. Drake," Hackley said shortly.

"Drake," Mason added, "is a detective."

"Oh," Hackley announced, "it's got that far, has it?"

"That's right," Mason told him, "where do we talk?"

"Come in and sit down."

Hackley held the door open for the three, said, "Go right ahead through the first door to the left."

Della Street led the way into the room which had been fitted up as a library, evidently a somewhat hasty job of superimposing books and shelves over what had at one time been merely the conventional living room in a country house.

"Sit down," Hackley invited, making a sweeping inclusive gesture.

The party seated themselves.

"All right," Hackley said, "now let's hear what you have to say."

"You're getting the cart and the horse all mixed up," Mason said. "*We* want to hear what *you* have to say."

"I have nothing to say."

"You knew Ethel Garvin."

"Who says so?"

"I say so," Mason said. "You knew her when she was in Nevada. You were quite friendly with her. You talked her out of getting a divorce from her husband. You told her that if she'd sit tight and let her husband think she'd secured a divorce, then when Edward Garvin had found some other interest he could be made to pay a lot of money for a settlement."

Hackley said, "I don't think I'm going to like you, Mr. Mason."

Mason met his eyes, said affably, "I'm quite sure you're not."

There was a silence for several seconds.

"Now, then," Mason went on, "Ethel Garvin came down to Oceanside at an early hour this morning. She stopped in here and had her gasoline tank filled. I don't know what she told you, or what you told her, but I *do* know that she started out from here, drove down the road about two miles, stopped her car in a parking place off by the side of the road and was murdered."

"I suppose," Hackley said, "all this is just a conversational background, a barrage of words by which you're trying to get me to commit myself. I'm quite certain that this Ethel Garvin, whoever she is, wasn't murdered. I think you're probably simply trying to get some admission out of me that I knew her in Nevada. Now, then, if you'll put your cards on the table and tell me what you want to know and why you want to know it, we may get along a lot better."

Mason said, "You have a telephone over there in the corner. Just ring the Oceanside police and ask them if Ethel Garvin was murdered at an early hour this morning."

Hackley promptly got up, crossed over to the telephone, smiled and said, "That's a very nice bluff you're running, Mason, but it isn't going to work because I'm going to call you cold. Whenever a man makes a pass at me, I call him."

He picked up the receiver, said, "I want the police station, please," and then after a moment said, "Can you kindly tell me whether an Ethel Garvin was murdered this morning somewhere near Oceanside? . . . Never mind *who* this is, I'm simply asking a question. . . Well, let's put it this way. I might be a witness in case there's anything to it . . ."

Hackley held the telephone in silence for several seconds, then said abruptly, "Thank you," and slammed the receiver back into place.

He turned and faced his audience, then started pacing the floor, eyes half slitted in thought, his hands pushed down deep in the side pockets of his double-breasted coat. Abruptly he turned, standing with his back to the wall. "All right," he said, "you win."

"What do we win?" Mason asked.

Hackley's smile was without mirth. "You've won your ante back, Mr. Mason, which is more than people usually win who start playing with me. Now you said this gentleman," nodding his head toward Drake, "was a detective."

"That's right."

"From Los Angeles, San Diego, or Oceanside?"

"Los Angeles."

"Connected with the homicide squad there, Mr. Drake?"

Drake glanced at Mason and hesitated.

Mason smiled and shook his head. "He's a *private* detective. I hire him."

"Oh," Hackley said, "and the charming young lady is your secretary?"

"Yes."

"And you?"

"I'm a lawyer."

"Indeed. And you're retained by someone I take it. You're hardly investigating this case as a matter of philanthropy."

"I'm retained by someone."

"His name?"

"Edward Charles Garvin."

"The husband of the woman who was murdered?"

"The ex-husband."

"I see," Hackley said. "Makes an interesting combination, doesn't it?"

"Very."

"All right," Hackley said, "you've sneaked up on my

130

blind side. You've caught me somewhat unawares and at a disadvantage. However, I'll make my statement. No, don't bother to take it down, Miss Street. I don't think I care to have a reported interview at the present time. I'll simply make a statement of fact that you people can have as the basis for whatever investigation you are making. I'll make that much of a contribution to finding out who murdered that woman."

He paused dramatically, said, "What I'm going to tell you is the whole truth."

There was another momentary pause, and then he said, standing with his back to the wall, his eyes, moving from face to face watching to see how they were taking it, "I own a ranch in Nevada. It's rather a large holding. I like it. I like to live there. I have never married because I don't care for marriage. I am not a hermit, I like women, but the idea of settled domesticity simply doesn't appeal to me, and never has.

"There's a guest ranch, a so-called dude ranch, adjoining my property in Nevada. I find some of the guests who stay there are rather interesting. As you can well judge, many of these guests are not there simply because they like the idea of recreation on a guest ranch in Nevada. They're there because they want to establish a six weeks' residence in order to get a divorce.

"I'm frank to admit that some of those women have taken something of an interest in me and I in them. The woman who severs her domestic ties goes to a state where she has no friends, and finds herself, perhaps for the first time in years, entirely on her own, is apt to be lonesome and is apt to be seeking companionship. I happen to have a ranch that is accessible. I happen to be available, and perhaps by some of them I am considered eligible.

"I had always lived on my ranch and enjoyed it until Ethel Garvin came to Nevada, to establish a residence on this adjoining dude ranch. I liked Mrs. Garvin. I enjoyed being with her, but gradually I began to realize that she was a very determined, and a very resourceful woman. I also began to realize that she had a very definite plan of operation, and that the plan in some way concerned my future.

"I waited until it became apparent that something had to be done. The situation was drifting to a point where I, for one, found it intolerable. I didn't want to hurt her feelings. We'd been too good friends for that. I didn't want to tell her simply and plainly that I was not going to be at home when she called. I chose the easy way. I had long been looking for the right sort of investment in California. My real estate broker found this place. It was offered at what I considered a bargain as prices go these days. I told my dealer to close the deal very quietly and as far as possible to keep news of it out of the papers.

"When he had the property all in escrow, I simply slipped away from my ranch in Nevada. I left word for Ethel that I had been called away very suddenly on business that would keep me out of the state for some time, that I would get in touch with her as soon as an opportunity presented itself, but that in the meantime I was working on a deal that was so confidential I couldn't take any chance of having any slip.

"Then I jumped in my own plane and flew to Denver. At Denver I put my plane in storage, took a passenger plane for Los Angeles and picked up a new automobile which had been ready for delivery to my order, and came here to this place.

"I was very careful not to let Ethel Garvin know where I was. The information that she is or was in California comes as a distinct shock to me, something in the nature of an unpleasant surprise. I had an idea she would think I was in Florida. I rather expected she would go there.

"Needless to say, she did not come here last night or any other time to have the gasoline tank of her automobile filled, and I haven't seen her since I left Nevada.

"The news that she was murdered early this morning is more than a shock. It fills me with a sense of anger. She was a very lovable woman . . . The only comment that I could make is one that I hardly care to make under the circumstances. I *will* state that I happen to know that, during her lifetime, Ethel Garvin had a deep-seated fear of her husband. She was planning something. I don't know exactly what it was but I do know that she was very much afraid of what her husband would do when she started to put her plan into execution.

"There are some things which I do not care to say here in the presence of witnesses but which I would tell the police if I were required to do so, things that would not put your client, Mr. Mason, in the most favorable light.

"And now I think that concludes any statement I care to make and terminates the necessity of prolonging the interview."

"Very interesting," Mason said. "You will appreciate the importance of telling us the absolute truth?"

"I am not accustomed to deviating from the truth."

"You are absolutely certain that Ethel Garvin did not come here at an early hour this morning, that perhaps she didn't fill the gasoline tank without your knowing she was on the premises?"

"Absurd, gentlemen. In the first place, the gasoline pump is locked up. In the second place, she had absolutely no idea that I was in California. I took elaborate precautions to see that she didn't know where I was."

"Had you," Drake asked, "made any attempt to find out when she left Nevada?"

"What makes you ask that question, Mr. Drake?"

"You were attached to your Nevada ranch. It is hardly conceivable that you intended simply to walk away and leave it. One would gather that when the embarrassment caused by the presence of Mrs. Garvin had passed you would return."

Hackley acknowledged the point with a slight bow. "I
133

see that you have a certain ability, Mr. Drake. I am quite certain that Mr. Mason finds you a valuable assistant. The question is well taken."

"And the answer?"

"The answer," Hackley said, "is that I couldn't have secured the information without having someone on the ground who would give it to me. That someone must necessarily have known where I was in order to communicate the information. I didn't care to let *anyone* know where I was. Therefore, while I would have liked very much to have had some source of information such as you have suggested, Mr. Drake, I did not. I came here, and no one, absolutely no one, knew where I was."

"How did you keep your ranch running?"

"My foreman and manager is a very close-mouthed individual. I appreciate both his loyalty and his integrity. I also appreciate the shrewd business acumen with which he safeguards my interests. He has a checking account in an amount sufficiently ample to enable the ranch to be run during periods of my absence.

"And now if you will excuse me, Miss Street, and you, gentlemen, I have other matters to attend to. I have given you all of the information which is available and I do not care to discuss the matter further."

"You were here last night?" Mason asked.

"I said that I didn't care to discuss the matter further," Hackley said firmly. "I've given you all of the information and now I am going to wish you a good night."

He strode past them, walked with calm deliberation through the door of the living room out into the hall, and opened the outside door.

Della Street caught Mason's eye and nodded. "Go ahead, chief," she said.

Della Street walked along the edge of the room inspecting the books in the bookcases, waited for Mason and Drake to leave the room first. Then she followed after a moment.

"Good night," Hackley said with some formality.

"Good night," Mason said.

Drake said nothing.

Della Street, looking very demure, caught Hackley's eye, gave him a very personal smile, and said, "Good night, Mr. Hackley, and thank you *so* much."

"It was a pleasure," he told her.

"Rex," Hackley said, "stay there. These people are leaving."

The dog, now much more obedient and less hostile, promptly settled down on his haunches, and looked to Hackley for instructions.

Mason led the way to the automobile, climbed in the driver's seat. Drake held the door open for Della Street, and she jumped into the car. Drake followed her with an apprehensive glance over his shoulder in the direction of the dog. He slammed the door shut with a quick motion of his arm.

Della laughed, "Still thinking about the dog, Paul?" she asked.

"You're damned right I am," Drake said.

Mason started the car. Hackley, standing motionless in the doorway, watched the car glide into motion.

Della Street caught his eye, waved her hand almost surreptitiously.

Hackley's grim mouth softened into a smile. The car swept along the graveled driveway.

"Well," Drake said, "I told you he was tough."

"He's tough," Mason said, "but we still have a few clues to run down which are going to be very interesting."

"Such as what?" Drake said.

Mason said, "You can see that dog is very well trained. He certainly didn't get the dog with the place, and he didn't pick up the dog in California. The dog was one that he must have had on his Nevada ranch and of which he must be very fond, otherwise he wouldn't have taken the animal with him while he was trying to make a get-away."

"All right, what does that add up to?" Drake asked.

"Hackley is afraid of something. He leaves the dog outside guarding the place. The dog is trained so that no one can come to the place at night."

"Well, what about that?"

Mason said, "We are now going to stop at the home of Rolando C. Lomax and find out if he heard the dog staging a particularly violent demonstration of barking at approximately one o'clock this morning."

Drake chuckled, "I'll hand it to you for that one, Perry. It's an idea."

Mason drove down the graveled driveway to the pavement, then turned the car to the right, stopped in front of the house of Rolando Lomax.

Lomax, answering their ring of the bell, seemed cordial enough.

He was a husky man nearing sixty, his heavy shoulders stooped from hard work, his skin tanned and wrinkled by exposure. His hair was turning gray, matted on his forehead and still bearing evidences of perspiration resulting from physical effort. The sleeves of his woolen shirt were rolled up disclosing hairy arms and huge powerful hands.

Mason said, "We're investigators checking up on something that happened in the neighborhood. Perhaps you've heard about it."

"You mean the woman who was killed down the highway?"

Mason nodded.

"What did you want to know?"

"You were here last night?"

"Yes."

"Did you," Mason asked, "hear anything unusual taking place up at the house back there?"

136

"You mean the one that's been bought by that tall dude?"

"That's the one."

"I heard the dog bark like hell last night," Lomax said. "I told my wife something must be wrong. The dog was really making a commotion."

"Do you know what time it was?" Mason asked.

"I know exactly what time it was. That is, I don't know exactly what time it started, but after the dog kept on barking for a while I thought there must be something wrong and got up and looked out of the window. My bedroom window looks right over towards the Hackley house."

"Yes, yes," Mason said eagerly, "and what happened?"

"Well, I looked at my watch. I thought something might be wrong over there. When I got up it was exactly twenty-four minutes past twelve."

"And your clock is right?" Mason asked.

"Just about right. I set it by a radio program every day. It isn't over a second or two off."

"And it was just about twelve-twenty-five?"

"Exactly twelve-twenty-four," Lomax said. "I made a note of the time."

"And how long did the dog keep barking?"

"Just about as soon as I got to the window, I saw lights come on over there in that house this Hackley had bought—and then all of a sudden the dog quit barking as though someone had told him to shut up. I waited for a while. The lights stayed on and the dog quit barking so I figured everything was all right and went back to bed. The dog must have been barking three or four minutes before I got up.

"If you ask me, that dog's a mean one, but I'm not saying anything—not yet, I'm trying to be neighborly. However, I've got chickens here and if he ever starts killing chickens I'm going to march right over there and tell Hackley that a dog like that is a city dog. He's got no

137

business being out here in the country. Never saw one of them yet that wasn't a killer when you get 'em out in the country. Damned shame too. The people who had that house used to be nice people. They were rich but neighborly. They'd do anything. I guess they were city people all right but they sort of fitted into a country background.

"Now you take this here Hackley, he's different. He's city from the word 'go' and he's one of these fellows that doesn't want to have any neighbors. He treats me as though I wasn't here. Just goes on by. Sometimes he'll nod, sometimes he won't. Never has stopped to pass the time of day.

"Out here in the country a man gets to depend on his neighbors and when you find a man who's unsociable like that it bothers you."

"It certainly would," Mason said.

"So I'm not under any obligations to put up with any monkeyshines from that dog. Don't like 'im. Had trouble with a dog like that once before."

"And the dog only barked once that night?"

"Just that one time," Lomax said.

"You didn't happen to notice a car going in or out of the driveway?"

"I didn't happen to notice any car," Lomax said doggedly. "When I go to bed, I go to bed to sleep. I've got a thirty-acre ranch here and it's a job working it. I'm pretty tired and ready for bed when it gets that time of day. I listen to the news broadcast at nine o'clock, and then I'm ready to roll in. I don't usually wake up until daylight. I'm up just about daylight and starting work. What's more, I'm not the sort that pries into the affairs of my neighbors and I don't want my neighbors prying into *my* affairs. I want to live and let live. That's the way we are down here."

"And you didn't see or hear any automobile?"

"I didn't see or hear anything until I heard that dog

barking and I got up then to see what it was all about. The way the dog sounded—well, it's the way a dog sounds when he's a little worked up over something. Pretty hysterical, if you ask me."

"You think somebody was over there?"

"I think the dog was pretty much worked up over something."

"You didn't see anyone over there?"

"It's just like I told you. I saw the lights were on in the house and after a while the dog quit barking. Then I went back to bed."

"And how long before you went to sleep?" Mason asked.

"How long before what?"

"Before you went back to sleep."

"I don't know," Lomax said. "I didn't have any stop watch. It might have been—I don't know. Hell, it might have been thirty seconds, maybe almost a minute."

"Thank you," Mason said, smiling. "Please don't mention anything about our having been here. I don't want Hackley to know we stopped in and I think that you and Hackley would get along better if he didn't know you've given us this information."

"I don't care what he knows," Lomax said. "I hew to the line and the chips can fall where they want to."

Mason wished him good night. The three trooped back to Mason's car.

Della Street said, "I committed a little petit larceny out there at Hackley's place."

"How come?" Mason asked.

She laughed and said, "Just my woman's eye. I don't suppose either of you noticed the woman's scarf that had been thrown in the corner back on top of the bookcase, did you?"

"A scarf?" Mason said. "Lord, no!"

Della Street reached inside of her blouse and pulled out a colored silken scarf, a scarf which was a blending

139

of pastel shades starting with a strip of green and merging gradually into a strip of deep violet.

"Do you," she asked Perry Mason, "smell anything?"

Mason raised the scarf to his nose, then gave a low whistle.

"Della! Is that the scent I think it is?"

"What is it?" Drake asked.

Mason said, "Unless I'm greatly mistaken, that is the perfume used by my friend Virginia Bynum."

Della Street said, "It's rather faint, probably nothing you could make stand up in court, but—well, it's a thought, chief."

"It's more than a thought," Mason said frowning. "It's a problem."

"And here," said Della Street, "is something else."

She pulled a flattened small woman's hat out from under her coat. "The scarf and the hat were together on the bookshelf in the corner. You'll remember Drake's man said he remembered Ethel Garvin was wearing a hat when she left her apartment."

Mason took the hat.

Drake emitted a low whistle. "Damn it, Perry, suppose *both* of those women were in love with Hackley!"

"And both here last night," Mason said significantly.

13

MASON, THE MORNING MAIL STACKED UNOPENED ON HIS desk, paced the floor, from time to time tossing comments to Della Street.

"The thing doesn't tie in," Mason said. And then after a moment, "The gas tank on that car of Ethel Garvin's was full . . . The windshield was dirty . . . She didn't get that tank filled at a service station unless she was in too big a hurry to wait to have the windshield cleaned. *That* doesn't sound reasonable."

Again Mason paced the floor, then tossed out a few more comments.

"We know that someone was at Hackley's at twelve-twenty-four in the morning. We *think* that Virginia Bynum may have been there but she *couldn't* have been there at that time because she was out on the fire escape watching Denby."

Della Street said, "Well, as far as I'm concerned, the one *I* would like to know about is Frank C. Livesey. I've known men just like him before. He's conceited, vain and, if you ask me, he's cruel."

"What makes you think he's cruel?"

"I know he's cruel. It's his way with women. He's a man who's been a playboy. He finds himself getting past the age of playing, but he's in a job where a certain class of girl is absolutely dependent upon him. Not for her bread and butter perhaps, but for her gingerbread and cake, and with that type of girl gingerbread and cake is really more important than the bread and butter."

Mason said, "That doesn't mean anything."

"The heck it doesn't," Della Street said. "A man of that type becomes arrogant. He . . ."

Knuckles sounded on the exit door of Mason's private office, one rap then a pause, three raps then a pause, then two raps.

"That's Paul Drake's code knock," Mason said. "Let him in."

Della Street opened the door. Paul Drake entered the office, grinned a greeting, said to Mason, "What are you doing, wearing holes in the carpet again?"

"That's right," Mason said. "I'm trying to get the thing straightened out."

"Well," Drake told him, "I have some news for you."

"What?"

"Police have located a man down in Oceanside by the name of Irving, Mortimer C. Irving . . . Now, get the time element of this thing, Perry, because it's important."

"Okay, shoot."

"Irving had been down visiting some friends at La Jolla. He was driving back to Oceanside and was a little worried about the time. As a matter of fact he'd evidently been in a poker game down in La Jolla and he didn't want his wife to find out about it. He had lost some money and was feeling pretty glum about it. He made a point of noticing the time because he was getting a story ready for his better half."

"Go on," Mason said.

"When he got to within about two miles of Oceanside he saw a car parked off to the side of the road. The lights were on. What's more they were on the bright beam so that even coming up the road the way he was, the glare bothered him."

"What time?" Mason asked.

"Well," Drake said, "the guy got home at exactly twelve-fifty. He looked at his watch and his wife also verifies that. Ten minutes to one in the morning."

"Go ahead," Mason said.

"Now the important point," Drake said, "is that this thing ties in with the testimony of a rancher who remembers that a car was parked for a while so that the lights shone into his bedroom. He didn't pay too much attention to it but he remembered that there was a car there somewhere around the middle of the night. He didn't look at his watch or a clock and therefore his testimony doesn't amount to much for practical purposes, but in any event we know that a car *was* parked there."

Mason nodded.

"Now this man Irving enters the picture and he could be a damned dangerous witness. He says that he wondered why a car was parked there with the lights on the bright beam and thought perhaps someone might be in trouble."

"Go on," Mason said. "What did he do?"

"Well, he brought his car to a stop but kept in the road. He has a spotlight on his machine and he swung that spotlight around and looked the car over. He said it was a big light or tan-colored convertible and that no one was in it. It was standing there with the lights on—and he looked it over pretty carefully. He couldn't see any sign of anyone anywhere around the automobile, just the car standing there. He didn't take the license number but he did give it a pretty good once-over. Now, then, get this, Perry, the description of the car is one that *could* match Garvin's automobile."

"Or any other convertible, for that matter," Mason said. "All the guy knows is that he saw a big convertible."

"Tan colored."

"Lots of them are that color," Mason said. "Mine is a light brown, Garvin's is a light shade of bluish gray that would probably look tan in the light of a spotlight. You see all sorts of convertibles in the light colors."

"I know it," Drake said. "I'm just telling you what the police have. Now by the time they get done with this witness he could be damned dangerous. You know what they'll do. They'll start coaching him and telling him what he saw until finally he'll become convinced that he actually saw Garvin's car. He'll even recognize any dents in the fenders. He might get to thinking he remembers the license number."

Mason nodded moodily and said, "It's a crime the way witnesses hypnotize themselves—sometimes with the aid of the police. I . . . ."

The door from the outer office opened and Gertie, the telephone operator and receptionist, came bouncing into the room only to stop short at sight of Paul Drake.

"Oh," she exclaimed, "I thought you and Della were alone."

"It's all right," Mason said. "What is it?"

"Mrs. Garvin is on the telephone, Mr. Mason. She's calling from San Diego, and she's all excited. She says she simply has to talk with you right away and—well, I thought perhaps you'd like to have me plug in both lines so Della could listen and perhaps take notes. She's . . ."

"Go ahead, do that, Gertie," Mason said, "and then put her on the line."

As Gertie turned and ran back to the outer office, Mason nodded to Della Street and said, "Take a notebook, Della. Make notes on what she says."

Della Street nodded, opened her notebook, waited until the jingle on the bell showed that Gertie had put the call on both lines, then she nodded to Perry Mason. They picked up the receivers on the two telephones simultaneously.

"Hello," Mason said.

Lorraine Garvin said hysterically, "Oh, Mr. Mason, I'm so glad I got you. I . . ."

"Take it easy," Mason said. "Tell me what's happened."

"They tricked us."

"Who did?"

"The police."

"What happened?"

"Well, the Mexican immigration authorities came to us and wanted to know how long we were remaining in Mexico and Edward told them he didn't know, that we might go down to Ensenada and that we might be there for two or three weeks, we might even be there longer.

"Well, they were very nice about it, but told us we'd have to get tourist cards. They said those tourist cards were good for six months, that they were issued at the immigration station at the border and that we wouldn't have to go across the border to the U. S. side to get them but could just have them issued on the Mexican side."

"All right, then what happened?"

"So we got in Edward's car and started for the border,

but when we got there, the officers kept pushing us over into a line of traffic that was off to the right. Ed tried to explain to them that he wanted to get tourist cards but they didn't talk English."

"All right, what happened?"

"Well, the first thing we knew we were in a line of traffic that was headed for the United States side and we couldn't get out of it. So Ed thought it would be best to just drive the car across and then swing right around and come back on the Mexican side. The cars were going right on through one right after the other, the officers at the border just looking to make sure there was no contraband and then motioning them on."

"You should have known better," Mason told her, frowning.

"We know better now," she told him. "Well, it was just a trap. We tried to pull out and a couple of U. S. traffic officers blew whistles and yelled at us to get back into line and Ed told them we just wanted to get tourist cards and they said we'd have to go across and come around now, that we couldn't get out of line. So we crossed over the border and the minute we did a car shot out from the United States side and drew alongside and that man Tragg grinned at us and said to Edward, 'I told you we'd do it the hard way if you didn't come the easy way,' and they took Edward to San Diego and put him in jail."

"Where are you now?"

"I'm at the U. S. Grant Hotel in San Diego."

"They didn't arrest you?"

"No, they were very nice to me. They told me how very sorry they were to inconvenience me and that I could go back to Mexico in the car and get our bags. And then they called again and asked me if I had any objection to letting them look the car over."

"Where's the car?"

"In the garage here at the hotel."

"Hadn't they looked it over before?"

"Well, they looked it over when they took us in, but now it seems they want to take it and have it searched for fingerprints or something. They said they'd have to have it for about three hours."

Mason said, "Where are the keys to the car?"

"In the car, I guess."

"When did the police telephone you?"

"Just now."

"What did you tell them?"

"I told them that I'd have to go across the border to get my bags and check out of that little hotel there in Tijuana. They told me that they'd give me a police car and . . ."

Mason interrupted to say hurriedly, "Now, do exactly what I tell you to. Get tough with them. Tell them that you certainly aren't going to be seen riding around in any police car; that you're going back to get those bags; that they can send an officer with you if they want, but you're going back in your own car and get those bags and check out of the Hotel Vista de la Mesa. Do you understand that?"

"Yes."

"And see that you do that," Mason said. "Don't let them get their hands on that automobile for at least an hour and a half or two hours. Delay the thing just as much as you can. Don't act as though you're trying to conceal anything, but simply be mad and hurt and annoyed and independent. Be sure that you don't tell the officers that they *can't* have the car. Tell them they can have it as soon as you get back from across the border. Do you understand?"

"Yes, but I don't see why . . ."

"You don't have to," Mason said. "Do exactly as I tell you and don't tell anyone you've been talking with me. Now you understand what you're to do?"

"Yes, but I . . ."

"Do it, then," Mason said. "Delay things so it's two

146

hours if possible before the police get hold of your automobile. I've got to get busy. Have confidence in me. Do exactly what I tell you. Good-by."

Mason hung up the telephone.

"What is it?" Drake asked.

Mason, on his feet, his eyes sharp with excitement, said, "Just as you said, Paul. You know what's going to happen? The police are trying to get hold of Garvin's car. They tricked him into going across the border, and then nabbed him. Now they want to get his automobile. You know what they're going to do with it? They're going to take that automobile up to Oceanside, show it to Irving, have Irving say that that's the car he saw, then let Irving look it all over carefully, and point out any little individual things he can find on the car—fender dents or dented hub caps or anything of that sort."

"Well," Drake said, wearily, "there's nothing you can do about it. After all, if Irving is the kind who falls for a deal like that . . ."

"They all fall for it," Mason said. "Don't be silly. You know what happens with witnesses."

"What happens?" Drake asked, lighting his cigarette.

Mason said, with feeling, "It's been demonstrated dozens of times that if you have a crime committed in front of a whole room full of witnesses and then call on those witnesses to make a written statement of what took place, the statements will contain all sorts of variations and contradictions. People simply can't see things and then tell what they've seen with any degree of accuracy."

"I suppose so," Drake said.

"Hell, it's been demonstrated time and again," Mason said. "It's a favorite stunt in classes in psychology in college. But what happens when you have witnesses in the trial of a case? They get on the stand one after another and tell a story that might have been written on a mimeograph. A witness sees something. He tells it to the police. The police point out little discrepancies between his story and that of the other witnesses. They point out what must have happened. Then they let the fellow think it over. Then they talk with him again. Then they let him talk it over with other witnesses. Then they take him to the scene of the crime. Then they get the witnesses to re-enact what happened. By the time a witness gets on the stand he's testifying to a composite of what he saw, what he thinks he saw, what the other fellow tells him *he* saw, and what he concludes he must have seen, judging from the physical evidence. Look at what's happening in this case right under our noses. They've found this witness. They're going to take Garvin's automobile and . . ."

"I know," Drake said, "but there's nothing we can do."

"The hell there isn't," Mason said. "You take Della in your car. Follow me just as fast as you can."

"What are *you* going to do, Perry?"

Mason said, "I'm going to take *my* convertible, drive it down to Oceanside, park it in just about the position the witness says that other car was parked. You and Della are going to get Mr. Mortimer C. Irving, tell him you want him to take a look at a car, and drive him down the highway. My convertible will be parked there and I'll bet you ten to one the guy identifies my convertible as the one he saw—if he sees it *before* he sees Garvin's car."

"And then what?" Drake asked dubiously.

"And then," Mason said, "we're going to come back home and Mrs. Lorraine Garvin is going to tell the police they can 'borrow' her car to look it over. The police will rush the car up to Oceanside and ask Irving to identify it. Irving will then tell them that isn't the car, that he's already identified the car, that it's a car with a certain license number."

"He won't identify it if he thinks it belongs to you and knows who you are," Drake said.

"He won't know who I am," Mason told him, "and he won't know whom the car belongs to."

Drake shook his head and said, "In the words of a

man who has a lot more sense than I have in such matters, 'include me out.' "

"Why?"

"It's too damned dangerous. You can get into trouble over that."

"What sort of trouble?" Mason asked. "All we're doing is asking a man to identify a car."

"And pulling a razzle-dazzle on him. You're making him think it was the same car he saw there shortly after midnight and . . ."

"And that's exactly what the police are going to be doing," Mason said. "The police adopt the position that it's all right when they do it, but illegal when someone else does it. The hell with that stuff! Are you coming or not?"

"Not," Drake said positively. "I have a license to consider. That's getting too close to . . ."

Mason glanced over at Della Street.

She pushed her chair back, started for the hat closet and said, "My car's in the parking lot, chief. It's all filled. I can't make quite as good time with it as you can with that big convertible of yours, but I'll be right on your heels if you keep anywhere near the speed limit."

Mason grabbed his hat. "Let's go," he said.

Drake said, "There'll be a hell of a squawk over that, Perry. They'll . . ."

"Let them squawk," Mason said. "I'm not going to sit tight and let them put ideas in the mind of that witness. I'm not going to let them hypnotize my client into a murder rap. If I have a right to cross-examine a man and ask him how he knows that's the car, *after* he's given his testimony in court, I have a right to cross-examine him before he testifies and demonstrate to him that he can't really tell one convertible from another. Come on, Della."

14

■

Perry Mason and Della Street stopped in front
of the unpretentious little house on a side street in Oceanside.

Mason, leaving Della Street at the wheel, left her car,
climbed the steps and knocked on the door.

A redheaded woman with a truculent manner jerked
open the door. Deep-set blue eyes sized Mason up from a
toil-worn face. She said, "We don't want anything," and
started to slam the door.

"Just a minute," Mason said, laughing, "I want to see
your husband."

"He's working."

"Can you tell me where?"

"At the Standard Service Station."

"He's told you about the automobile he saw when he
was driving back from La Jolla?"

"Yes," she said.

"I want to talk with him about it," Mason told her.
"Did he describe it to you?"

"All he could see was that it was a sort of a light-
colored convertible. There was no one in it. It wasn't the
car that woman was driving when she was killed."

"You know what time he got home?"

"I'll say I know what time he got home," she said. "Ten
minutes to one. Sitting down there with those fellows
swapping yarns and gambling money that he hasn't any
right to risk! He's a lousy poker player, always trying to
bluff when he doesn't have a good hand—coming back
with a lot of stories and . . ."

"We'll find him at the filling station?"

"That's right."

Mason thanked her, walked rapidly back to the automobile, and had Della Street drive him to the filling station where he inquired for Mortimer Irving.

Irving, a tall, slow-moving, genial individual with twinkling eyes who managed somehow to look a lot younger than his wife, grinned at them and said, "Yeah. I saw this car down there—didn't think anything of it at the time but—well, you know, I saw the lights on and—oh, I don't know, I just sort of wondered. I thought maybe some girl was having a little difficulty and had switched on the lights hoping it would attract attention and—shucks, I don't know, I just turned my spotlight on it."

Mason said, "Could you get away from here for about half an hour?"

"Nope."

"If I gave you ten dollars?" Mason asked.

The man hesitated.

"And another ten that you could slip to your buddy who's on duty to take care of all the customers who came in while you were gone?"

Irving tilted back his hat and scratched his head, thinking the matter over.

"How much did you lose at the poker game?" Mason asked, his voice friendly.

"A little over fifteen bucks."

"Why didn't you say so in the first place?" Mason asked. "I'll give you twenty dollars, another ten for the man who's on duty with you, and another five for the boy who's running the washrack to come over and help out in case cars get jammed up here. Then you can go ahead and tell your wife that you really made a profit on the trip to La Jolla, after all. You lost fifteen or sixteen bucks and got twenty back."

Irving said, "You sure do know how to sell a bill of goods, mister. If I could talk like that I'd be the top salesman for the whole United States. Just a second and I'll go talk to the boys."

"Here's the thirty-five dollars," Mason said, counting out a twenty, a ten and a five. "You won't be gone more than a few minutes."

Irving went over and talked with his assistant, then with the man at the grease rack. He came back with a grin, opened the rear door of the car, climbed in and said, "Now this is *really* going to be fun. I'll enjoy going home tonight and meeting the wife. I was thinking I'd rather take a beating than to go back and hear about that money I lost in the poker game. Now I'm going to enjoy it."

Mason nodded to Della Street who drove the car rapidly down the highway.

"You think you'd know this convertible if you saw it again?" Mason asked.

"Well, to tell you the truth, I didn't take a look at it so much to see what make and year and model and all that stuff it was. I just looked it over the way a person would to see if people were in it. I was a little worried about—oh, I don't know, I was thinking that some girl had maybe got out with a wolf who was getting a little too rough or something, and . . . shucks, I don't know, I just saw the lights and I stopped and turned my spotlight on the car, that's all. At night that way when you turn a spotlight on an automobile, the light brings the car out sharply against a dark background, but there aren't any shadows or anything. It's what you'd call a flat picture if you were talking about it in terms of photography."

"I see you play around with a camera," Mason said.

"I do when I can get enough money to buy film. I get a great kick out of it."

"Well," Mason said, "we'll see if we can't get you some film. What size does your camera take?"

"Six-twenty."

"We'll see what we can do about that," Mason told him.

Della Street started slowing the car.

"Now, then," Mason said, "there's a convertible parked over there. Is that about the same position that the car was parked when you . . ."

"That's just about the same position and that's just about the same kind of car. Just about that size and . . ."

"And as nearly as you can tell," Mason said, "that's the same car. In other words, it has the same characteristics, generally, as the car you saw. It could be the same car."

"It *could* be," Irving said.

Della Street stopped the car, surreptitiously picked up a notebook and balancing it on her leg started taking down the conversation.

"In other words, from your best recollection of the car that you saw parked here early in the morning when you were returning from La Jolla, you couldn't say definitely that this car you're looking at now is that car, and you couldn't say that it isn't that car."

"I'll say it *looks* like the car," Irving said. "In fact, from all I can tell from here, it *is* the car.'

"You didn't notice any distinguishing features?"

"Just that it was a light-colored convertible and it was just about the same size and color and just about the same shape as this one. I—what do you want me to say? That this *is* the car?"

Mason grinned and said, "I just want you to tell me the truth. I'm investigating the case and trying to find out in good faith just what type of car it was and just how well you saw it and how well you can identify it."

"Well, to tell you the truth," Irving said, "just looking that thing over . . . Look, I was coming from the other direction. Suppose we go down the road a little bit, turn around and come back."

Mason, nudging Della Street, said, "All right, I'll drive, Della."

He got out and walked around the car to slide in behind the steering wheel. Della Street, still keeping her notebook out of sight on her lap, slid over to the right-hand side.

Mason drove the car down the road, made a U-turn, then came on back, driving slowly.

"Stop just about here," Irving said. "Now let me take a look . . . Shucks, that could be the same car as far as I'm concerned. It has the same lines and—and it's standing in just about the same place. Right about here is where I stopped my car. I saw that other car from just about this angle. As far as I'm concerned that could be the same car. You understand I can't identify it and say it *is* the same car, but I sure can't say it *isn't*."

"That's fine," Mason said. "That, I think, covers it. That seems to me to be a pretty fair statement of facts. As nearly as you can tell that could be the car standing right there."

"That convertible standing right there," Irving said.

"By the way," Mason said, "my eyes aren't too good. Can you read the license number on it?"

"Move back just a little bit," Irving said, "and I think I can."

Mason backed the car.

Irving read the license number, "9 Y 6 3 7 0."

"That's fine," Mason said, then added, "I guess that covers it."

He started the car, drove rapidly back to Oceanside, stopped at the service station, let Irving out, then made a turn back down the highway.

Della Street smiled and said, "Now *there's* a fair-minded witness."

"He is now," Mason said, "but by the time the police got done putting ideas in his mind, he would have felt certain the only car that would have answered the description of the one he saw there was the convertible belonging to Edward C. Garvin."

Mason crowded the speed limit until he had left Oceanside, and then really stepped on the gas. "I want to get there and get that convertible out of the way before the police arrive," he said.

Half a mile from the place where he had parked the car, Della Street said, "It looks as though you're too late, chief."

Mason exclaimed under his breath as the glare of a red spotlight shone in the distance on the highway. Then the sound of a siren reached their ears.

A big police car, followed by a man driving Edward Garvin's convertible, slid rubber as they braked to a stop in front of the place where Mason's car was parked.

"Might just as well go through with it," Mason said with a grin, and turning off the highway drove up to a point beside his convertible.

A man, whose vest had a shield bearing the words SAN DIEGO COUNTY, DEPUTY SHERIFF, accompanied by Sergeant Holcomb, came striding across from where the police cars were parked.

"What's the idea?" Holcomb demanded belligerently.

"Just parked my car here for a while," Mason said.

"*Your* car?"

"That's right."

"What are you trying to do?" the deputy sheriff inquired.

Mason said, "I'm trying to find out who murdered Ethel Garvin. I understand my client has been taken into custody and charged with that murder."

"Come on," Holcomb said belligerently, "what's the idea of parking your car here?"

"Any law against it?" Mason asked.

"I want to know what the idea is."

Mason's face was a mask of cherubic innocence. "Well, gentlemen," he said, "I'm going to be frank with

155

you. I'm trying my best to uncover evidence as to the real facts in the case. I understood there was a man here in Oceanside by the name of Irving who had seen a car parked here. Now, just to show you my willingness, to co-operate, I'm going to tell you all about him. His name is Mortimer C. Irving. You'll find him at the Standard Station—the first one on the right-hand side as you go in to town. He's a likable chap, and he was down at La Jolla playing poker the night the murder was committed.

"He was driving back and he saw a car parked there. It had the lights on. Now, quite definitely it wasn't the car in which the body of Ethel Garvin was found. It was a different type of car. As nearly as he can remember it was a convertible.

"I'd like very much to find out something more about that automobile but unfortunately Irving can't tell us very much about it. All he knows is that it was a big convertible. He thinks that it was just about the color and size of this car of mine that I left parked here so he could look it over."

"In other words," Holcomb said, "you forced an identification on him. Is that right?"

"I didn't force any identification on anybody on anything," Mason said.

"The hell you didn't," Holcomb blazed. "You know as well as I do the only way for a man to make an absolute identification of an automobile or a person is to pick one out of a line-up. You planted *one* car there in the same position and . . ."

"And by the way what were *you* intending to do with Garvin's car?" Mason asked.

"We're looking it over for fingerprints," the deputy sheriff said.

Mason bowed and smiled. "Well, don't let me interfere, gentlemen. If Mr. Garvin let you have the automobile I'm quite certain you'll find he's only too glad to co-operate in every way that he can.

"Incidentally, Mr. Garvin has a perfect alibi for the hours during which the murder was committed . . . And now, if you'll pardon me, gentlemen, I'll be getting back to my office."

And Mason moved over to his convertible, opened the door, slid in behind the steering wheel, turned on the ignition, started the motor, and purred away, leaving the two officers standing there, watching him with angry eyes, but hardly knowing exactly what to say under the circumstances.

15

HAMLIN L. COVINGTON, THE DISTRICT ATTORNEY OF San Diego County, sized up Perry Mason as the defense lawyer entered the courtroom, then turned to his chief deputy, Samuel Jarvis.

"A good-looking fellow," Covington whispered, "but I can't see that he's any wizard."

"He's dangerous," Jarvis warned.

Covington, a dignified, tall, powerfully built man, said, "Well, there's certainly no need to be afraid of him in *this* case. He probably makes a lot of fast maneuvers, and gets those boys up north all worked up trying to follow him. I'm not going to be tricked into trying to follow him. I'm going to maintain a solid position against which that damned shyster can dash himself with no more effect than the ocean smashing spray against the Sunset Cliffs."

Sam Jarvis nodded, and then grinned, triumphantly. "If Mason only knew what we had waiting for him," he gloated.

"Well," Covington said, with a certain self-righteous dignity, "after all, he has it coming to him. He likes to pull fast ones in court. We'll cure him.

"And," Covington continued, "he's going to get a citation to appear before the grievance committee of the Bar Association on that automobile identification business. *That's* going to slow him down some on cross-examination. The more he tries to mix the witness up, the more he's going to give the Bar Association a foundation for its complaint."

Covington chuckled with satisfaction. "We'll show him that we do things a little differently in *this* bailiwick, eh Jarvis?"

"You bet," Jarvis agreed. "When he hears . . ."

Abruptly the door from the judge's chambers opened, and Judge Minden entered the courtroom.

Lawyers, spectators and courtroom attaches stood in a body as the judge walked over to the bench, hesitated a moment, then nodded gracious permission to the crowd to be seated.

The bailiff, who had pounded the court to order with his gavel, intoned, "The Superior Court of the State of California, in and for the County of San Diego, Honorable Judge Harrison E. Minden, presiding, is now in session."

"People of the State of California versus Edward Charles Garvin," Judge Minden said.

"Ready for the prosecution," Covington announced.

"And for the defendant, Your Honor," Mason said, smiling urbanely.

"Proceed with the impanelment of the jury," Judge Minden told the clerk.

Covington whispered to Samuel Jarvis, "You go ahead and impanel a jury, Sam. I'm going to keep myself in reserve . . . Sort of a big gun to blast Mason out of the water. Only we won't need to do much blasting in this case."

"He'll be blasted all right," Jarvis said, "whenever we get ready to press the button."

Covington stroked his gray mustache. His eyes twinkled with appreciation of the picture his assistant created.

Judge Minden said, "As the names of prospective jurors are called, you will come forward and take your place in the jury box. Mr. Clerk, draw twelve names."

Judge Minden made a brief statement to the jury impanelment concerning their duties, called on the district attorney to advise the jurors of the nature of the case, asked the prospective jurors a few routine questions, then turned them over to the attorneys for questioning.

Mason varied his usual courtroom technique by asking only the most vague and general questions.

District Attorney Covington, suddenly suspicious, whispered a warning to Jarvis, forced Jarvis to continue with a long line of searching questions until gradually it dawned on Covington that the district attorney's office was apparently being maneuvered into the position of try-trying to get a hand-picked jury, while the defense seemed casually willing to accept any twelve men who were fair.

Questions concerning the death penalty removed four jurors from the box, but their places were filled, and Mason, smiling, seemed to treat the entire matter as being a mere procedural formality preliminary to an acquittal.

Nettled, District Attorney Covington took over some of the examination himself, and finally, late that afternoon when a jury had been impaneled, the thoroughly exasperated district attorney realized that Mason had outgeneraled him, because the lawyer, swiftly exercising those peremptory challenges for which no reason need be given, showed that he had somehow acquired a thorough knowledge of the characters and backgrounds of the prospective jurymen.

159

"Do you care to make an opening statement, Mr. District Attorney?" Judge Minden asked.

It had been understood that Jarvis was to make the opening statement, but Covington, angry and flustered, was on his feet in front of the jury, telling them that he expected to prove that the defendant, Edward Charles Garvin, had, as the result of an illegal divorce, found himself faced with a bigamy prosecution, involved in a hopeless maze of domestic entanglements, and so had conceived the idea of extricating himself by the simple but deadly expedient of pulling the trigger of a revolver.

"I expect to show you, ladies and gentlemen," Covington said, his voice crisp with denunciation, "that this man deliberately lured his wife into a midnight appointment, an appointment from which he had carefully planned she should never return alive. A cold-blooded, deliberate, well-planned, skillfully executed murder which might never have been uncovered had it not been . . ."

A tug at his coattail from Samuel Jarvis made Covington realize suddenly he was telling too much. He paused, cleared his throat, said, "had it not been for the efforts of the police of this county, working in friendly co-operation with those of Los Angeles County.

"I shall not, however, ladies and gentlemen, dwell at any great length upon the evidence. I propose to show that the defendant fled from the United States to Mexico, where he sought haven and sanctuary from a charge which his wife had placed against him, and . . ."

"Just a moment," Mason interrupted cheerfully. "Your Honor, I object to any attempt on the part of the prosecution to introduce evidence of any other independent crime for the purpose of discrediting the defendant, and charge the remarks of the district attorney as prejudicial misconduct. I ask that the Court admonish the jury to disregard the remarks."

"If the Court please," Covington said angrily, "this is an exception to the general rule. This is a case where the charge of bigamy which was placed against the defendant by his wife is the motive for the murder. That is something counsel for the defense knows very well. It is a case where we are permitted to introduce evidence of another crime. We are forced to do so in order to prove our motive. It was because of this crime that the defendant fled to Mexico and because of it that he decided to murder his wife, and make himself a widower, so that he could then go through another marriage ceremony with the woman with whom he had become infatuated."

"Same objection," Mason said, cheerfully, "same assignment as misconduct."

Judge Minden said, testily, "Well, of course, Mr. District Attorney, I don't know what the evidence is going to disclose, but it would seem to me that you're anticipating a legal point. Wouldn't it be better to reserve this matter until the time comes when you wish to put in your evidence, and then we can have an objection from the defense, the jury can be excluded during argument, and the Court can then make an intelligent ruling? This is, in a way, approaching the subject by the back door, and the Court is hardly in a position to make an intelligent ruling. It may be part of the *res gestae* but in order to determine that point we should first find out *what* the circumstances are.

"I think it would be much better if you simply stated to the jury what you expected to prove in regard to the motions and activities of the defendant at the time the murder was committed and then left these legal questions to be disposed of in an orderly manner."

"Very well, Your Honor," Covington conceded with poor grace. "If the Court wishes me to adopt that procedure, I shall do so."

"Under the circumstances," Judge Minden said, "and for the purpose of protecting the rights of the defendant, the Court will admonish the jury not to pay any attention to any remarks which have been made *at this time* by the district attorney concerning the commission of another crime."

Covington, angrily realizing that he had been placed in a position where it looked as though he had attempted improperly to influence the jury, blurted, "That is about all, ladies and gentlemen. I am going to prove beyond all reasonable doubt that this defendant committed the murder, that it was a dastardly, premeditated, cold-blooded murder, and I'm going to ask for a conviction of first degree murder without recommendation. In other words, I'm going to ask for the death penalty for this defendant."

Covington turned and glowered in anger at Edward Garvin, then at Perry Mason. He sat down abruptly, whispered to Jarvis, "Damn his supercilious smirk! I'll make him take this case seriously before so very long."

"Proceed with your case," Judge Minden said, "or does the defendant wish to make an opening statement at this time?"

"Oh, if the Court please," Mason said, casually, "I'll make a very brief opening statement."

He got up from his chair, walked over to the rail in front of the jury box, glanced impressively at the jurors, and took a deep breath as though about to launch upon some elaborate summation of the case.

The jurors, aware of Mason's reputation as a trial lawyer in another jurisdiction, many of them seeing him for the first time, surveyed him with friendly interest.

Mason said, "If the Court please, and ladies and gentlemen of the jury." He paused dramatically for a moment. Then his face softened into a smile and he said, "He can't prove it."

And then, before the jurors or the district attorney realized that this was all of his opening statement, Mason turned and walked back to the defense table.

One or two of the jurors smiled. A slight ripple of

mirth developed in the courtroom and was silenced by the judge's gavel.

"Proceed," Judge Minden said to the district attorney, but those who noticed the judge's countenance saw there was a slight twinkle even in His Honor's eye.

Covington leaned over to Sam Jarvis. "You go ahead and prove the *corpus delicti,* Sam," he said in a hoarse whisper. "I'm going out and get some air. We're going to tear this damned shyster limb from limb. When he gets done with this case the reputation he's built up as being a legal wizard will be as tattered as a rag doll that a dog has been shaking to pieces. You go ahead, Sam, and —dammit, rip the sawdust out of him."

Then Covington, striding with the outraged dignity of a man who has seldom encountered anyone with sufficient temerity to stand up and encounter his wrath, barged down the aisle of the courtroom, while his assistant started in with the long line of preliminary proof.

Knowing that the witness who had found the body was one of Drake's men, realizing that he would, if given the opportunity, slant his testimony so that it would be as advantageous as possible to Mason's side of the case, the deputy district attorney handled the man with gloves.

He merely asked him if he had found, on the date in question, an automobile parked by the side of the road, had had occasion to investigate the car, and whether he had found in it the body of a woman. He brought out that the witness had found a revolver on the ground by the car and had notified the police and subsequently had seen the body at the time of the coroner's inquest and that it was the same body.

Abruptly Jarvis tossed the ball to Perry Mason.

"You may cross-examine," he said.

"No questions," Mason said.

Jarvis was visibly surprised. He had expected Mason would try to lay the foundation for his defense through this witness.

The next witness was the chief of police of Oceanside.

With this man Jarvis was much more relaxed, much more at home. The police officer testified to having been summoned to the scene, to having notified the coroner and sheriff of San Diego, of having "looked the ground over" and later on, of having attended the inquest where the identity of the murdered woman was established.

Feeling his way cautiously, Jarvis sought to qualify the man as an expert in studying tracks in connection with crime. Then, awaiting Mason's objection, the deputy showed what he could about the position of the automobile, the tracks which had been found on the ground.

Hamlin Covington returned to the courtroom, making his entrance as impressive as possible. He sat down beside his chief trial deputy, listened for a few moments, then leaned over and whispered to Jarvis, "Go ahead. Ask him what the tracks showed. Let's put Mason in the position of objecting, of trying to keep out the evidence. Smoke him out. Get him on the defensive."

Jarvis whispered, "We haven't qualified him as much of an expert. Mason will rip him to pieces. He'll take him on voir dire and rip him to pieces."

"Let him try," Covington said. "At least we'll start him objecting. We'll get him where he has to take the case seriously."

"All right," Jarvis whispered, "here goes." He rose to his feet, said to the chief of police, "Now, Chief, just what did these tracks show in regard to two cars having been parked parallel to each other?"

Then Jarvis half turned to Mason, waiting for the indignant objections. Mason might not have heard the question.

"Well, it seems this car where the body was found," the chief said, "had been parked right next to another car that had been left there, and . . ."

"Just a minute," Judge Minden said. "I'd like to have that last question read again, Mr. Reporter."

The court reporter read the question.

Judge Minden glanced expectantly at Mason.

Mason remained silent.

"Go ahead, answer the question," Covington rasped at the witness.

"Well, it was this way," the witness said. "The car that the body was found in had been driven right up next to another car that had been left parked there. You could see where the car that had the body had been inched around until it was in just the right position, and then the murderer just stepped across into the other car, dragged the body of the victim over behind the steering wheel and drove away. That's the way it was done."

"Cross-examine," Jarvis said triumphantly.

"Let's see if I get this," Mason said, his manner showing that he was merely interested, but indicating a wish to see that the jury understood the situation. "You did some tracking there, Chief?"

"I did."

"Now, you say that the car which had the body in it had been '*inched*' into position."

"That's right. I have to explain something of the nature of that ground. It's a sort of sand and decomposed granite that packs hard as concrete. You can sort of make out tracks but not tire patterns, at least not plain enough to do much with them.

"You could see where the front wheels of Ethel Garvin's car had wobbled around a little bit as the driver tried to get the car in just exactly the position he wanted. He'd even backed once in order to slide it right up next to another set of tracks that had been made by a car that had been left standing there."

"Yes, yes," Mason said, his manner showing breathless interest. "Now you say that other car had been left standing there."

"That's right."

"Then the woman wasn't killed while she was driving the car."

"No, sir, she wasn't. You can tell from the blood spatters and the position of the clotted blood that she had been over on the right-hand side when she was shot. The man who was driving the car had pulled the trigger on the gun and then he'd driven the car with the body in it right up to this point where he'd left the other car. He only had to step across from one car to the other. Then he dragged the body across behind the steering wheel and drove away."

"I see," Mason said. "Now you say the tracks showed where this other car had been left there, waiting?"

"That's right. Yes."

Mason didn't change the tone of his voice in the least, but as though passionately interested in the answer, said, "Just what was there about the tracks, Chief, that showed the car had been *waiting?*"

"Well, you could see the tracks where the car had stood there and then driven away."

"How did that show the other car had been *waiting?*"

"Well, it went in straight, and then—well, when it went out it curved back to the highway. The tracks showed that."

"I see," Mason said, "and if the tracks hadn't curved, Chief, where would the car have gone?"

"Well, it would have gone straight ahead."

"And what was straight ahead?"

"Well, it couldn't have gone straight ahead."

"Why not? What was straight ahead?"

"The Pacific Ocean."

"Oh, I see. Then the car *had* to turn."

"Of course it had to turn."

"Yet you say the only way that you knew the car was left *waiting* there was because the tracks curved?"

"Well, the car was waiting there. You could tell by

166

the way the tracks were of the car where the murdered woman was found."

"That's it," Mason agreed enthusiastically. "Now you're getting the point I want. Just what was there in the tracks of this car to show you that it had been left *waiting?*"

"Well, you could see where the tracks of Ethel Garvin's car had been manipulated around to get in just the right position."

"Then it wasn't anything in the tracks of the car that had been left *waiting* that showed you what had happened, but something you'd deduced from the tracks of an entirely different automobile."

"Well if you want to put it that way, yes."

"My dear man," Mason said, "it's not the way *I* want to put it. *You're* doing the putting. Just put it your own way, but kindly try and put it right."

"Well, that's the way it was."

"Then you were mistaken when you said you could tell from the tracks of the getaway car that it had been left waiting there?"

"No, you could tell it from the tracks like I explained to you."

"But what was there about the tracks of the car that had been left waiting that showed *it* had stood there?"

"Well, it—well, you could see from the way the other car had been sidled up to it."

"You mean the car containing the body of the murdered woman?"

"Yes."

"Try and understand the question," Mason said. "Was there anything in the tracks of the car that you say had been left waiting there that showed it had been left waiting—in the tracks of that one particular car?"

"Well, no," the chief said, and then added, by way of explanation, "naturally there couldn't be. You can't tell from car tracks whether a car just drove in and then went right out, or whether it stopped for an hour, or two hours, or four hours, unless you had some change in condition, such as a rainstorm while the car was parked there or something."

"Oh," Mason said with a disarming smile, "then you *were* mistaken in stating to the jury when you gave your testimony on direct examination that the tracks of the *parked* car showed it had been left there for a while?"

"Sure. There was nothing in *those* tracks," the man said. "It's the way you have to reconstruct the whole picture from the tracks of that other car."

"So you *were* mistaken?" Mason said.

"Well—I . . . I guess so."

"I knew you were," Perry Mason said, smiling disarmingly, "I just wanted to see how difficult it would be to make you admit it. That's all, Chief. Thank you."

"Just a minute," Covington shouted, getting to his feet. "You *weren't* mistaken in stating that the murderer left his car there while he went out and committed the crime and then drove the other car up to the position immediately parallel to his parked car, were you, Chief?"

"Come, come," Mason said, smilingly. "I'll have to object to counsel leading his own witness. I can ask leading questions on cross-examination but counsel can't ask them on direct or redirect."

"The question is leading," Judge Minden said. "The objection is sustained."

"Well, what did happen?" Covington asked.

"While the witness was present, of course," Mason amended.

"Well, he can tell what happened from an examination of the tracks."

"He tried to tell," Mason said. "He's given some conclusions from two sets of tracks. I take it no photographs were made of those tracks?"

"They were all tramped out before our photographer got there," Covington said.

"Well, of course, the *defendant* isn't responsible for that," Mason reminded him.

"Well, tell us about those tracks. What do they show?"

"Objected to as calling for a conclusion of the witness," Mason said. "No proper foundation has been laid."

"Sustained," Judge Minden snapped, but then he added somewhat acidly, "the witness has certainly given his conclusions previously as to some phases of these tracks, and without objection."

"Quite right, Your Honor," Mason said, smilingly. "And then admitted he was mistaken."

"Well, he wasn't mistaken about what happened," Covington snapped.

"The witness admitted he was mistaken," Mason said.

"Very well," Covington said sneeringly. "You may have your technicality, but I think the jury understands."

"I'm quite certain they do," Mason said.

"Your next witness," Judge Minden said to Covington.

A bailiff entered, walked over to Perry Mason, handed him a folded paper.

The lawyer unfolded it, read it.

It was a citation asking him to meet with the grievance committee of the Bar Association two days later at eight in the evening for a discussion of charges that he had tampered with a witness in a manner that resulted in changing the testimony of the witness.

Mason refolded the paper, slipped it into his pocket.

Covington watching Mason's expressionless face said to Jarvis, "Damn him, *that* will fix him. He's trying to pretend he doesn't give a hoot, but he's now in a hell of a spot.

"If he tries to break Irving down on cross-examination tomorrow, he'll be cutting his own throat. If he lets his testimony stand without trying to impeach the witness, he'll be cutting his client's throat.

"We'll teach that fellow he can't pull his fast ones when he's dealing with us."

"Come, come gentlemen," Judge Minden said irritably, "let's get on with the case."

Samuel Jarvis called a surveyor, introduced maps and diagrams. He called the autopsy surgeon. He called a friend who identified the body, then said, "If the Court please, it's approaching the hour of adjournment."

Judge Minden nodded. "I think we've made very good progress today," he said. "I'm not going to have the jury confined, but the jurors are admonished not to discuss the case among themselves or with anyone else, and I'm going to ask the jurors not to read the newspapers, to carefully avoid reading anything concerning this case. You will not discuss the case with anyone nor permit it to be discussed in your presence. You won't form or express any opinion until the case is finally submitted to you. Court's adjourned until ten o'clock tomorrow morning!"

Walking out of the courtroom and down the long corridor, Covington said to his assistant, "I can see how Mason has built up a reputation for himself. He's a grandstander, he's smart, and he's always putting on a show for the jury. Tomorrow I'm going to have the great pleasure of knocking the wind out of him. We're going to smash that poise of his like a gunner smashes a clay pigeon."

"With both barrels," Samuel Jarvis agreed, feelingly.

"With both barrels," Hamlin Covington promised.

Back in the courtroom, Mason turned to reassure his client. "Keep a stiff upper lip, Garvin."

Garvin smiled wanly. "What was that paper the officer served on you? Does it concern me?"

"Not in the least," Mason assured him. "It concerns *me.*"

16

WHEN COURT RECONVENED THE NEXT MORNING, HAMLIN
L. Covington, having slept on the events of the previous
day, and having made his first appraisal of Mason's
character, was warily watchful as he proceeded to lay
the foundation for his knockout punch.

Records were introduced showing the marriage of Edward Charles Garvin to Ethel Carter. Then by witnesses Covington proved the Mexican divorce and the
marriage to Lorraine Evans. Then Covington sought to
introduce certified copies of the records showing the filing
of the complaint charging Garvin with bigamy, the warrant which had been issued for his arrest.

"Now then," Judge Minden said, as Covington handed
up the certified copies of the records which he proposed
to introduce in evidence, "I take it this is the point at
which we can argue the matter which was touched on in
the district attorney's opening statement. I presume you'd
like to have the jury excluded, Mr. Mason, while you
make your objection and argue it."

"On the contrary," Mason said, smiling at the judge,
"after having thought the matter over, and in view of the
manner in which the evidence has now been introduced,
I think that it is a proper part of the district attorney's
case. It would go to show motive, under the hypotheses
claimed by the district attorney, so I'll make no objection
whatever."

Covington, who had been eagerly looking forward to
a courtroom battle wherein he could best Mason on the
lawyer's legal objection, yielded with bad grace. "You

made enough commotion about it when I merely touched on it in my opening statement," he said.

"That was before you had offered orderly proof," Mason told him in the manner of a teacher rebuking an ignorant and presumptuous pupil. "As the Court pointed out to you, the matter should have been handled in this way. Now that you're following this procedure I have no objection whatever, Mr. District Attorney."

"Very well," Judge Minden said quickly, forestalling the angry reply which was quite evidently trembling on Covington's lips, "the documents will be received in evidence. Proceed, Mr. District Attorney."

And Covington proceeded. Slowly, remorselessly, he built up a wall of evidence.

Virginia Bynum testified to having left the gun on the fire escape. Livesey told of bringing it in, handing it to Garvin; of being instructed to put it in the glove compartment of Garvin's car and of doing so.

George L. Denby told of the gun being brought in and handed to Garvin.

Mason seemed utterly detached, didn't even bother to cross-examine either Virginia Bynum or Livesey. He did ask Denby on cross-examination, "How do you know it was the same gun?"

"It had the same number, sir."

"Did you write the number down?"

"No, sir. I looked at it."

"And remembered it?"

"Yes, sir, I have a photographic memory for numbers. I deal in them so much I get to remember them."

"That's all," Mason snapped.

Covington grinned over at his assistant. "Dropped that one like a hot potato, didn't he?"

"I'll say," Jarvis gleefully agreed.

Covington went on with the building of a deadly wall of evidence. He showed that Edward Garvin and the woman whom he claimed as his second wife, Lorraine

Evans, had stopped in the hotel at La Jolla. Calling the woman who ran the hotel, he showed their abrupt departure; showed that immediately after driving out for dinner they had returned, packed and hastily checked out, and at that time another person had been with them, a visitor who was also driving a convertible somewhat similar in size, color and appearance to Garvin's automobile.

Covington built to his dramatic climax. "Do you," he asked the woman who managed the hotel, "know the identity of that other person?"

Mason said quite casually, "Why you don't need to waste time with that, Mr. District Attorney, *I* was the driver of that other car. I'm quite willing to admit it."

Realizing that the testimony had been robbed of much of its dramatic value, Covington, nevertheless, managed to turn Mason's admission to good account. "Exactly," he said smiling, "and immediately after your visit, the defendant, and the person to whom he then claimed he was married, went dashing off to Mexico."

"Do you," Mason asked, "want to be sworn as a witness and state that as a fact?"

"No," Covington said, smiling serenely at Mason. "I will prove it by a competent witness whom you may cross-examine Mr. Mason. Call Señora Inocente Miguerinio."

The fleshy, good-natured proprietor of the Vista de la Mesa Hotel rolled seductive hips as she walked to the stand, readily identified the defendant and the auburn-haired woman who was seated in the chair beside him; told how the pair had come to stay at her hotel on the night before the murder.

Covington looked at the clock so that he could explode his bombshell in time for the afternoon editions.

"Call Howard B. Scanlon."

Howard Scanlon, a spare, rangy man in the early fifties, whose face with high cheekbones, long, determined mouth, and faded blue eyes, showed a singular lack of self-consciousness, came striding forward, held up his hand, and was sworn.

Covington glanced at the clock, then settled back in his chair.

Scanlon gave his name and address to the court reporter, then looked up to face Covington, awaiting the opening of his questioning.

Covington managed to make his manner elaborately casual. "What's your occupation, Mr. Scanlon?"

"I'm a painter, sir."

"Exactly. And on the night of September twenty-first, where were you?"

"I was in Tijuana, staying at the hotel Vista de la Mesa."

"Anything in particular that fixes that time in your mind, Mr. Scanlon?"

"Yes, sir."

"What?"

"I'd been looking for the right kind of a job. My wife was in Portland, Oregon. That's where I'd been before I came to Southern California, and I made up my mind that if I could get the kind of a job . . ."

"Now just a moment," Covington interrupted with fatherly benevolence, "don't tell us what you thought, don't tell us anything about your own business problems, Mr. Scanlon, just try and answer the question. Is there anything that fixes the night of the twenty-first day of September in your mind?"

"Yes, sir."

"Now just what is it? Just tell us what fixes the date in your mind."

"Well, I tried to telephone my wife to get her to come down here."

"I see. Now, where was your wife?"

"In Portland, Oregon."

"And you were trying to place a telephone call to her?"

"Yes."

"At what time?"

"Well, I'd been calling her all during the evening, but she hadn't been home. She was out with friends at a movie and . . ."

"Now just don't testify to anything that you don't know. Nothing that your wife may have told you later, Mr. Scanlon, just what you *did*. Now you have stated that the date is fixed in your mind because you were trying to telephone your wife."

"Yes, sir."

"Did you talk with your wife?"

"Yes, sir."

"What time?"

"That was at about ten minutes past ten when my call came through."

"Now did you notice the time?"

"Yes, sir."

"Now while you were waiting for that call to come through, immediately prior to ten-ten, where were you?"

"I was in the telephone booth."

"Where?"

"At this hotel, the Vista de la Mesa, in Tijuana."

"There's more than one booth there?"

"Yes, there is."

"Now, how long did you wait before your party came on the line?"

"About five minutes, I think."

"And during the time you were waiting there, did some-one have occasion to enter the other telephone booth?"

"Yes, sir."

"Where?"

"There in the hotel in Tijuana."

"At what time?"

"Just before ten-ten. I'd guess about ten-five, something like that."

"You know that it was before ten-ten?"

"Yes, sir, because my call came through at ten-ten."

"And how long was it before your call came through that someone entered the other booth?"

"Not over five minutes."

"Now did you see this person?"

"Not then. I did later."

"How much later?"

"About two or three minutes later when he left the booth."

"You did see him then?"

"When he was leaving the booth, yes, sir."

"Who was he, if you know?"

The witness raised a pointing forefinger. "That man sitting there."

"You are pointing at Edward Charles Garvin, the defendant in this action?"

"Yes, sir, that man sitting right beside Mr. Mason, the lawyer."

"And you saw this man Garvin emerging from the adjoining booth?"

"Yes, sir."

"And what did he do while he was in there, if you know?"

"He put through a long-distance call."

"How do you know?"

"I could hear him."

"You could hear his voice coming through the partition from the other booth?"

"That's right. I was sitting there right next to the partition and . . ."

"And what did he say?"

"I heard him say that he wanted to place a long-distance call. I remember he said he wanted to talk with Ethel Garvin at the Monolith Apartments in Los An-

176

geles, and then a moment later I heard him put in money, and then start talking, and he said: 'Ethel, this is Edward. There's no use our throwing a lot of money away on lawyers. I'm down in Tijuana now and you can't touch me here. I'm going to drive up to Oceanside. Suppose you jump in your car and drive down there and meet me. We'll talk things over, and work out something that'll be satisfactory.' And then he was silent for a while and then he said: 'Now don't be like that. I'm not a fool. I wouldn't be calling you unless I had plenty on you. Remember that man you were playing around with in Nevada? Well I know all about him. I know where he is right this minute.' And then he went on to tell her where this man was and how to get to his ranch. I've forgotten just what the directions were, but it was some place out of Oceanside."

"Did he mention the name of this man?"

"No, sir, I don't think he did. If he did, I don't remember that. Just the man she had been playing around with in Nevada."

"And then what did he say, if anything?"

"He said: 'You better come to Oceanside. I'll meet you on the lot we used to own there, the place where we were going to build our house. I'll drive up there and meet you. I'll be there with my car, and I'll leave the lights on so you'll know it's me.'"

"And then what else did he say?"

"Nothing. He just said he was glad she was being sensible and hung up."

"And then what?" Covington asked.

"And then the man walked out of the booth."

"Cross-examine," Covington snapped at Perry Mason.

Mason looked at the clock. It was eleven-thirty-two, too early to ask the court to take a noon adjournment. Too late to suggest that the court might give him a few minutes by way of recess.

Mason managed a smile which masked his feelings,

said casually, and in a voice which was so low as to be hardly audible, "Rather keen of hearing, Mr. Scanlon?"

"Yes, sir, I am," Scanlon said, "I always have been. I could hear things pretty well."

"Now when you repeated what this man said," Mason said, "you quoted his exact words."

"Well, I can't say they're his exact words, but that's about what he said."

"You've talked with Mr. Covington, the district attorney, before you came to court?"

"Yes, sir, I have."

"And did you discuss your testimony with Mr. Covington?"

"Yes, sir."

"Several times?"

"Yes, sir.

"Was that the way you repeated the conversation when you *first* talked with him—the way you're telling it now?"

"Well, he told me I had to say what the man said. He said I couldn't just say the general effect of what he said, that I had to use the man's exact words as nearly as I could remember what they were. So that's what I tried to do."

Mason said, "You were spending the night at the Hotel Vista de la Mesa?"

"Yes, sir."

"How long had you been there?"

"Two days."

"In other words this conversation took place on the second night that you stayed there? . . . Or was it the third?"

"It was the second."

"Now you had been trying to get your wife earlier in the evening?"

"Yes, sir."

"Was there any particular reason why you hadn't called her earlier during the day?"

"Yes, sir, there was. I had work in San Ysidro but I couldn't find a place to live. I simply couldn't find a house either to buy or rent. Then I found out that I *might* be able to live across the border in Tijuana and commute back and forth.

"I went across the border and stayed at this hotel while I was looking around for a place that I could rent. I had to get permission from the Mexican authorities and I finally had things all fixed up, so I wanted to telephone my wife and tell her to bring our things down. Naturally I wanted her to get started just as soon as possible, because I couldn't maintain two homes and I wanted to be reunited with my family."

"I see," Mason said. "So you went in there to the booth to telephone her?"

"That's right."

"Now, did you hear the clock chime?"

"Yes, sir, there was a clock that chimed."

"Did you hear the clock chime at ten o'clock?"

"I did, yes, sir."

"Where were you at that time?"

"I was just coming down the hall to the telephone booth. I'd called my wife earlier in the evening—oh, three or four times, and no one had answered. I felt certain she would be back by ten o'clock, so as it approached the hour of ten I decided to go telephone once more."

"Now the lights were burning brightly in the lobby at that time?" Mason asked conversationally.

"No, sir, they were not."

"They weren't?" Mason asked, apparently surprised.

"No, sir, those lights were turned off sometime shortly before ten o'clock when the woman who runs the hotel rented the last room."

Mason said with a smile, "Just what you *know*, please. Don't testify to what she subsequently told you. You don't know of your own knowledge why the lights were turned off."

"Yes, sir, as it happens I do. I was in the lobby when the last room was rented. A young woman traveling by herself rented the room and I heard the conversation at the time when the Mexican woman who runs the place told her that this was the last room in the house, and she was going to close up the place and turn off the lights. I actually saw her turn out the lights."

"What time was that?"

"It was just—well, I don't know. It was a few minutes before ten o'clock. Oh, perhaps ten or fifteen minutes, something like that. I can't be certain of the time. I was sort of killing time waiting for ten o'clock to come. I made up my mind that I'd try to put through my call again at ten o'clock."

"Well," Mason said, as though Scanlon's testimony had ruined his last chance of cross-examination, "apparently you had every occasion to remember everything about the events of that evening."

"I did, yes, sir."

"So the lights were turned out sometime before ten?"

"That's right."

"No lights at all in the lobby?"

"Oh, yes, there was a night light. It was rather dim."

"I see," Mason said casually. "Then you saw this man who had put in the telephone call from the booth next to you as he left the booth. Is that right?"

"Yes, sir."

"You remained in the telephone booth?"

"Yes sir."

"Opened the door and looked out?"

"Yes, sir, that's right."

"Didn't open it all the way?"

"No, sir, just a crack."

"Now, do you mean just a crack or do you mean several inches?"

"Just a crack."

Mason smiled and said, "You're certain of that?"

"Yes, sir."

"Now if the door was only opened a crack," Mason said, "it would have been possible for you to have seen through that crack with only one eye, whereas if it had been opened several inches you could have seen with two eyes. Now think very carefully. Was it merely a crack, or was the door open several inches?"

"Just a crack."

"Then you only saw this figure leaving the telephone booth with one eye. Is that right?"

"Well, I guess so, yes. I hadn't stopped to consider it before, but I remember I had the door opened just a crack. I guess I only did see him with one eye."

"And this man left the booth and then went down the corridor toward the rooms?"

"No, sir, he didn't. He went out of the front door."

"*What* door?"

"The exit door, out to where the cars were parked, and drove away."

"How do you know he drove away?" Mason asked.

"Well, I . . . I guess I don't actually *know* that he drove away but I saw him walk out, and just a few seconds after that I heard a car being started out there in the driveway. Then headlights came on and shone in the lobby for a second or two and furnished a bright illumination. Then the car swung around and the beam of light from the headlights swept across the lobby and disappeared."

"And you didn't see that man again until you entered this courtroom today to testify?"

"Yes, sir, I did."

"*Where* did you see him?"

"The officers arranged to put him in a place where I could see him."

"After he was arrested?"

"Yes, sir."

"Anyone else with him?" Mason asked. "Did the officers use a line-up so that there were several men in your line of vision and then ask you to pick out the man you had seen?"

"No, sir, they didn't. There was just this one man there, but they contrived to have him walk around so I could see the way he walked, his gait, and his general build, and things of that sort."

"By the way," Mason said casually, "do you know what color clothes the man had on when you saw him leaving the booth? Was it a brown suit?"

"Sort of a brown, I think, yes, sir."

"What color shoes?"

"Dark, I think."

"And his necktie?"

"His necktie was . . . let me see. No, I never saw his necktie."

"You don't know whether he had a necktie on or not?"

"No, sir."

"Why not?"

"Because I never had a front view of this man."

"You didn't see his features then?"

"No, sir."

"Was he wearing a hat?"

"I . . . I can't remember."

"You don't remember whether this man was wearing a hat?" Mason asked.

"No, sir."

"You know what color socks he had on?"

"No, sir," Scanlon said, smiling.

"Or the color of his shirt?"

"It was—I think it was . . . No, sir, I don't know."

"So," Mason said, "you are identifying a man whom you saw with one eye through a crack in the door in a dark lobby, a man whose face you had never seen in your life until the police pointed him out to you in the jail and . . ."

"No, sir, that's not right. *I* pointed him out to the police."

"In the jail?"

"Yes, sir."

"You were with the police at the time?"

"Yes, sir."

"How many other prisoners were in sight?"

"Just this one. There were no others in the place where I saw this man."

"And yet you say the police didn't point him out to you?" Mason asked sarcastically. "They did tell you they were going to show you a man they wanted you to identify, didn't they?"

"Well, they said they'd like to have me look at this man and see if I *could* identify him."

"And then this one man was brought in to the yard or shadow box or whatever place it was where you were given an opportunity to look at him?"

"Yes, sir."

"And do you mean to tell me that one of the police officers didn't say to you at that time in effect, 'There he is. Take a good look at him. Look at the way he walks. Look at him when his back's turned'?"

"Well, yes, they did say something like that."

"And you identified this man *before* the officer said that?"

"No, sir," Scanlon said. "It was afterwards."

"How long afterwards?"

"After he'd walked around for a little while."

"I see. Just as soon as the officer told you that he wanted you to identify this man you pointed your finger and said, 'That's the man,' didn't you?"

"No, sir, I didn't. I looked him over a good long while before I identified him."

"A *long* while," Mason said scornfully, "ten or fifteen or twenty seconds, I presume."

"No, sir," Scanlon insisted, "it was a minute or two."

"As much as two minutes?" Mason asked.

"Yes, I'm certain it was."

"Could it have been longer than that?"

"It could have been."

"As much as three minutes?"

"I'll say it could have been. I think perhaps it was. I wanted to be sure."

"In other words," Mason said, "it took you three minutes of careful study of this defendant under conditions of good visibility to make up your mind that he was the man."

"Well, it could have been three minutes."

"Now, when you saw this man whom you observed in Tijuana that night," Mason said, "you saw him after he had left the telephone booth and while he was walking across the lobby?"

"Yes, sir."

"How fast was he walking? Was he moving rather rapidly?"

"Well, he was walking right along."

"And you didn't see him until after he had passed a few feet from the telephone booth?"

"Yes, I guess so."

"Ten feet?" Mason asked.

"Perhaps."

"And you couldn't see him after he had passed through the outer door and gone out into the yard where the cars were parked?"

"No, sir."

"Now, how many feet is it across that lobby?"

"Oh, I'd say it was perhaps twenty-five feet."

"So you only saw this man while he was walking rather rapidly for a distance of fifteen feet?"

"Yes, sir."

"And you observed him with one eye?"

"Yes, sir."

"In semi-darkness."

"Yes, sir."

"With his back turned toward you."

"Yes, sir."

"And that's why it was so difficult for you to be absolutely certain when you made your subsequent identification, wasn't it?"

"What do you mean?"

Mason said, "That's why you studied the matter for some three minutes before you were able subsequently to identify this man and say to the officers, 'Yes, that's the man.'"

"Yes, sir, that's right."

"Now, how long do you suppose it took that man to walk the fifteen feet?" Mason asked.

"I don't know. I hadn't figured it. A little while."

"Do you know how many miles an hour a man covers at an ordinary walk?"

"Well, if you want to put it in miles an hour," Scanlon said, "while he was going that fifteen feet I'd say he was walking—oh probably three miles an hour."

"All right," Mason said, "let's do a little mathematical computation."

He whipped a small slide rule from his pocket, manipulated it quickly, said, "For your information, Mr. Scanlon, a person walking one mile an hour covers about 1.46 feet per second, so at the rate of three miles an hour that man would cover approximately 4.4 feet per second."

"I'll take your word for it," Scanlon said, smiling.

Mason said, "So in walking fifteen feet at the rate of speed you mention, the man would have covered the distance in something less than three and one-half seconds. Therefore, unless you are mistaken, you saw this individual for approximately three and one-half seconds with one eye under conditons of dim light."

"Well, I guess that's right if you say so."

"I'm simply making the necessary mathematical computations from what you yourself have told me."

"Yes, sir."

"And you now think that's right, do you, Mr. Scanlon, that you saw this man for about three and a half seconds?"

"Well, I thought it was longer than that but if that's the way it figures out why I guess that's right."

"Saw him three and a half seconds under conditions of very poor visibility with one eye, looking at his back," Mason said, "but when you wanted to identify him for the police, when you wanted to be sure, *it took you three minutes under conditions of broad daylight looking at him where you could see his face, his figure and everything about him?*"

"Well, I wanted to be sure."

"So in order to be sure of the man's identity you had to look at him for three minutes with both eyes and in full daylight?"

"Well, to be *absolutely* certain."

"Then," Mason said, with a friendly disarming smile, "when you saw him under conditions of poor visibility for only three and a half seconds looking at him with only one eye, you naturally weren't absolutely certain of his identity, were you? Not at that time, at the end of the three-and-a-half-second interval?"

"No, I wasn't *certain* of it then," Scanlon conceded, "not absolutely. But I was after I saw him there in the jail."

"I thought so," Mason said, with a smile. "Thank you, Mr. Scanlon, that's all."

"That's all," Covington snapped angrily.

Judge Minden looked at the clock. He said, "It appears to be approximately the hour for the noon adjournment. We'll take our usual adjournment until two o'clock this afternoon. The jury will remember the admonition of the Court and refrain from discussing the case or permitting it to be discussed in their presence, nor will they form or express any opinion concerning the guilt or innocence of the defendant until the case is finally submitted.

"Court will take a recess until two o'clock."

Edward Garvin reached out and caught Mason's arm. His fingers pressed into the flesh of the lawyer's arm. "Mason," he said, "for God's sake I . . ."

Mason turned to smile reassuringly at his client, but the smile was only on the lawyer's lips. His eyes were cold and hard.

"Smile," Mason said.

"I . . ."

"Smile, damn it," Mason said in a low half-whisper, "smile."

A travesty of a grin twisted Garvin's features.

"Do better than that," Mason said, "smile and keep that smile on your face until the jury have filed out."

Mason watched expression struggling on Garvin's face, laughed good-naturedly, patted Garvin on the shoulder, said, "Well, let's get some eats," and turned casually away.

"Mason, I've *got* to see you," Garvin whispered.

Mason said over his shoulder in a low voice, "Try to see me now and with the jury looking at you, and with that expression on your face, and you'll be buying a one-way ticket to the death cell in San Quentin."

And with that the lawyer walked casually out of the courtroom, his brief case tucked under his arm, an expression of smiling unconcern on his countenance.

Della Street joined Perry Mason in the corridor. "Good Lord, chief," she said in a whisper, "could he be telling the truth?"

"I don't know," Mason said. "I'm going to find out later, but I don't dare to let the spectators or the jurors see me holding any hurried conference with my client at this moment."

"What do we do now?" she asked.

"Get Paul Drake and eat," Mason said. "It's all we *can* do."

Drake came pushing his way out of the crowd milling around the door of the courtroom, a crowd that looked curiously at Mason.

Drake grabbed Mason's arm and squeezed it. "Boy," he said, "you did a great job of cross-examination there, Perry. You made the guy admit that it took him three minutes to identify a man under good light and yet he only saw him three seconds when he was looking at his back in the dark."

"Just the same," Mason said, "there's something about that witness that bothers me. He's prejudiced, he's testifying to a composite of what he thinks he saw, what he thinks he remembered, and what he thinks must have happened, and he's now testifying positively; but somehow there's a certain underlying sincerity, a rugged sense of fairness the guy has that bothers me."

"You don't suppose your client *did* go out and do any nocturnal wandering around, do you?"

"How the devil would I know?" Mason said. "Every so often a client lies to you. But in this case we have an ace up our sleeve."

"You mean his wife's testimony?"

"That's right. Of course the jury will probably figure she'd back her husband regardless, but they're not going to send a newlywed to San Quentin and leave a beautiful bride languishing for her lover if they can avoid it. I'm hoping that Mrs. Garvin's alibi will overcome Scanlon's testimony."

"She's certain of the time?" Drake asked.

"Sure she is," Mason said. "That's the advantage of having a clock that chimes."

"Loud chimes?"

"Sure, I heard it. I heard it chime ten o'clock that night when I went to bed. I . . ."

He broke off as he saw Señora Miguerinio emerge from an elevator and come rolling down the corridor with an enormous clock under her arm. She flashed a good-natured smile at Perry Mason, and said, "How do you theenk, Meester Mason? Does the husband come back to his wife and again make the honeymoon in my little hacienda, no?"

"Oh sure," Mason said, with an air of great confidence. "What are you doing with the clock, Señora?"

"The deestrict attorney he wants thees clock."

"Why?" Mason asked.

"Because he ees to show heem to the jury."

"What clock is it?" Mason asked, keeping his manner exceedingly casual.

"Thees ees the clock from my hotel, the clock that I have to tell the time."

"The one that strikes the chimes?" Mason asked.

"Sure, strikes the chimes," she said, and then added, "during the day it strike the chimes."

"During the *day?*" Mason inquired.

She nodded. "Sure, during day, yes. During the night, no. He wake the guests up. People like to hear the chime of the clock in Mexico during the daytime but at night the chimes go off, no?"

"And what happens to the chimes during the night?" Mason asked.

"Thees ees electric clock," she said, "weeth chimes. Here ees a sweech on the side of the clock. When you don't want the chimes you pool thees sweech like thees and the chimes go off, no?"

"You mean when you pull this switch the chimes don't sound any more?"

"That's right. You pool the sweech and the chimes he don't go until you pool the sweech back up. Every night when I go to bed, just before I go into my bed, I pool

189

the sweech down and the chimes he don't sound no more. Then in the morning when ees time for people to get up and ees nice and sunny and warm, why then I pool the sweech up and the chimes start once more."

"So the district attorney wants to see the clock?"

"Sure, the clock ees to be sold to the government. He shows heem to the jury and then have to put heem in court and the law ees going to buy me a new clock to take the place of thees one. I tell them I am a poor widow woman and I cannot afford to buy a new clock, I cannot bring thees clock in unless I have one for my hotel. You cannot run a hotel without a clock. No?"

"Certainly not," Mason said.

"Well," she said, "I have to go see the deestrict attorney. He tole me to come just as soon as court ees out because he wants to talk weeth me about my testimony. I have to go back on the weetness stand weeth the clock."

"Well," Mason said, *"we'll* go on to lunch."

"You enjoy your lunch, Señor," she said.

"Oh sure," Mason told her, "we will. Thank you."

They turned and resumed their walk down the corridor. Drake muttered an exclamation under his breath.

"Good heavens, chief," Della said in a hushed whisper.

"Enjoy your lunch," Mason repeated sarcastically.

17

MASON, PAUL DRAKE, AND DELLA STREET SETTLED BACK on the cushions of the booth in the restaurant.

"I don't think I can eat a thing," Della Street said. "It's ghastly."

Mason, a confident smile on his face, said, "Don't do

that, Della. People are sitting all around us, watching us, wondering what we're talking about, how we're feeling. Keep smiling, keep confident, keep happy, make an occasional joke, and discuss what's happening in low tones."

"Exactly what *is* happening, Perry?" Paul Drake asked.

"I don't know for sure," Mason told him. "I'm afraid that the testimony of this man, Scanlon, is going to stampede that jury. I personally think Scanlon . . ."

"You surely don't think Garvin actually did place that call, then get in his car and drive to Oceanside?"

Mason said, "I think Garvin was fool enough to get in his car and go *somewhere*. When you've cross-examined a lot of people on the stand over a period of years, you form an impression as to whether a man is telling the truth or lying just by the way he answers questions. Now, I'll admit that while I managed to put Scanlon in a somewhat disadvantageous position, and while the police didn't play fair in not having a line-up, the fact remains Scanlon is trying to tell the truth, and he gives me that impression.

"Now let's suppose that he did have some difficulty in recognizing the man who was in that telephone booth putting through the call. Nevertheless, he isn't at all dubious about the conversation which took place, and I know from experience the walls between those two booths are paper-thin. And the police must now have the record of that telephone call and it must have been to Ethel Garvin.

"Now let's suppose for the moment Scanlon didn't recognize Garvin when Garvin left the booth. Who else in that hotel could possibly have put through such a call to Mrs. Garvin?"

"When you look at it that way," Drake admitted, "it's pretty tough."

Mason said, "I recognized at once that the weak point in Scanlon's testimony was the statement he made concerning his recognition of the party he had seen leaving the telephone booth. Therefore, I concentrated on that.

But you'll note that I was particularly careful not to cross-examine him about the conversation itself. Naturally, I picked on the weakest link in the chain."

"Well, for my part," Drake said, "when Mrs. Garvin gets on the stand and swears absolutely that her husband was with her all night, I'd say the jury would be pretty apt to believe her."

"Of course," Mason pointed out, "you get into more trouble there. She's fixing her time by the chimes on the clock and . . ."

"Didn't she say she looked at her watch once?"

"Yes, but she definitely stated that she heard the chimes. Now suppose the chimes weren't sounding. That, of course, brands her testimony as false right there."

They gave that matter thoughtful consideration for a moment.

Mason threw back his head and laughed.

They looked at him in surprise.

"Come on," Mason said, "a smile at least! Let's pretend there's been a joke about something."

The others tardily joined him in half-hearted merriment.

"On the other hand," Mason went on after a moment, smiling as though amused at some funny story he was telling, "the deadly part of the thing is that the question of whether there were chimes, or whether there were not chimes, depends entirely upon the testimony of the Señora Miguerinio. It all depends on what she *thinks* she did. Just as a person will quite frequently forget to wind the clock when he goes to bed, just as he will forget to put the cat out, so Mrs. Miguerinio may have forgotten to shut off the chimes on that particular night. If only I hadn't gone to sleep at ten o'clock—if I had only stayed awake another half hour even, I could have told whether her testimony about shutting off the chimes was true."

"That's what comes of having a clean conscience,"

Drake said. "You . . . wait a minute, Perry, here comes one of my men."

One of Drake's operatives stood in the doorway looking over the diners.

Drake held up his hand with his index finger extended, saying, as he did so, to Mason, "I told him I'd be here. He's got a pipe line into one of the court attaches, who doesn't have any idea this man is one of my operatives. He wouldn't be coming here to look for me unless it was important."

The man caught Drake's signal, nodded, then walked casually back toward the men's room.

Drake excused himself, and followed.

As Drake left the table, Della Street said to Mason, "Let's hope this is a lucky break."

"Let's hope it is," Mason said. "We can use a little luck."

They waited tensely until they saw Drake returning.

Mason took one look at Drake's approaching face and shook his head.

"What is it?" Della Street asked.

"Paul Drake has a mask of gloom an inch and a half deep all over his countenance," Mason said.

Drake approached the table, and as he started to slide in on the bench Mason said, "Smile, Paul."

Drake's lips twisted in a mirthless smile.

"What is it?" Mason asked.

"You're licked," Drake said.

"How come?"

"The D. A. has a surprise witness he's going to throw at you. A service station attendant in Oceanside who put gas and oil in Garvin's car."

"What time?" Mason asked.

"Around eleven-thirty. Garvin was nervous and tense, pacing up and down, and while the car was being serviced, Garvin walked over toward the curb and watched the cars that were coming along the road headed south.

He seemed to be looking for someone, and seemed to be as taut as a violin string. The service station attendant noticed him particularly."

"How good is the identification?" Mason asked.

"One hundred per cent," Drake said. "The man identifies the car, and he identifies Garvin. He noticed him particularly."

"Well," Mason said, "that's certainly piling it on."

"Why didn't you ask Garvin about this?" Drake asked.

"I didn't dare to."

"Why not?"

"The prisoners are given lunch in the jail by the sheriff. The deputy sheriff is supposed to whisk Garvin out of court immediately after the noon adjournment. He brings him back about five minutes before two.

"I didn't dare to risk a conference with Garvin while the jury were there in the room, or while the spectators could see us. To have conferred with Garvin immediately following that testimony from Scanlon would have emphasized the disastrous nature of that surprise testimony. And having Garvin brought back to court early is about as bad. I can have a *casual,* whispered conference with him at about five minutes to two, and that's all I dare to do."

"Can't you get an adjournment? Some sort of . . ."

"To try that would be considered as a confession of panic," Mason said. "I've simply got to go into court, sit there with a smile on my face, and take it."

"You're going to have to take a lot," Drake said.

"Well," Mason told him, "I've dished out a lot in my time, so I guess I can sit there and take it if I have to. The grievance committee of the Bar Association wants to talk with me tomorrow night about my tactics in getting Mortimer Irving to identify *my* car as the one he saw parked by the side of the road. All in all, it's a great life."

"Can they do anything to you about that identification business?"

"I don't think so. I contend I was absolutely within my rights. I had a right to talk with that witness, and I had just as much right to park one single car there by the side of the road and ask him whether that was the same car he had seen, as the police did to take Howard B. Scanlon to some position of vantage, and ask him whether or not the single man he saw walking back and forth in the jail yard was the man he had seen emerging from the telephone booth there at the hotel the night of the murder . . . Well, I guess there's nothing much we can do here except put on an act of being carefree and happy. Then we'll go up to court early. I'll have a chance to ask Garvin a couple of apparently casual questions in the five minutes I'll see him before court opens.

"All right, Paul, do you know any funny stories? People are watching us."

18

MASON STROLLED INTO THE CROWDED COURTROOM AT seven minutes before two o'clock. He lit a cigarette, settled down in his chair at the counsel table, smiled confidently at some half dozen members of the jury who had arrived early and were occupying their seats in the jury box. He seemed completely relaxed, a man who had just finished a good lunch and was mentally and physically contented.

At four minutes before two o'clock the deputy sheriff brought Edward Garvin into the courtroom.

Garvin leaned over to whisper in Mason's ear. "Mason, for God's sake let me talk to you."

Mason smiled up at him and said, "Sit down, Garvin.

I'll talk with you in a minute. Now, whatever happens, don't make any move to talk to me. Just sit there."

Mason watched Garvin sit down, pinched out his cigarette, dropped it in the large brass cuspidor, stretched, yawned, and watched the courtroom clock tick away the precious seconds.

Then, as though just happening to think of something, he turned with a smile, leaned toward Garvin, and said, "Just answer questions. Keep a smile on your face. Did you telephone Ethel Garvin?"

Garvin tried to smile but couldn't. "Mason, listen to me. I did telephone her. I did walk out and take my car up there. The man is telling the truth. But Lorraine is willing to stay with her alibi. She woke up and found me gone. She said what she did because . . ."

Mason interrupted to say, "Don't talk so fast. Don't talk so much. Now, settle back as though you hadn't a care in the world. I'll talk with you again in a minute."

Mason straightened up in his chair, looked around the courtroom casually, as though looking for Della Street, then glanced once more at the clock, yawned again, then turned toward Garvin and said, "All right. Let's have the rest of it."

Garvin said, "I went up there to meet her, Mason, but she didn't show up. I waited around for a while and then went to Hackley's road. I parked my car and reconnoitered through the field. After a while, a damn dog heard me and started barking. After he quieted down I worked my way to the house again. Ethel's car came out of the driveway. I recognized the car. I couldn't see whether she was alone or not.

"I ran back to get my car and I found I'd got myself good and lost. It took me almost a quarter of an hour to get my car. I drove down to the place where I was to meet her. Her car was there. She was in it, dead. I was smart enough not to go near the machine, not to touch anything, and not to leave any tracks. I drove back to Tijuana."

"What time did you get there?" Mason asked.

"I don't know. I didn't look at my watch, but I told Lorraine I was in a jam. I woke her up and told her what had happened. I told her she was going to have to give me an alibi. That's the whole truth, Mason. I'm sorry I lied to you. I . . ."

There was a sudden rustle of motion as the spectators stood up. Judge Minden emerged from his chambers, took his place on the bench. Sounds of motion and scraping chairs caused momentary confusion as the spectators regained their seats.

Garvin said, "I'll pay anything, Mason. I'll add ten thousand dollars or twenty thousand dollars or . . ."

"You haven't half enough money to pay for what you've done," Mason whispered angrily. "You've double-crossed me, but I won't double-cross you. Now sit back, damn you, and shut up."

"Who's your next witness?" Judge Minden asked Covington.

"Call Mortimer C. Irving," Covington said.

Irving came forward and took the stand. He avoided Covington's eyes, caught Mason's eyes for a moment, grinned somewhat sheepishly, then settled himself in the witness chair.

He gave the statistical information concerning his name and address to the court reporter, then looked up as Hamlin Covington arose from his chair and strode impressively forward.

"Early in the morning of September twenty-second of this year, did you have occasion to travel along the road between La Jolla and Oceanside, and at a point some two miles south of Oceanside?"

"Yes, sir."

"What time?"

"At about twelve-fifty A.M."

197

"I will call your attention to the map which has been introduced as People's Exhibit A," Covington said. "Can you orient yourself on that map, that is, can you look at it and understand what it is, what it shows?"

"Yes, sir."

"Are you familiar with the territory of which that map is a scaled reproduction?"

"I am. Yes, sir."

"On that map can you point to anything unusual which you saw at the time you were so traveling along the highway between La Jolla and Oceanside?"

"Yes, sir."

"Please do so."

Irving walked over to the map, placed a finger on it, and said, "I saw an automobile parked at just about this spot."

"Anything unusual about that automobile?" Covington asked.

"Yes, sir. It was parked there with the lights on and as nearly as I could see no one was in the car."

"Now, what time was this, as nearly as you can recall?"

"About twelve-fifty."

"Did you do anything with reference to making an examination of that car?"

"Yes, sir."

"What?"

"I stopped my car. I turned my car's spotlight on that automobile and looked it over rather carefully. I thought that perhaps . . ."

"Never mind what you thought. Just tell us what you did."

"Yes, sir. I turned the spotlight on the car and looked it over rather carefully to see whether there was anyone in the car."

"Did you notice the license number of the automobile?"

"I didn't at that time. No, sir."

"Now can you describe that car to us?"

"Yes, sir. It was a convertible automobile of a light color. It was a large automobile. The top was up and the headlights were on. It had, as I remember it, white-walled tires."

"Were any of the doors open?"

"No, sir, the doors were all closed."

"Mr. Irving, I am going to ask you if since that time you have had occasion to see the automobile of Edward Charles Garvin, the defendant in this case?"

"Yes, sir, I have."

"Can you tell us whether or not that was the automobile you saw parked there at that time?"

"It was an automobile very similar to that."

"Thank you. That's all. You may cross-examine, Mr. Mason."

Covington strode back to his chair and sat down.

Mason said, "Two days later, and while this matter was fresh in your mind, Mr. Irving, you talked with me about what you had seen, did you not?"

"If that's an impeaching question," Covington said, "I object on the ground that . . ."

"It's not an impeaching question. I'm simply asking him whether he had such a conversation. The question can be answered yes or no."

"Did you have a conversation with Mr. Mason?" Judge Minden asked. "Just answer yes or no."

"Yes."

"And, following that conversation, did you ride with me down the road shown in this map?"

"Yes, sir."

"And at that time there was an automobile with License Number 9Y6370 parked at about this position, wasn't there?"

"Yes, sir."

"And did you at that time identify that automobile with the California State License Number 9Y6370 as the automobile which you had seen at twelve-fifty in the morning of September twenty-second of this year?"

"Well, I didn't *identify* it. I said that it looked something like the automobile I'd seen."

"This automobile that I am referring to now is a light-colored convertible?"

"Yes, sir."

"And you looked it over rather carefully?"

"Yes, sir."

"And didn't you at that time and place identify that automobile as being the one you had seen?"

"Well, I said I thought it was the one I had seen."

"You *thought* so then?"

"Yes, sir."

"But you *don't* think so now?"

The witness ran his fingers through his hair. "Well, to tell you the truth," he said, "I . . ."

"That's what you're here for," Mason said as the witness stopped, "to tell the truth."

"Well, of course I couldn't make a *positive* identification of the car I saw there that night. I can only tell what it looked like and the general kind of a car that it was. I . . ."

"You're not answering my question," Mason said. "You thought at the time you were with me that this car I have referred to was the same car you had seen there, didn't you?"

"Well, of course, I can't identify an automobile absolutely when I just see it at night on . . ."

"Just answer the question," Mason said. "Did you or did you not at the time you were with me think that was the car you had seen?"

"Yes, sir, I did," the witness blurted.

"And now," Mason said, "at this time, when the occasion is not as fresh in your mind as it was then, do you want this jury to feel that you have changed your mind?"

"Well, I realize now that I couldn't identify any car positively and absolutely."

"Specifically," Mason said, "what has occurred between the occasion when you identified that car with me, two days after the time you had seen it, and the present time to make you change your mind?"

"I didn't say I'd changed my mind."

"You have changed it, haven't you?" Mason snapped.

"Well, I don't know that I have."

"In other words," Mason said, "you still *think* that the car you saw two days later with License Number 9Y6370 was the car you saw there at twelve-fifty in the morning of September twenty-second, don't you, Mr. Irving?"

"Well," Irving admitted, "I've been led to realize how impossible it would have been to have made an identification at the time I first saw the car parked there."

"Who led you to realize the impossibility of making such an identification?"

"I just kept thinking the matter over and . . ."

Mason said, "You specifically stated, Mr. Irving, that you had been *led* to appreciate the impossibility of making such an identification. Now who led you?"

"Well, I don't know. It could have been just the way I thought things over."

"Someone *led* you," Mason said. "Who was it?"

"I didn't say that anyone led me."

"You said you had been led. Who led you?"

"I . . . well, I had several talks with Mr. Covington, the district attorney."

"In other words, Mr. Covington led you to believe that you couldn't make a positive identification of the car you saw there that night. Is that right?"

"Well, I don't know that I'd express it that way."

"*I'm* expressing it that way," Mason said. "Answer the question. Did or did not Mr. Covington lead you to the belief that you couldn't identify that car under those circumstances?"

"Oh, Your Honor, I object. After all, this cross-examination is . . ."

"Overruled!" Judge Minden snapped.

Irving hesitated.

"Answer the question," Mason said.

"Well, I guess he did."

"That's all," Mason said smiling.

"Call Harold Otis," Covington said.

Otis, a young, well-knit individual, took the witness stand, gave his name and address to the court reporter, and in response to questions by Covington, testified that he was employed in a service station in Oceanside, that he had worked on the twenty-first of September from the hour of four o'clock in the afternoon until midnight; that sometime before midnight, as nearly as he could place it, at about half an hour before he had left work, he had seen the defendant, Edward Garvin; that the defendant had driven up to his service station in a convertible automobile; that the witness had taken the license number of the automobile; that he had noticed it particularly; that he had filled the automobile tank with gasoline at the request of Mr. Garvin and had washed the windshield; that while he was serving the car Garvin had been exceedingly nervous and restless; that he had gone over to stand by the curb where he could watch the automobiles which were traveling south on the highway.

Covington produced a photograph of Edward Garvin's car and the witness identified it as being the car Garvin had driven on the night in question. He identified the license number; identified the make, model and year of the car.

"Cross-examine!" Covington said triumphantly to Perry Mason, and strode back to his seat beside Samuel Jarvis at the prosecution's counsel table.

"After you serviced the car, what did the driver do?" Mason asked.

"He drove away."

202

"In which direction?"

"North."

"Toward Los Angeles?"

"Yes."

Mason smiled enigmatically as though this information was destined to wreck Covington's case. "And you didn't see him drive back, did you?"

"There are hundreds of cars an hour pass that service station. I don't try to check up on all the cars that are using the road."

"Certainly not," Mason said. "But you didn't *see* his automobile come back down that road, did you?"

"No, sir, I didn't, but . . ."

"Never mind the reasons," Mason said. "I'm simply asking you whether you did or did not see that automobile returning?"

"No, sir."

"And," Mason announced triumphantly, arising and pointing a finger at the witness, "you went off duty at midnight that night, didn't you?"

"Yes, sir."

"So that in the event that car had returned *after* midnight, considerably after midnight, perhaps as late as three o'clock in the morning, you wouldn't have been there to see it, would you?"

"Certainly not, but I wouldn't have seen it anyway. I wouldn't have noticed cars going along the highway. That's not my business."

"Do you mean to say," Mason said, "that you *never* notice automobiles going along the highway?"

"Well, I don't look at them particularly."

"Exactly," Mason said, "but you do notice automobiles from time to time going along the highway, don't you?"

"Well, I guess so, yes."

"Now then," Mason said, "your attention had been attracted to this automobile because you thought the driver was unduly nervous and restless. Is that right?"

203

"Well, he looked as though he was looking for . . ."

"Never mind drawing any conclusions," Mason said. "Simply answer the question. Your attention was attracted to this particular automobile because the driver was nervous and restless. Is that right?"

"Yes, sir."

"So you looked the automobile over pretty carefully?"

"Yes, sir."

"And so you could remember the license number?"

"Yes, sir."

"Therefore, having remembered what this car looked like, if you had seen it again you would have noticed it, wouldn't you?"

"Well, perhaps I would."

"And if that car had been driven from your service station into Los Angeles, and hadn't returned until three o'clock in the morning, so that the defendant couldn't possibly have been anywhere near the scene of this murder at the time the crime was perpetrated, you wouldn't have known it, would you?"

"Well . . ."

"Yes or no!" Mason thundered at the witness.

"Well, no."

"That," Mason announced triumphantly, "is all."

Covington regarded Mason with a puzzled frown, then he slowly got to his feet. He was trying in vain to conceal the fact that Mason's hint of a Los Angeles alibi for Garvin had him worried. "Your Honor," he said, "I had intended to wind up my case very shortly with the records of the telephone company on that long distance call to Ethel Garvin from Tijuana, but I would like to have an opportunity to perhaps call one more witness who is not at the moment immediately available. If it would be possible for me to have an adjournment until tomorrow morning . . ."

Judge Minden shook his head. "I feel that would be

an unreasonable request, unless, of course, the defendant should consent to it."

Mason said, "No, Your Honor, we want this case to proceeed as rapidly as possible."

"But Your Honor," Covington persisted, "there is at stake a matter of some considerable importance which I am not now at liberty to explain."

Mason, on his feet, said with sudden graciousness, "All right, we'll consent to a continuance. Go ahead. If you think you can find any evidence proving that this defendant was in the immediate vicinity of the crime at the time it was committed, we're willing to help you. We'll *consent* to an adjournment."

And Mason sat down.

"I've proved it already!" Covington shouted. "What more do you want? I've proved he was . . ."

"Gentlemen, that will do!" Judge Minden said, pounding his gavel. "In view of the fact that counsel for the defense has consented to a continuance, Court will at this time take a recess until tomorrow morning at ten o'clock, during which time the jury will remember the admonition of the Court. They will not converse about the case; they will not read the newspapers; they will not form or express any opinion, nor will they permit any person to discuss the case in their presence. Court is adjourned."

Mason arose, stretched, walked over to where Paul Drake and Della Street were standing, and whispered, "Gosh, was that a break! I certainly wanted that adjournment, but I was afraid to admit it. The district attorney threw it right in my lap."

"Better watch that boy," Drake said. "He's dangerous. He's looking for something."

"He's worried," Mason said, and then added, "but he isn't half as worried as I am. However," he added, "there's one thing we're going to do, right now."

"What?" Drake asked.

"That witness, Irving," Mason said. "I tricked him into making an identification of my car."

"That sure was a smart trick," Drake said.

"It may have been just a little *too* smart."

"What do you mean, Perry?"

Mason said, "Let's go look over my car. That man Irving is an honest witness."

Mason led the way down to where his car was parked, opened the door and started looking it over carefully.

"Take a look at the rubber footmat in front here, Paul," he said.

"What the devil are you getting at?" Drake asked. "Do you mean that . . ."

Mason suddenly gave an exclamation, bent over the car, then started tugging at the rubber mat.

"What is it?" Drake asked.

Mason pointed to a brownish stain.

"Paul," he said excitedly, "we're rushing this to the best crime laboratory available. We're going to find out if that's human blood."

"Human blood!" Della Street exclaimed.

"Exactly," Mason said.

"What the devil are you getting at?" Drake asked.

Mason said, excitedly, "I'm getting at the facts of the case. Mortimer Irving was telling the truth. *My* car *was* the one he saw parked there."

"Your car?"

"Sure," Mason said. "Remember that Garvin got in his car and drove away. My car was parked there right beside his. The keys to the ignition were in the drawer in the office of the hotel."

Drake gave a low whistle.

Della Street said, "Then you mean . . ."

"I mean," Mason said, "that there was absolutely nothing on earth to have prevented Lorraine Garvin from getting up, dressing, borrowing my automobile, driving up the coast road, killing Ethel Garvin, and then driving my car back to Tijuana. In other words, that gun really was in the glove compartment all the time. When Lorraine opened the glove compartment to look for Garvin's sunglasses she found the gun. She didn't say a word. She handed Garvin the sunglasses, and at the first available opportunity took that gun out and put it in her purse."

Drake looked at Mason in open-mouthed amazement. "I'll be damned!" he said.

"And now," Mason told him, "the only thing we're going to have to do is find some way of proving all of that and doing it within the next few hours. Come on, Paul, you're going to get busy."

19

UP IN PERRY MASON'S SUITE IN THE U. S. GRANT HOTEL in San Diego, Lorraine Garvin looked across the table at Perry Mason. Her eyes were desperate, angry, and defiant.

In the chair at Mason's right sat Paul Drake, watching her with shrewd eyes while Della Street was taking down in her shorthand notebook every word that was said.

"I tell you I *didn't* leave that hotel," Lorraine said desperately.

Mason's eyes were cold and hard. "You *had* to leave that hotel," he said. "Of all the people who were there, there were just two persons who were interested in Ethel Garvin. You and your husband.

"Now then, thanks to the testimony which has been dug up by the district attorney we can prove that your husband got up, took his car and drove away. It would not have been possible for him to have changed automobiles. He was seen in his *own* car at Oceanside. He was seen there at a time that indicates unmistakably he must have been driving his own car from the time he was seen to leave the Hotel Vista de la Mesa in Tijuana. Now then, here's what happened. You knew what he was going to do. He'd been discussing it with you. When he left you knew that he was going up to see his ex-wife. You knew that you were in the position of being a bigamous wife until you could get her out of the way and have a legal ceremony."

Her lips clamped in a firm line. "I'm not going to sit here and talk with you any longer," she said. "I'm going to see *my* attorney."

"I think you'd better," Mason said. "You know what happened. You got up, dressed hurriedly, went out to the office, got the keys to my car, jumped in, crossed the border, and drove like a bat out of hell. You passed your husband before he had gone halfway to Oceanside. You made contact with Ethel, murdered her . . ."

"I tell you I *didn't!*"

"And I say you must have. You didn't care too much whether you merely got her out of the way so your husband would be free to remarry you, or whether you caused him to be suspected of the murder and had him disposed of via the gas chamber, which is what you are trying to do now with your fake alibi."

She pushed back her chair, got to her feet, and said, "No one can force me to stay here and listen to these insults. My husband asked me to lie to give him an alibi. I did. Now I'm going to consult an attorney who will represent me."

In silence they watched her sweep across the room and go out and slam the door behind her.

Mason said, "Well at last we know what happened, but we have no way of *proving* it. That blood could have been placed there at any time. All the district attorney needs to do is adopt the position that we planted the bloodstain by cutting a finger and getting a few drops of human blood on the rubber mat."

"Then what would happen?" Della Street asked.

"Then," Mason said, "our whole case against Lorraine Garvin would blow up and we'd be licked."

Mason got to his feet, started pacing the floor, frowning. The others watched in silence.

Then suddenly, Mason paused, whirled, looked at Paul Drake.

"What's the matter?" Drake asked.

Mason said, "There's another possibility we haven't explored, Paul."

"What is it?"

Mason said, "This thing has developed so darned fast, Paul, that we haven't had time to think it out to a logical conclusion, but when you come right down to it, how did Lorraine Garvin make contact with Ethel?"

"Well, it's a cinch she did it somehow," Drake said.

Grabbing his hat, Mason said, "Come on. We're going to drive to Tijuana. Bring a shorthand notebook, Della."

The others followed Mason down to the garage where Mason jumped in his car and made time to Tijuana. They found Señora Inocente Miguerinio surrounded by newspapers, ensconced behind the desk in the hotel, her face beaming with pleaure over the realization that the trial of the millionaire miner had given her hotel a great deal of free advertising.

Mason said, "Good afternoon, Señora."

"Buenas tardes, Señores, and you, too, Señorita," she said smiling, "and how goes eet weeth the case? You 'ave got your client acquitted, no?"

"No," Mason said, "and I want to ask you a couple of questions. What about the last room you rented the night of the murder? Who rented it?"

"Eet was a señorita, a nice, sweet girl, with so beautiful curvas," and Señora Miguerinio swept her two hands in a series of curves indicating the contours of a feminine body.

"What color hair?" Mason asked.

"A beautiful blonde. The blonde that ees like platinum, no?"

Mason said, "Did she register? What name did she give?"

"I weel look up the register," Señora Miguerinio said, and turning the pages of the register, said, "She was the Señorita Carlotta Delano, from Los Angeles."

"When did she come in?"

"I do not know the time, Señor. After all, here in Mexico we do not make so much importance of the time as do you yanquis. Eet was just before I turn out the lights and go to bed."

Mason turned to regard Paul Drake with frowning concentration.

"What the devil," Drake asked, "are you getting at?"

Mason said, "Let's consider the time element, Paul. I left my room and went down to Edward Garvin's room. During the time I was in his room, Señora Miguerinio must have rented the last room to this blonde señorita. She then turned out the lights and went to bed. By the time I retraced my steps back to my room, the lights were out—but some girl was in the adjoining telephone booth putting through a phone call. As I remember it now, there was something significant about that phone call. Now it's reasonable to suppose that this woman who was putting through the phone call was the woman to whom Señora Miguerinio had rented the last room."

"Si, si, Señor, that ees eet! She asked about the telephone and how she could make a call to Los Angeles."

"Now then," Mason said to Drake, "just suppose that this woman was actually our mysterious friend with the gun, the beautiful legs, and the habit of prowling the fire escape. Suppose this was Virginia Bynum telephoning to

Los Angeles for instructions. Come on, Paul, we're going to find out about that telephone call."

Forty minutes later they had their answer. The call had been placed at nine fifty-five. A woman who gave her name as Miss Virginia Colfax had placed a call to Frank C. Livesey in Los Angeles.

Drake, regarding the sheet which contained the information, gave a low whistle.

Mason said, grimly, "Okay, Paul. Now I'm beginning to see daylight. I think I know who borrowed my automobile."

20

GARVIN, BROUGHT TO THE CROWDED COURTROOM BY THE deputy sheriff who had him in charge, whispered angrily to Mason, "What the hell is all this about you trying to frame my wife?"

"Shut up," Mason whispered peremptorily.

"I won't stand for it," Garvin said. "I'll ask permission of the Court to have another attorney substituted. Damn it, Mason, you can't . . ."

Judge Minden entered, rapped court to order and gazed out over the crowded courtroom in which every available seat was occupied, every inch of standing room taken.

"People versus Garvin," he called. "Are you ready to proceed, gentlemen? And is it stipulated that the defendant is in court, and the jurors are all present?"

"So stipulated," Mason said.

"So stipulated," Covington agreed.

Judge Minden looked at Covington, who started to get

to his feet, but before he could address the Court, Mason said, hurriedly, "If the Court please, there are one or two questions I would like to ask of Frank C. Livesey. May I be permitted to have him recalled for additional cross-examination?"

"What do you want to cross-examine *him* about?" Covington said sneeringly. "He was only called in a routine way in connection with the handling of the gun."

Mason smiled, "Then there certainly should be no objection on the part of the district attorney to having him recalled."

"There isn't," Covington said.

"Mr. Livesey, take the stand again for additional cross-examination," Judge Minden said.

Livesey arose from the back of the courtroom, walked to the witness stand, his face twisted in a grin.

Mason waited until Livesey had seated himself, then said, suddenly, "Mr. Livesey, do you know Virginia Bynum?"

Livesey frowned, "I've told you before, Mr. Mason, that I know so many people that I . . ."

"Yes or no?" Mason asked. "Do you or do you not know her?"

Livesey looked into the lawyer's eyes, squirmed uncomfortably, said, "Yes, I know her."

"Now then," Mason said, "answer this question yes or no. Did you or did you not have a telephone conversation with Virginia Bynum shortly before ten o'clock on the night of September twenty-first of this year?"

Covington was suddenly on his feet, his expression puzzled, but his instinct as a trial attorney making him realize that some dramatic development was impending, a development which might bode no good for his side of the case. "Why, Your Honor," he said, "this is not a routine cross-examination. This is going far afield. This is taking up matters which were not covered in the direct examination."

"It is for the purpose of showing the interest of the witness," Mason said.

"Well," Judge Minden said, dubiously, "it seems to the Court the inquiry is certainly far afield, but counsel should have the widest latitude in a case of this kind, when it comes to showing personal interest or bias. I will overrule the objection and permit that question, but I warn counsel that I don't intend to permit any fishing expeditions."

"I'm not fishing," Mason said.

"Very well, answer the question, Mr. Livesey."

Livesey twisted his position in the witness chair, glanced appealingly at Covington, ran his hand over his bald head.

"Yes or no," Mason said crisply. "Did you or did you not have such a conversation?"

Livesey cleared his throat, started to say something, then paused thoughtfully.

"Did you or didn't you?" Mason thundered.

"Yes," Livesey said, after a moment's hesitation.

"Yes," Mason said. "And at the time of that conversation Virginia Bynum was in Tijuana, wasn't she?"

"Oh, I object, Your Honor," Covington said. "That plainly calls for a conclusion of the witness. He couldn't know where a party was telephoning from. All he could possibly know is what the other party said, and that would be hearsay."

"Sustained," Judge Minden said, but he was leaning forward now, looking over the edge of the bench, regarding Livesey with a thoughtful frown.

"And did you, over the telephone at that time, give Virginia Bynum susbstantially the following instructions? Did you tell her to take my automobile, which was parked at the Vista de la Mesa Hotel, and drive it to Oceanside?"

"Oh, Your Honor," Covington said, "this is completely far afield. If Mr. Mason wants to make Mr. Livesey his own witness that's one matter, but I only called Mr. Livesey in connection with a routine matter and . . ."

"Nevertheless, this might show his bias, his personal interest in the outcome of this trial," Judge Minden said. "I may say that the Court is very much interested in hearing the answer to that question. Answer it, Mr. Livesey."

Livesey's hand was stroking his bald head now with rhythmic regularity.

"Yes or no," Mason said. "Did you give her substantially those instructions?"

Livesey sat on the witness chair, his hand keeping an even tempo as it moved slowly and rhythmically across his forehead, back up over his head, down to the back of his neck, then back to his forehead again.

The silence in the courtroom was ominous and tense.

"Did you or didn't you?" Mason asked.

There was no answer.

"Answer the question," Judge Minden snapped.

Suddenly Livesey turned to the judge. "I refuse to answer that question," he said, "on the ground that the answer would incriminate me."

It took Judge Minden more than a minute to silence the courtroom. When he had restored order, he said, "The Court will take a fifteen-minute recess. At the end of that recess the spectators who return will be restricted to the number of spectators for whom there are chairs available. And the first sign of disorder will result in the courtroom being cleared of *all* spectators. The jury will heed the previous admonitions of the Court. Court is now adjourned for fifteen minutes."

Mason grinned at Paul Drake. "Things are beginning to look up, Paul."

"Darned if they aren't," Drake said.

21

■

WHEN COURT RECONVENED AND LIVESEY WAS BACK ON the stand, he amplified the previous statement he had made by reading from a piece of paper which he held in his hand. "I wish to state that I have now consulted counsel. I have been advised not to answer any questions concerning any of my relations with Virginia Bynum and I refuse to answer any further questions on the ground that the answers may incriminate me."

Covington, on his feet, protested vehemently, "Your Honor, this has all the earmarks of a cheap frame-up. By having a man refuse to answer questions, an attempt is made to lead the jury to believe this man may be mixed up in the murder of Ethel Garvin. I charge that it's a cheap piece of trickery."

"You made the charge," Mason said. "Now go ahead and prove it."

"I can't *prove* it. You know that. This matter has taken me by surprise."

Judge Minden banged his gavel. "Counsel will refrain from personalities," he said. "The Court is met with a most peculiar situation."

"I'll say it's most peculiar," Covington said irritably. "It's *too* peculiar. I personally happen to have reason to believe this is simply a matter of trickery. Virginia Bynum was out on the fire escape watching the offices of the Garvin Mining, Exploration and Development Company at the time counsel is now charging, at least by inference, that she was in Tijuana. However, by making these statements in front of the jury in the form of highly significant and leading questions, and then having a really friendly witness refuse to answer the questions on the ground that the answers might incriminate him, counsel has drawn a very neat red herring across the path of the prosecution.

"The jury are apt to attach undue significance to what the witness is saying. I claim it's a deliberate frame-up. Remember this man holds his office at the pleasure of the defendant. By the time the smoke all blows away, it will probably appear that this whole thing has been carefully rehearsed; that the only crime Livesey could possibly have committed is that of speeding in an automobile, or some relatively minor crime which, while technically a crime, is one which has no relation to the case we are here investigating.

"This cheap trickery is entirely on a par with . . ."

"Just a moment," Mason interrupted. "You keep on making those charges and I'm going to hold you personally responsible. You . . ."

"Gentlemen," Judge Minden said, "we will have no more personalities, and we will have no more speculation as to the reason for the statement made by this witness. Mr. Livesey, do I understand that you're going to refuse to answer any more questions concerning your relations with Virginia Bynum?"

"Yes, sir."

"How about what happened on the night of September twenty-first and the morning of September twenty-second? Will you answer questions . . ."

"I refuse to answer any questions concerning what happened on the night of September twenty-first or the early morning of September twenty-second on the ground that such answers might incriminate me."

"I want a four-day adjournment," Covington said angrily, his face flushed. "I'll have the grand jury in session and we'll get to the bottom of this. We . . ."

"In the meantime," Mason said, "I would like to recall George L. Denby to the witness stand for a brief question or two and then I will have no objection to the Court granting the request of the prosecution for continuance."

"Very well, take the stand, Mr. Denby," Judge Minden said.

Denby came walking to the witness stand, quietly efficient, gravely dignified. He took his position in the witness chair, placed the tips of his fingers together and looked inquiringly at Mason.

Mason said, "Mr. Denby, I would like to get the time element straight here. You have stated that you were working in the office of the Garvin Mining, Exploration and Devlopment Company all during the night of September twenty-first and the morning of September twenty-second."

"Yes, sir."

"Now then, are you acquainted with Virginia Bynum?"

"No, sir, I am not—that is, in the sense you probably mean. I met her in the offices of the corporation when she inquired about a stock certificate. That, I believe, is all."

"Now you know that the gun which was found on the fire escape was the weapon that has been introduced in evidence here in this case."

"Yes, sir."

"And how do you *know* it was the same weapon?"

"By the number, sir."

"What is the number?"

"S64805."

"You remembered that number?"

"Yes, sir, I remembered the number on that murder weapon."

"Why?"

"Because I thought it might be significant."

"You didn't make any notes?"

"No."

"Do you want the jury to believe that you can remember a number which you have seen as casually as the number which you saw on that gun?"

"Yes, sir, I have a photographic memory for numbers. I very seldom forget a number once I have seen it."

Mason approached the witness, took a wallet from his pocket and took from it a card. "What is this, Mr. Denby?"

"It seems to be a driving license made out to Mr. Perry Mason, an attorney at law."

"And have you ever seen that before?"

"This driving license?" Denby asked puzzled.

"Yes."

Denby shook his head. "No, I have not seen it."

"When was it issued?"

"On June fourth, nineteen forty-seven."

"When does it expire?"

"June fourth, nineteen fifty-one."

Mason walked up, took the license from Denby's hand, turned back toward the counsel table, then suddenly paused and said, "Very well, if you're so efficient in remembering numbers and have such a photographic memory for retaining numbers in your mind, what's the number of that driving license?"

Denby's cold eyes held a mildly contemptuous smile. "The number of the driving license, Mr. Mason," he said, "is 490553."

Mason glanced at the driving license.

"Is that right?" Denby asked.

"That," Mason told him, "is right."

There was a ripple of surprised approval from the spectators.

"Now, then," Mason said, whirling suddenly and pointing his finger at Denby, "if you have such a photographic memory for numbers how does it happen that when I first asked you, you were unable to remember who it was that owned Certificate Number 123 in the corporation?"

"I can't carry in mind the figures on every bit of stock in the corporation."

"I see," Mason said. "That's all."

"We will adjourn, until Monday morning at ten o'clock," Judge Minden said. "The jury will remember the admonition of the Court."

22

MASON, DELLA STREET AND PAUL DRAKE SAT IN MA-son's suite at the U. S. Grant Hotel.

Across the table from Perry Mason a tear-stained Virginia Bynum tried to meet the lawyer's eyes and failed.

Mason said, "Virginia, you're mixed up in a nasty mess. Whether you can get out of it with a whole skin depends entirely on whether you tell the truth. We now know that you were lying about being out on the fire escape the night of the murder. You can be prosecuted for perjury. We know that you took my car from Tijuana. We know that you drove it to the scene of the crime. The way things are right now you can be arrested for murder. You'd be tried and probably convicted—but somehow I don't think you're guilty of that murder, so suppose you tell us the truth."

She hesitated, looked from Mason's steady eyes to Drake's cold, accusing face, looked to Della Street for sympathy.

Della Street crossed over to pat her shoulder. "Why don't you tell the truth, Virginia?" she said. "You know Mr. Mason will give you the breaks—if he can."

Virginia suddenly threw back her head. "All right,"

she said, "I'll tell you. I see no reason for trying to protect people who aren't protecting me.

"It all happened when I fell for Frank Livesey. I was a party girl. He was in a position to make me or break me. He sold mining stock and threw one party after another. I don't know all the deal, but as nearly as I can find out Livesey and Denby had been looting the corporation. Denby would juggle papers around and take certain papers out of the files whenever an audit was expected.

"They had things going nicely when it suddenly began to appear that someone was tampering with the files in the corporation. They couldn't, either one of them, imagine who it was. However, by leaving certain traps they became convinced that this person was getting into the office at night, so they delegated me to wait in the office and see who it was. I kept the window onto the fire escape open. They told me whenever anyone started to open the door of the office I was to step out of the window to the fire escape, wait until I saw who was in there and what was being done. They said I could work my way down the fire escape where I wouldn't be seen.

"I liked Frank Livesey. He did a lot of entertaining and—well, I was living by my wits. I wasn't selling anything I didn't want to sell, but these stock buyers could make me a lot of money. Well, naturally I was under obligations to do just about as he wanted.

"You know what happened. Mrs. Ethel Garvin used a key she had when she was a secretary to get into the office. I ran down the fire escape. You caught me. I managed to make my escape in a taxicab, but I came back to the building and had the taxicab wait. When I saw this woman who had been in the office leave the building I had the cab follow her. I found out she was living at the Monolith Apartments. I recognized her as soon as I saw her enter the office because I'd seen her when she and Mr. Garvin were still married."

"And you reported all this to Livesey?" Mason asked.

"That's right."

"And what happened?"

She said, "Livesey and Denby bribed the switchboard operator at the Monolith Apartments to listen in on any conversations that came over Ethel Garvin's telephone and advise them. They found out then what she was up to; that she was substituting proxies and trying to control the stockholders' meeting. By this time they had reason to believe she had found out about the shortage of cash in the treasury of the corporation.

"Edward Garvin had gone away with his new wife and no one could find him, but Frank Livesey had the idea you would manage to find him and that when you did locate him you'd advise him to go across the border into Mexico. So he stationed me at the border in Mexico to let him know if Garvin crossed over to Tijuana.

"You know what happened. Garvin crossed the border. You followed him in your car. I got a taxi and followed you to the hotel. Garvin didn't know me, but you did, so I had to keep out of sight. However, after I thought you'd gone to bed, I got a room in the hotel so I could watch what was going on, without having the possibility of trouble with some night watchman. It turned out to be the last available room. I telephoned Frank Livesey as soon as the lights were switched off. I had a front bedroom. Frank told me not to go to bed but to sit up where I could look out of the window and make absolutely certain that you people didn't sneak away in the night. He said you were sharp and that he thought you might be pulling some trick.

"I hadn't been by the window over a few minutes when Mr. Garvin came out, jumped in his car, and drove away. I had to do something fast. I knew that the keys to the cars were in the drawer in the office all properly labeled. I knew your car when I saw it. I knew it was a fast car and I felt that it was the car to take. I ran into the office, opened the drawer, found the keys that

221

had the name 'Mason' tied to them, got in your car and followed Mr. Garvin. He went to Oceanside. He stopped several times and then had his gas tank filled. When he drove out of the service station I followed him out on the Fallbrook road near to the place I since discovered belonged to Mr. Hackley. He parked his car on the main road, locked the ignition, got out and took off across the field. I thought that was my best chance to telephone and was starting back to Oceanside when I saw a car turn in the road which went to Hackley's place. That was Ethel Garvin's. There was another car shortly behind it. That was Mr. Denby, driving his own car.

"Mr. Mason, I had no idea what he was planning. He listened to what I had to say, then told me that he was going to borrow your car for a while and that I was to take his car and try to find out what was going on in the house that was down at the end of the driveway. The clerk at the Monolith had told him of Garvin's call to Ethel Garvin.

"I moved along into the fields and worked up close to the house. I could see a light go on and could see Ethel Garvin and a tall man. The man was talking with her. He filled the gas tank on her car, then they went into the house. I kept working closer and then almost died of fright when I saw a dark shadowy figure—then I realized it was Mr. Garvin. He was moving toward the house, trying to get a look at what was going on, but a dog started to bark and kept barking and Mr. Garvin had to get away in order to be far enough away so the dog wouldn't bark.

"After a while, Mrs. Garvin came out, got in her automobile and drove away. Mr. Garvin tried to follow her, but he'd been so close to the house that by the time he ran the three or four hundred yards across the field to the road, she'd got away.

"I got in Mr. Denby's car and, to tell you the truth, I was pretty nervous. I'd been out there in the dark trying to find out what was going on in the Hackley house. I was afraid of the dog and afraid of someone jumping on me. I at one time had to run through some brush, and lost my scarf. I also snagged my stockings and—well, I'm afraid I looked a mess.

"I got in Mr. Denby's car, drove to Oceanside, couldn't find any trace of Mr. Garvin, and was wondering what to do when Mr. Denby showed up driving *your* car. He seemed very nervous and excited. He said, 'Here, quick! Jump in Mr. Mason's car. I want you to beat Garvin back to Tijuana. Make it just as fast as you can.

" 'As soon as you get back to Tijuana, park the car. First thing in the morning I want you to check out, leave the hotel where you're staying, take a plane to Los Angeles, go to your apartment and stay there. If anyone asks you where you were, tell them that you were sitting out on the fire escape watching the office and that I was working *all* night. Be sure to say that I was dictating a lot of cylinders on the Dictaphone dictating machine. That's all you need to know.'

"And," Virginia went on, "that was all I did know. I just jumped in the car and did exactly as he told me."

Mason looked at Della Street. "Got it all down, Della?"

Della looked up from her shorthand notebook.

"I guess that does it," Mason said, grinning at Paul Drake. "You can see what happened, Paul. Because Garvin told his wife to meet him there at the site of the property they had once owned, Denby knew right where to go. He knew where that property was located. He drove my car down there and parked it by the side of the road. He then probably walked back forty or fifty yards and waited. When Ethel saw a car parked there she naturally supposed it was her husband's car. She slowed down. Denby stepped out of the shadows. He had Virginia Bynum's revolver in his hand. He killed Ethel, pushed her body over to the right-hand side of the car, drove her car alongside of my car, stepped out into my car, pulled

Ethel's body over behind the steering wheel, dropped the gun on the ground, got in my car, drove back to Ocean-side, changed cars with Virginia and beat it back to Los Angeles.

"He'd been arranging an alibi for a long time. There's nothing about a dictated Dictaphone record that shows *when* it was dictated. He'd been carefully saving up a supply of dictated cylinders dealing with a lot of technical phases of the corporation's business which would sound as though they'd been dictated the night before the stock-holders' meeting. All he had to do was to get back to the office long enough to pick up those records and put them on the desk of his transcribing secretary. Of course, she would be firmly convinced he'd been working all night."

Mason turned to Della Street, "Della, call the secretary of the Bar Association. Get him on the line for me."

When Della Street had the call through, Mason, grinning, said, "This is Perry Mason talking. Your grievance committee wants to have me appear tonight to explain how it happened that I tricked Mortimer C. Irving into identifying my car as the car he saw parked on the road by Oceanside when the murder was committed. You are kindly advised that it *was* my car Irving saw parked there. Now, if you can tell me any rule which makes it unethical or illegal for me to persuade a witness to tell the truth you're welcome to disbar me."

And Perry Mason, winking at his attractive secretary, hung up the telephone.